Praise for the Bay Island Psychic Mysteries

"The future shows much success for this series! Fun, vibrant characters (as well as a sexy smolder or two for good measure) give the novel just the right tone."

— *RT Book Reviews*

"I loved the protagonist, Cass. She and her friends were very well developed and felt like a group of people I'd like to get to know."

— *The Book's the Thing*

"The book starts off on a fast pace, and is a quick page-turner. Readers will love the charm, wit, and feelings that these characters show."

— *Bibliophile Reviews*

"It has so many great characters and just enough intrigue to keep me on the edge of my seat. The setting was quaint and the author made me want to live there. The mystery is well written and keeps readers guessing till the end."

— *Texas Book-aholic*

"I love a good cozy book right before bed, and this charming story about psychic shop owner Cass Donovan did not disappoint. I stayed up far too late into the evening because I couldn't put it down. A well-crafted mystery with a quirky cast of characters, and plenty of twists and turns to keep you guessing to the end."

— *The Mysterious Ink Spot*

"This engaging series just keeps getting better!"

— *Cozy Up With Kathy*

Books by Lena Gregory

Bay Island Psychic Mysteries

Death at First Sight
Occult and Battery
Clairvoyant and Present Danger
Spirited Away

All-Day Breakfast Café Mysteries

Scone Cold Killer
Murder Made to Order
A Cold Brew Killing

SPIRITED

AWAY

A BAY ISLAND PSYCHIC MYSTERY

LENA GREGORY

BEYOND THE PAGE
PUBLISHING

Spirited Away
Lena Gregory
Copyright © 2019 by Denise Pysarchuk.
Cover design by Dar Albert, Wicked Smart Designs

Beyond the Page Books
are published by
Beyond the Page Publishing
www.beyondthepagepub.com

ISBN: 978-1-950461-06-6

SPIRITED

AWAY

Chapter One

"Oh, please . . ." Bee Maxwell leaned closer to the window and fingered the blue silk scarf he'd spent five minutes arranging just so to achieve that casually draped look. "Don't even tell me Aiden Hargrove is taking a sudden interest in the occult."

"What are you talking about, Bee?" Cass Donovan had no time for Bee's theatrics. She was minutes away from having a full house for her group reading, and Emmett still hadn't fixed the air-conditioning. She nudged Bee aside and looked out the upstairs window into the parking lot.

Sure enough, Aiden was just climbing out of his shiny black Lexus.

Bee straightened. "I'd love to know where that man gets his money from."

"According to pretty much everyone, he's never worked a day in his life." Cass shrugged it off. She couldn't work up the same level of interest in gossip that Bee had mastered, and she had no patience for it today. "Must have family money."

"I knew his parents. Nicest people you ever want to meet, but Joe the plumber and soccer mom all the way." Bee frowned. "At least, she would have been if Aiden played soccer, which by all accounts, he didn't."

Cass turned away from the window to stare at Bee.

He lifted one bushy brown eyebrow, giving the illusion of a caterpillar crawling up beneath his bleached blond bangs, and shrugged. "What? I can't help it if people tell me things."

Cass laughed. She couldn't help it. He wasn't lying; people did tell him things, mostly because he was the biggest gossip Bay Island had ever known, and he wanted info on everything and everyone. Plus, he always had good dirt to trade.

"Besides, word has it Mr. Hargrove is looking for a new fashion line to invest in, evening gowns, if the Bay Island gossip mill can be believed. And he's looking for a designer." Bee grinned. "And you know how much I love designing gowns."

Bee's shop, Dreamweaver Designs, sat just down the boardwalk from Mystical Musings and catered to a well-to-do clientele. Though his annual fashion shows brought buyers from New York City trickling to Bay Island each autumn, Bee still struggled incredibly hard to make a name for himself and his designs. Backing from someone with unlimited funds like Aiden Hargrove could be just the career boost he needed.

Cass glanced out the window again. Something niggled at her. She squinted, focusing on Aiden as he rounded the back of the car and approached the passenger side. As quickly as the feeling had come over her, it disappeared.

"Hey, if he believes in all this psychic mumbo-jumbo, a suggestion from you to invest in a local designer sure wouldn't hurt." Bee waggled his eyebrows.

Cass pinned him with a glare.

"What?" Hope slid from his eyes, and he started to sulk. "Just sayin'."

"Cass?" Emmett Marx stood at the top of the spiral staircase in the upstairs reading room he'd built for her, mopping sweat from his forehead with one of the red shop towels he always had hanging from his back jeans pocket. "We have a problem."

That was the last thing she needed, especially when pretty much everything had gone wrong since she'd gotten out of bed that morning. "Please, don't tell me that. I'm minutes away from a packed house. I don't have time for problems."

Emmett winced. "Gonna have to make time."

The tinkle of wind chimes from downstairs signaled the arrival of her first guests, presumably Aiden Hargrove and whomever he'd brought with him.

"I'll take care of it." Bee's expression brightened as he squeezed her arm on his way past, then headed down the stairs, most likely to get on Aiden's good side.

"Okay." She sucked in a deep breath and blew it out slowly. "Hit me with it. What's the problem? The short version."

Not that Emmett ever elaborated on anything. Getting information out of Emmett was akin to pulling teeth, but her nerves were shot.

"You need a part." He stood stock-still, staring at her.

No one to blame but herself; she *had* told him she wanted the short version. "And?"

"I don't have it."

"Can you get it?"

"Yup." He stuffed his hands into his pockets and rocked back on his heels.

"So, what's the problem?" Cass wished she could bite back the words, or at least the tone, even as they shot off her tongue. "I'm sorry, Emmett. I'm just having a bad day."

If that wasn't the understatement of the year.

"Don't worry about it." Emmett shrugged. "I can get the part but not until tomorrow."

"Why not today?" She was perilously close to whining.

"Everything's closed."

A quick glance at the driftwood clock hanging between the front windows confirmed his statement. Quarter to seven on a Sunday evening. Not only was everything closed, but her group reading was due to start in fifteen minutes, so she couldn't even call everyone and cancel. Most of them would already be on their way. "Okay. All right."

Emmett waited.

She'd have to make the best of it. Maybe Stephanie could run to the convenience store and get an extra case of water. If she ever got there. Stephanie never showed up this late for a group reading. She usually hurried straight to Mystical Musings as soon as she finished working, which should have been almost two hours ago since she'd only been handling a small job on her day off. "Could you help me open the windows, please, Emmett?"

"Sure." Emmett moved through the room opening windows on the front wall while Cass opened those on the back wall facing the beach, allowing for as much cross-ventilation as possible.

Any other time, the bay breeze would have cooled the room right down, but the heat wave currently suffocating the island only brought more heat and humidity into the room—unless you counted the putrid odor of low tide.

Why me?

"Howdy, stranger." Luke Morgan rounded the top of the stairs and strolled toward her, but even his slow Southern drawl, which usually sent shivers skittering up her spine, only brought annoyance.

"No kidding," she snapped.

Luke stopped short and frowned. "Something I said?"

"Oh, I don't know, Luke. You supposedly moved to Bay Island to be closer to me, and when was the last time I saw you? A week ago?" She shoved her sweat-soaked hair behind her ear, dangerously close to falling apart completely.

"Uh . . . um . . . okay, then." Emmett cleared his throat and backed toward the spiral staircase, his cheeks flaming bright red. As soon as he reached the wrought iron railing, he turned and bolted down the stairs.

Great. She hadn't even gotten to ask if he was staying for the reading, though she couldn't blame him if he didn't.

Luke frowned and inched closer. "You okay?"

"Honestly?" She threw her hands in the air. "I have no idea."

True enough. Problem was, she couldn't figure out what was wrong. So, the air conditioner was on the fritz. So what? And Stephanie, whom she counted on to help prepare everything for the readings, hadn't shown up yet. She'd be there. She'd never missed a reading. And Bee had pitched in to make sure everything was done.

But something was wrong. Something had been eating at her since she'd opened her eyes that morning. She just couldn't put her finger on it yet. Maybe she should call Stephanie and make sure she was all right.

"Hey?" Luke stood facing her and rubbed his hands up and down her arms, a gesture of friendship, nothing more.

Not exactly the relationship she'd been hoping for when he'd taken the position as Tank's partner and moved to Bay Island.

He tilted his head and studied her more closely, his deep blue eyes more keenly observant than she'd have liked. Luke Morgan didn't miss much. "You all right?"

"I guess." She waved him off and stepped back. It was either that or give in to the desire to curl up in his arms.

He lowered his hands to his sides. "I'm sorry I've been so busy lately."

"It's fine." They did need to have this conversation, but not here and not now. She turned away and looked out the window. Cars had already filled the small gravel lot. Bee must be keeping everyone downstairs. No surprise, if Emmett had told him what happened.

"No, Cass, it's not fine." Luke moved behind her and wrapped his arms around her waist, then rested his chin on her shoulder. "I moved to Bay Island to be closer to you, to see if we could make a go of this, but lately I haven't had a free minute."

She nodded. What could she say? It was true.

But if she were going to be honest, neither had she. Summers on Bay Island had been different during her childhood. She remembered long walks on the beach, playing in the surf with friends, picnics beneath the lighthouse. So far this summer, she hadn't managed one beach day. Actually, she hadn't even managed a day off since before Memorial Day had brought flocks of tourists to Bay Island, many of whom visited her boardwalk shop or came in for readings.

Luke sighed. "This art theft case has everyone working overtime."

"You haven't said much about it." Cass tried to slip out of his grip and turn to face him.

"I haven't had time." He pulled her tighter against him, cocooning her in a warm embrace that should have brought comfort but only made her more aware of the sweat soaking her back.

The minute hand on the clock clicked, breaking the strained silence. She was going to have to get started. "And, unfortunately, right now *I* don't have time."

He kissed her neck and stepped back. "I know."

"Can we talk about it after the reading?"

"That's actually what I stopped by to tell you; I can't stay for the reading tonight. I'm sorry. We might have a break in the case, but Tank and I have to meet with someone tonight. I'm not sure how long it'll take."

Disappointment surged. It would be the first reading he'd missed since moving to Bay Island. Not that she expected him to show up for every group reading, but tonight of all nights she'd wanted him there. "Do you want to get together afterward? Maybe go to the diner or something?"

"I wish I could, but I have no idea how long this'll take. What do you say we meet up for breakfast in the morning? Pancakes?" He smiled, the setting sunlight streaming through the windows sparkling in the depths of his blue eyes.

She softened and brushed his shaggy dark hair away from his

face. He obviously hadn't had time for a haircut either. "Where do you want to meet?"

"How about at the hotel?"

The Bay Side Hotel, where he'd been staying every night since he'd moved there.

"It's more private than the diner," he added.

Uh-oh. Did he mean more intimate private, or did he mean I can dump you without the whole town watching private? "Sounds good."

He dropped an innocent peck on her cheek. "Good luck tonight."

"Yeah, thanks." *Somehow, I have a feeling I'm going to need it.*

Once he left, she stared out the window, taking the moment to herself. The low-tide stench was starting to get to her, and her stomach rolled over. Or maybe it was the thought of losing Luke that was churning in her gut. Maybe that was the source of the impending sense of doom that had been hounding her all day. No. It didn't seem right. Something else. Something hovering just out of her reach.

"You ready?"

She jumped, startled by the intrusion.

Bee stood at the top of the stairs, one foot still on the top step, hand clutching the railing, tensed to bolt at the slightest provocation.

How in the world was she going to pull this off tonight? She plastered on a smile. "Sure, go ahead and send everyone up."

Bee sighed and crossed to her, the thump of his platform shoes against the hardwood floor pounding through her head. He hugged her, then tucked a long strand of stringy damp hair behind her ear. "You don't have to pretend for me, honey. I can always tell when you're hurting. I just wish I knew why."

Cass wrapped her arms around him and rested her cheek against his broad chest. "So do I, Bee."

He dropped a kiss on top of her head, then set her back. "Why don't you go freshen up while I get everyone seated?"

She laughed. "That bad, huh?"

"Weeell . . ." Bee winced and fluffed her hair a bit, but the long blond waves fell limp the instant he let go. "Oh, honey, I can't lie to you. You're pretty much a hot mess right now. Why don't you try putting your hair up tonight? It'll be cooler anyway. Or better yet, wear the sash."

Yikes. If Bee was suggesting she cover her hair with the silk sash she sometimes wore around her head for individual readings, she must be in worse shape than she thought. "Thanks a lot, Bee."

He obviously missed the sarcasm, because he smiled and nodded. "That's what friends are for, dear. Now, shoo. It's getting late, and people are testy enough down there without having to wait any longer in the stifling heat."

"What do you mean testy?" Her group readings had turned into social events as much as psychic ones, and everyone was usually in a good mood.

Bee fanned himself with his scarf. "Seems Aiden brought a friend, and she's already managed to insult at least three people that I'm aware of. Speaking of which, I'd better get back down there before anything else happens. Are you good now?"

"Yeah, I'm fine. Is Stephanie here yet?"

Bee caught his bottom lip between his teeth and shook his head.

"All right. Go. Get everyone up here and settled as fast as possible, and make sure you offer them cold drinks." She hurried toward the small office Emmett had built for her behind the stairway. She'd fix herself up and get this over with as fast as possible. Maybe then she, Stephanie, and Bee could go to the diner and try to figure out what her problem was. She had a sneaking suspicion she needed to know, and sooner rather than later.

Chapter Two

Cass smoothed her sweat-soaked hair back and wrapped it into what she hoped would be a bun but ended up more a sloppy knot at the back of her head. Maybe Bee was right. Maybe she did need the sash, but to get it she'd have to go against the flow of clients ascending the stairs to the reading room. No way was she trying to go downstairs for the sash. It wasn't worth it, since it probably wouldn't help anyway.

She lifted the small makeup mirror off her desk and tried to survey the damage. As if the lopsided bun wasn't bad enough, tendrils had escaped and plastered themselves against her face and neck.

Murmurs sifted through her closed office door: ". . . believe how hot it is in here . . . might need to leave early . . . better be all she's cracked up to be . . . that smell?"

"It'll be worth it . . ." an unfamiliar voice interrupted. "Trust me, Cass is amazing."

Though she couldn't make out who the woman's voice belonged to, the sentiment brought the boost to Cass's confidence she needed to make this work. It reminded her that she loved what she did and that people loved her in return. They counted on her. Even though many of the clients—probably most—who attended her readings came searching for entertainment and social interaction, there were always a few who came seeking help and guidance. Cass had a responsibility to them.

She tamed the lumps of hair plastered against her head with a comb, added a little blush to cheeks that were way too pale for summer on an island, and smoothed on coral lipstick.

Okay, you can do this.

She shoved to her feet and started toward the door, then thought better of the idea and returned to her desk. She stuffed the makeup back in its case and stuck the case and the mirror into her desk drawer, then slid the chair into place beneath the desk. No sense leaving a mess she'd have to tend to later when her need for order reared its ugly head.

With one last glance around the office to make sure everything was in place, she headed toward the door again, then reached for the door handle and paused. She let her hand drop to her side. Who was she kidding? She was in no shape for this tonight. Whatever had been haunting her all day had begun to . . .

Wait. A thought trickled in, slowly, cautiously. Her mind resisted. Not *whatever*—

A woman's voice teased her, whispering, on the outside edge of her awareness, just out of her reach.

The office door shot open and smacked her in the forehead. She staggered back, tripped on the edge of the oriental rug, and went down hard on her butt. Her teeth clacked together, catching the inside of her cheek between them, and the coppery taste of blood filled her mouth.

"Oh, man, Cass." Bee rushed toward her and crouched at her side. "Are you all right? Are you hurt? I'm so sorry. I was in a hurry, and I didn't look before I—"

She held up a hand to stop the flow of words. "It's okay, Bee. I'm fine."

He grabbed her arm and hauled her to her feet. "Are you sure you're okay?"

"I'm sure. I'm fine."

He brushed off her shorts. "You'd better hurry up and get dressed if you're going to get this done."

"What do you mean?" She looked down at her khaki shorts and maroon silk camisole. "I am dressed."

Bee stepped back and eyed her up and down with a sneer, as if she were wearing a ratty bathrobe.

She huffed out a breath, in no mood for his theatrics. "What's the problem, Bee?"

"Oh, dear, nothing. I mean . . ." With a nod toward her hair, he sighed. "If you're sure that's how you want to go out there."

"I don't have time for this." Granted, he was right, but that didn't matter. She always dressed for her readings—not too fancy, but in something other than shorts and a camisole, usually a skirt and top. Today, though, well . . . her attire was the least of her problems. She started toward the door. "It's like a hundred and ten degrees in here, I'm going to be lucky if I even get through this."

"Hey." Bee grabbed her arm and spun her to face him. His big brown eyes bored through her, and he frowned. "Are you sure you're all right?"

"I'm fine." She blurted out the answer more harshly than she'd intended.

He narrowed his eyes. "This is me you're talking to, honey, and you are not fine. What's going on?"

She shook her head and lowered her gaze from the intensity of his stare. Bee knew her too well to miss the distress she'd seen in her own eyes reflected in the mirror. "I'm not sure, but could we talk about it later? Right now, I just need to get this done. Afterward, maybe we can go to the diner and talk. Okay?"

He squeezed her arm and deliberated a moment longer, then relented and let her go. "Sure, come on. But I'm eating light tonight."

Cass flipped the light switch off as they headed out of the office toward the reading room. "Are you feeling okay?"

"Yeah, but . . ." Bee patted his stomach. "In case you hadn't noticed, I've put on a few pounds."

"Are you kidding me?" Bee was one of those rare people who could eat like a horse and never gain a pound. Usually, but now that he mentioned it, she had noticed he'd gained a bit of weight recently, even though it seemed to have settled in all the right places, giving him a more muscular build than he'd already had. "You look amazing, Bee."

"Thank you, dear, but if I don't get it in check now, it'll get out of control. Better to be on top of it." He gestured her into the reading room ahead of him.

A number of familiar faces greeted her, as well as several newcomers she didn't recognize.

Aiden Hargrove slouched in a seat toward the front of the room, his arm slung over an empty chair next to him. If his bored expression was any indication, he had no interest at all in being there. Seemed Bee's hopes of any sort of psychic intervention would be short-lived, not that she'd ever lead someone like that. It would feel too much like taking advantage. Despite Bee's apparent hopes to the contrary, he knew that.

On Aiden's other side, a woman perched on the edge of her seat, red hair piled atop her head in some dramatic updo that had probably taken hours and cost a small fortune. Diamonds dripped from her neck and arms. She grinned widely when Cass walked in, gripped Aiden's arm and shook him.

Aiden shot her a half grin, nodded, then rolled his eyes as soon as she turned away.

Cass recognized the woman from the shop. She'd definitely been in a few times before, though Cass couldn't recall offhand what she'd come in for. Not a reading, that was for sure. She always remembered her reading clients.

Bee may have been right. The silk camisole might not have been the best idea. Sweat already had it clinging uncomfortably to her damp skin. She pulled the front away from her body and fanned herself as discreetly as possible.

Stephanie smiled at her from the front of the room and picked up the microphone.

And, that easily, everything fell into place. Maybe her unease did have something to do with Stephanie. She'd have to examine that later. Cass smiled back and waited through Stephanie's introduction, then strode through a smattering of less-than-enthusiastic applause to the front of the room and took the microphone Stephanie held out to her. She leaned over and whispered, "Thanks."

Stephanie winked, then dimmed the lights and retreated to the back table to sit beside Bee.

The burgundy curtains hung limp, framing the open windows. Usually, she'd have closed them to darken the room, set the atmosphere. Candles flickered amid the centerpieces on each table. She probably should have skipped those. Additional heat was the last thing they needed. A stack of papers sat perfectly still where Bee must have forgotten them on the bookshelf earlier, not so much as a flutter from the softest of breezes. If she made it through this reading, she would have Emmett install ceiling fans throughout the shop as soon as humanly possible.

"I'd like to thank you all for coming tonight." A bead of sweat trickled down the side of Cass's face. "I have to apologize for the heat. I expected the air-conditioning to be fixed before we started."

A few weak chuckles filled the room.

"Some psychic!" a man yelled from the back of the room and laughed, long and loud, as he looked around the room, the robust laughter of a bully searching for support.

Someone cleared their throat. A chair scraped along the floor as a gentleman Cass didn't recognize pulled himself closer to his table and propped his elbows on the blue cloth. Clothing rustled as people shifted uncomfortably and looked around at one another.

Cass's gaze shot to the back wall where Tank and Luke usually stood, arms folded across their chests, skeptical, since neither of them believed in her abilities, but supportive just the same.

Emmett slid his chair back two tables over from the smart aleck, but Cass discreetly shook her head, and he froze. Better to ignore someone like her heckler, not feed into his aggression.

Bee coughed. He waited for her gaze to find his, then widened his eyes and rolled a finger for her to get moving.

How was she going to salvage this mess?

She swiped the side of her face, shook her head, and smiled as she searched the room for a place to start. "I'm sorry, the spirits seem to be restless tonight as well. Must be the heat bothering them too."

A few more people laughed. This time, a little more genuinely.

Cass shook off the heaviness that seemed to be weighing her down. She had a feeling it was something more than the oppressive heat and humidity nagging at her. Whether it was some actual psychic sixth sense or just her natural intuitiveness screaming at her something was wrong, she had no idea. She did know she couldn't stand there all night and do nothing. "Um . . ."

Hot air bathed her neck, as if someone was breathing right behind her. She whirled around but found nothing, then sucked in a deep breath. Her chest ached with the effort.

Bee coughed again.

I know, I know. She didn't even bother looking at him.

A young couple sat at a small round table toward the back corner, heads together, smiling down at the cell phone the guy held between them.

Cass focused on them and approached slowly, giving them time to shy away if they weren't interested in being singled out, giving herself a moment to collect her thoughts.

The woman looked up as Cass approached. Her eyes widened a bit, but her smile remained firmly in place as she stared at Cass.

Her companion looked up a moment later. Since neither of them seemed distressed by her attention, she continued.

A glint of fading sunlight flashed from the diamond on the woman's left ring finger.

Cass leaned against an empty table beside them and tried to relax. What could they want to know? It seemed they were already happily engaged, which meant the man wasn't looking to see if his intended would say yes if he popped the question—a common enough reason young men sought her services, insecurity.

No, this couple seemed quite comfortable with one another, more friends than anything else . . .

She ignored her gut instinct. She had to get this reading going. "You were friends before you were lovers."

The man shoved his seat away from the woman, tipped the chair, and almost landed on the floor before catching himself and shooting to his feet. The woman leaned back as far away as possible, staring at the man with her mouth open, clearly horrified by the prospect.

Backing away from the table, the man held his hands up in front of him as if Cass were holding him at gunpoint. "Oh, no. No way. I think you got the wrong impression."

The woman looked around the room and laughed uncomfortably, then gestured toward her friend. "My sister's husband and I came together because my fiancé and my sister couldn't make it. My fiancé got called into work at the last minute, and my sister is home with her dog who's giving birth."

"We were just looking at a picture my wife sent of our Shelby and her new pups," the man babbled as he snatched the phone off the table and held it up for everyone to see.

Heat blazed in Cass's chest and spread to her face. That's what she got for not trusting her gut. "I'm sorry. The friendship part came through loud and clear, but the rest of the message was kind of foggy."

Several people shifted and averted their gazes. A woman sitting alone at the table next to them smirked as she twirled a lock of long dark hair around her finger, clearly enjoying the fiasco.

Now what? Should she try to salvage this mess or move on?

"Must be the heat causing all that fog, huh?" Her heckler laughed out loud and slapped the table.

The brunette's smirk widened to a full-blown grin, showing off a line of perfectly aligned, shockingly white teeth.

She ignored both of them. Better to focus on anything else. Giving them a wide berth, she scanned the room, desperate for some way to salvage the situation.

A snort from the front of the room caught her attention, and she whirled toward it, grateful for any distraction.

"The heat sure is messing with those pesky spirits. What do you suppose they'll screw up next?" her heckler yelled.

Aiden Hargrove, who'd been lounging nonchalantly until then, sat up straighter in his chair, crossed one leg over the other, and applauded loudly.

Cass homed in on him. Just what she needed, someone to take her frustration out on. Arrogant Aidan Hargrove would make the perfect target. She sauntered toward him, taking her time, studying both him and his companion, searching for something to grasp hold of, ignoring the warning screaming in her head, begging her to back off.

Her foot caught on a chair leg, and she stumbled but caught herself against a table before she could fall. Great, seemed the heat had fried any cognitive awareness Cass might once have had and left her with nothing more than a wicked headache and a roomful of strangers staring at her, waiting to be enthralled.

For a fraction of a second, Cass considered trying to convince Aiden to invest in a line of gowns with Bee, but her conscience wouldn't allow it, not even under the most dire of circumstances. Besides, he obviously didn't believe in her skills, so it would probably only hurt Bee more than help at that point. One glance at Bee frantically shaking his head no convinced her she was right and helped focus her, despite her humiliation.

She took a deep breath and rolled her shoulders, focusing instead on Aiden's date.

The woman still sat on the edge of her seat, but now she held her bottom lip caught between her teeth, casting nervous glances at her companion. It hit Cass where she'd seen her before. The woman had come into the shop not that long ago seeking a love potion. Her hair had hung in waves around her face at that time, and Cass hadn't immediately recognized her with it piled atop her head, but the leather cord holding the small bag of crystals Cass had given her hung around her neck and disappeared into her blouse.

Cass forced a smile. "You're in love."

The woman cast her gaze down, but a smile flickered as she shot another glance in Aiden's direction. The most likely question the woman would want answered would be if her love interest returned her feelings.

Cass studied Aiden.

A lock of blond hair fell in a stylish wave across his forehead. He kept his gaze carefully focused on his perfectly manicured hands folded on the table in front of him. A touch of color spotted his cheeks.

Warmth invaded her mind, her heart. "He's in love too."

Aiden jerked his head up and shot a look over his shoulder at the brunette seated alone across the room, still twirling her hair around her finger.

"But with someone else." Cass tried to bite the words back even as they came out of her mouth. "I'm sorry . . . I . . . uh . . ."

Aiden shoved his chair back from the table and lurched to his feet. "I've had enough."

Tears shimmered in his date's eyes.

"Wait, please, I'm sorry. I didn't mean—" Cass held up her hands, wishing desperately she could unsay the words.

"We're out of here." He grabbed his date's arm and yanked her to her feet. "Didn't I tell you this woman was nothing but a fraud? Let's go."

The woman followed meekly, staring at the floor as Aiden weaved between tables toward the stairs. She spared the dark-haired woman a seething glance on her way past.

Cass's heckler laughed out loud as he called after Aiden, "Hey, buddy, where ya goin'? Why don't ya stick around, and maybe she'll tell you who ya really got a hankerin' for?"

Emmett shoved his chair back and surged to his feet, fists clenched. "That's enough, Dirk!"

Stephanie went after Aiden and his date, hopefully trying to do some kind of damage control.

Bee's attention swiveled between Cass, Emmett, and Dirk as he stood beside his table, clutching the chair back.

"I ain't even gotten started yet, Emmett." Dirk jumped to his feet and waved his hand in the air. "Hey, Cass. Do me next, will ya?"

Bee's gaze settled on the continuing confrontation between Emmett and Dirk.

Somehow, Cass needed to get control of this mess before someone got hurt. "All right. Let's all calm down. Please."

Dirk scoffed.

As Emmett rounded the last table between them, he pointed a finger at Dirk.

With one last glance at Cass, Bee went after him.

"Please, everyone. I have to apologize . . . Please . . ." Cass held her hands up for quiet.

"You'd best put that finger down, Emmett," Dirk demanded, taking a step toward him.

Emmett clenched his teeth but lowered his hand. A man of few words, he stepped back and gestured toward the stairs. "Just go, okay? I don't want no trouble here."

"You never want trouble, do ya, Emmett? But it always seems to find you." Dirk took a swing, landing a solid blow to Emmett's chin.

Emmett staggered back but shook it off and swung back, catching Dirk square in the nose.

Two women screamed and ducked away from the fight.

Chaos ensued as people scrambled to get out of the way, and Beast barked wildly from his room downstairs.

Dirk lifted a fist to take another shot at Emmett, but Bee hooked his arm from behind and swung him around, pinning him face-first against the wall.

Thankfully, Emmett stepped back. His girlfriend, Sara Ryan, held a hand flat against his chest, whispering urgently in his ear.

Some customers fled down the stairs, while others backed out of the way but stayed to witness the action.

The sound of sirens wailed in the distance. One of her customers must have called the police.

And worst of all was Cass's grim premonition; the worst of it was yet to come.

Chapter Three

The police officers who'd shown up at Mystical Musings—with Luke and Tank noticeably absent—had given Emmett and Dirk a stern warning about any further public confrontation and demanded they both go straight home and cool off.

Thankfully, the diner was open twenty-four hours a day during tourist season, and Cass, Bee, and Stephanie had cleaned up the mess at Mystical Musings, then agreed to meet up after Cass spent some time soothing Beast and settling him at home.

Cass second-guessed that decision as she strode across the diner parking lot with Bee and Stephanie on either side of her. Streetlamps bathed the parking lot in a soft welcoming glow, and a warm drizzle barely cooled her burning face. "Are you guys sure this is a good idea?"

Bee hooked an arm through hers. "Better to face the masses and get it over with than allow the gossip mill to get up and running without you making a public appearance first."

"I guess." She took a deep shuddering breath and braced herself. "Was that as disastrous as I think it was?"

Bee and Stephanie glanced at each other but neither answered.

Cass cringed. "Yeah, that's about what I expected. Do you think there's any way to salvage my reputation?"

"I don't see why not." Bee shrugged. "Look on the bright side. At least you finally got something right when you said Aiden was in love with someone else."

A small seed of triumph tried to surface. "You think?"

"Are you kidding me?" Bee harrumphed. "Did you see the look on his face when he stared longingly across the room at that other woman?"

The beginning of Cass's good mood deflated. "Yeah, but did you see the look on his date's face? I feel horrible for hurting her, and I honestly didn't mean it. I don't even know why I blurted that out."

Bee jogged up the steps to the entrance and held the door open for Stephanie and then Cass.

Cass stopped beside him. "I'm sorry if I ruined your chances of working with Aiden."

"No worries, hon. You mean way more to me than Aiden Hargrove ever could, even if he is supposedly worth millions." He winked and let the door fall shut as he propelled her into the crowded diner.

Only one thing could explain such a sizeable crowd at that time on a Sunday night, even during the peak of tourist season: good dirt. Since Cass recognized several customers from her reading, she also had to assume she was the night's headline.

The look of sympathy in the hostess's eyes as she greeted them with a huge smile only confirmed Cass's suspicions that, despite Bee's hopes, the Bay Island rumor mill was already up and running. "Hi, guys. Just the three of you tonight?"

"Yes, thanks, Gabby, and would you mind giving us a booth in the back?" He pointed toward the room at the back of the diner, separated from the main dining area by a glass wall with a lighthouse scene etched into it.

Cass shot him a grateful look.

"No problem." She gestured for them to follow her. "We opened the back room about a half hour ago."

Not long after the police were called to the shop. Apparently, rumors flew fast and furious on Bay Island.

Gabby led the way through the diner.

Customers looked up as Cass crossed the room, some averting their gazes, others offering a smile or a wave. None approached them, which wasn't entirely unusual, but Cass couldn't help feeling the undercurrent buzzing through the room. She'd be happy to escape to the small room behind the glass wall. At least there were only a handful of tables back there, of which only three were occupied, by people who paid no attention to them.

"Here you go." Gabby seated them in a corner booth and laid their menus on the table. "Enjoy."

Stephanie and Cass slid into one side of the booth, facing a view of the parking lot through the rain-spattered window. Bee took the other side, his attention focused out over the room and through the doorway into the main part of the diner, no doubt trying to assess the damage done to her reputation. Bee could home in on gossip like a bloodhound on a steak.

"Do me a favor, guys. Order me an omelet or something. I want to run to the ladies' room." Cass started to slide out of the booth.

Stephanie lay a hand on Cass's, a bit too perceptive, as usual. "Want me to go with you?"

"Thanks, but I'll be okay." She hurried across the room to the restrooms in the far corner. If the restroom had been on the other side of the diner, she probably wouldn't have braved the stares to go, but as it was, she needed a minute to herself.

Thankfully, all three stall doors stood open and the restroom was empty. Cass dropped onto one of the two chairs in the sitting area and stared into the mirror. Her appearance definitely reflected her mood.

A shelf holding tissues, baby wipes, and a basket filled with trial-size soaps, lotions, and hand sanitizers ran along the wall beneath the mirror. She yanked a baby wipe out of a half-filled package and swiped the smears of black mascara and eyeliner from beneath her eyes, then rummaged through her bag for blush. As it was, she looked about as pale as the ghosts she supposedly talked to.

Not that anyone would believe she could communicate with spirits after word spread about tonight's debacle.

After a few swipes of blush, she smoothed gloss on her lips, then gave up. It would have to do. She left her hair alone. No sense even trying to comb out the knotted mess. At least the sloppy knot toward the back of her head appeared somewhat stylish. If she attempted to do anything with it, she'd probably only make matters worse.

She threw her stuff back into her bag, turned away from the mirror, and pulled out her cell phone. Not that she expected Luke to answer, but she could really use a little comfort just then, and the sound of his deep Southern drawl would offer that.

After three rings, the call went to his voice mail. She started to hang up but didn't want him to think anything was wrong. "Hey, Luke, it's me. Just wanted to say hello and let you know everything was all right at the shop. I figured you'd hear about the incident there and didn't want you to worry."

After a moment's hesitation, she hung up. What else could she say?

The restroom door swung open and a woman strode through holding a little girl's wrist, trying to avoid hitting anything with the child's ketchup-covered hand. She shot Cass an exasperated smile and headed for the sink.

Since Cass couldn't think of any other way to procrastinate, she hauled herself to her feet, lifted her chin, and headed out to face the inevitable stares and whispers. She couldn't avoid it, not in a town as small as Bay Island, so she figured she may as well face it head-on and move past it. Hopefully, the next juicy tidbit would come along soon, and her troubles would be forgotten. Then she could work on restoring her reputation.

She offered Bee and Stephanie her best smile as she returned to the booth.

"There you are." Bee leaned back and hooked his arm over the seat back. "I was beginning to think I'd have to come looking for you."

Cass lifted a brow. "In the ladies' room?"

"Honey, there is nowhere I wouldn't go if you needed me."

And just like that, everything was okay. She would need to work hard to restore her good name and keep Mystical Musings up and running, but the people—and puppy—who truly mattered would love her and stand by her no matter what. "You're the best, Bee."

"Yeah, well, don't you forget it." He patted her hand and winked at Stephanie. "We ordered you a vegetable skillet with a side of fries and rye toast. I hope that's okay."

Her stomach churned. She'd be lucky to get anything down. "It's perfect, thanks."

"So . . ." Stephanie shifted to face her more directly. "What happened tonight?"

Cass lifted her hands. "I have no idea."

But that wasn't true. She'd been off even before she'd started the reading, should really have canceled.

"I'm sorry I was late. I had to meet with a potential client, and he was only here for the day." If her eye roll was any indication, she wasn't too excited about the prospect.

Stephanie didn't usually have trouble with clients. Most, especially those native to Bay Island, trusted her. "You don't think it'll work out?"

"Well, he hired me, so that's a start." She laughed. "But if the interview was any indication about what it'll be like to work for Calvin Morris, he won't last long."

"So, why'd you agree to take him?" Bee asked.

"Adoption is more expensive that we realized." Her big brown eyes sparkled, as they always did when she spoke of the baby she and her husband, Tank, were trying to adopt. She pulled her long brown hair back off her face. "So I'm taking on whatever extra work I can get."

"How's everything going?" Cass traced a finger around Mystical Musings' ad on her place mat. Many clients said they'd seen her ad there. Maybe she should splurge for a bigger ad, something more noticeable.

"Slow." She laughed. "Adoption is definitely more of a process than I realized, but it'll be so worth it."

"Of course it will, dear," Bee said. "The things we treasure most are the things we've worked the hardest to achieve."

"Very true," Cass agreed. "And there's never a need to apologize about being late, Steph. I appreciate that you make it to every reading."

"I wouldn't miss a single one."

Cass slouched lower in the seat. "If there are any more after tonight."

"Are you kidding me?" Bee leaned forward, clasped his hands on the table, and lowered his voice. "After tonight, you'll probably have standing room only at your next reading. No one will dare miss it."

That could be true. It was always possible people would show up just to see if she'd mess up again. At least then she'd have a chance to prove herself. "I hope you're right."

"Of course I am. I'm always right."

Stephanie pointed a finger at him. "Okay, now you're pushing it."

He shot her a grin. "I was wondering which one of you would call me on it first."

The waitress arrived with their food. "I heard about what happened tonight, Cass. I'm sorry."

Cass leaned back so Elaina could put her plates in front of her. What could she say? "Thank you."

Thankfully, Bee saved her having to say anything more. "So, tell me, how bad is it?"

Elaina shrugged and slid a plate with a burger and a huge pile of fries in front of him. "Mostly people are talking about Emmett and Dirk going at it again."

"What do you mean, again?" Cass had grown up on Bay Island but had left to go to college and had lived in the city for seventeen years, so she wasn't as up-to-date on the regular goings-on as she could be.

"Those two go at it every once in a while. I don't know what started the feud between them, I was too young at the time, but supposedly it had something to do with Emmett's wife."

"That's what I heard too," Bee said. "Though nothing specific. No one seems to know the gritty details."

Elaina set Stephanie's grilled cheese sandwich down, asked if they needed anything else, then excused herself and hurried off.

Bee slid some of his fries over and poured a big puddle of ketchup on his plate.

Cass frowned. "I thought you were eating light tonight."

He lifted his top bun. "Do you see bacon on this burger, hon?"

Nope. No bacon, but the two fat, greasy, fried onion rings adorning the burger weren't part of any diet Cass had ever heard of. "You're out of your mind, Bee."

"So I've been told." He took a big bite, chewed and swallowed. "Now, what was going on with you tonight?"

"I already told you I don't know." She pushed a couple of home fries around her dish with her fork.

"I know." Bee slid the salt and pepper across the table to her and gestured to her plate. "I mean before the reading. Something was bothering you."

With her stomach still in knots, Cass set her fork on her plate. "I don't know what's been bothering me lately. It's like I have a bad feeling in my gut."

Stephanie stopped with her hand partway to her mouth and lowered her sandwich back onto her plate. "Like when the shadows have crossed your vision in the past?"

The few times a shadow had crossed her vision during readings in the past, a death had soon followed. "Not exactly, but something . . . I don't know. It's like a premonition or something. A feeling in my gut. Ever since I woke up this morning, it feels as if . . .

something's trying to get through to me. If I didn't know better, I'd think someone was trying to contact me."

"Hold up." Bee held his hand out in front of him, palm toward her. "You can just stop right there."

Cass paused.

"You mean contact as in . . ." Bee wiggled his fingers. "Woo-woo contact? Because if that's the case, I do not want to hear another word."

Cass couldn't help laughing. For someone who didn't believe in the supernatural, Bee would go ten miles out of his way to avoid it. "I can't make any sense of it, but I do know something is wrong."

And it involves me. Or, at least, it will.

Of that, she was absolutely certain.

Chapter Four

Cass sat in her car at the diner parking lot exit debating which way to go. She should go straight home. At the same time, she really wanted to see Luke. The nagging sense that something was wrong begged her to check on him. She'd just left Bee and Stephanie, and they were fine, and she'd only dropped Beast off at home a little while ago, and he'd been his usually happy self once she'd spent some time soothing him after all the excitement. Of course, he could probably have eaten half the kitchen in less than the hour and a half she'd been gone, but still . . .

Her gut was begging her to swing past the hotel, and she'd gotten very good at trusting her instincts since she'd come back to Bay Island. She'd already left Luke a message, but he might think it was too late to call her back. She'd go by the hotel and see if his car was there. If it was, she could decide whether or not to call him. If she was going to get dumped, she didn't need to wait until morning. She could just get it over with tonight and sleep in.

With that decided, Cass turned up the air-conditioning, flipped the radio to a soft rock station, and headed toward the Bay Side Hotel. She navigated the dark road carefully, enjoying the drive, not in any real hurry since she was too jittery to go home and go to bed. She probably should have declined that cup of coffee after dinner.

Moonlight glinted off the bay, rippling across the surface wherever the thick stand of woods opened up enough to allow a peek. A bright glow lit the night ahead of her, and Cass slowed. She couldn't remember ever noticing the glow from the lighthouse on that end of the island from this section of road. Of course, she didn't often drive that stretch of road at night. But, what else could it be?

The moon wasn't that bright, and she wasn't yet close enough to see the lights from the hotel parking lot, but there wasn't much else around — other than Emmett's garage across the street from the hotel.

As she crept closer to Emmett's shop, pulses of blue and red light streaked the night, dashing all hopes that the light was radiating from any innocent source. She rounded a curve, and his parking lot came into view. Police cars, their lights flashing in a dizzying strobe effect, filled the lot. An ambulance stood idling nearby, its lights off. Fear for Emmett and his teenage son, Joey, sat like a rock in her gut.

Cass pulled off the road and parked on the shoulder. She ripped the keys out of the ignition as she swung her door open and pocketed them as she ran across the street searching frantically for any sign of Emmett or Joey. She weaved between the police cars, all Bay Island had from the look of it, as well as a variety of cars Emmett had lined up throughout the lot—some belonging to customers, a few for sale.

As she rounded the front of the ambulance, she spotted Emmett toward the back of the parking lot, in what would have been a dark corner if the entire place wasn't lit up like Grand Central Station. He stood with Luke and Tank, gesturing wildly.

When Luke caught sight of her hurrying toward them, he frowned then checked his watch and held up a finger for her to wait a minute.

She stopped and leaned against an aging station wagon, her heart hammering painfully.

Three people she couldn't recognize with their backs to her clustered around a sedan with its trunk open, not far from where Luke and Tank were deep in conversation with Emmett. One of the men snapped a few pictures, then squatted down, pointed at something near the back tire, and shot off another series of pictures.

Another of the men leaned into the trunk, but Cass couldn't tell what he was doing, and she couldn't see into the trunk from where she stood.

Emmett's raised voice pulled her attention from the car, the anger in his tone carrying to her across the lot but the words lost somewhere along the way.

She inched closer, searching the area for a familiar face, anyone who might be willing to tell her what was going on.

Emmett ripped off the red baseball cap he always wore and shoved his wild mass of graying hair away from his face. "I already told you! My dogs started barking. I came out to see why. He was out here looking for a fight, but I didn't give him one. If I got arrested, Joey would be left alone, so I turned my back on him and went inside. That's it."

Tank said something Cass couldn't make out, the volume of his voice much lower than Emmett's.

Emmett slammed the hat back on his head, smoothed his hand over his goatee, then propped his hands on his hips and stared straight at Tank. "Why would I have called the cops if I killed him?"

That brought Cass up short. Killed whom? Thoughts of Joey flashed through her mind, but there was no way in the world Emmett would be standing there so calmly if something had happened to his son. While his anger was unmistakable, Emmett showed no signs of grief.

Tank shrugged and mumbled something else too low for Cass to hear.

Giving up on creeping closer discreetly, and tired of waiting for Luke to get around to her, Cass headed toward them.

Emmett shook his head and reeled away from Luke and Tank. When his gaze fell on Cass, his eyes widened, and he pointed toward her, turned back, and said something.

Cass looked over her shoulder to see if someone had come up behind her. Nope. She whirled back toward Emmett in time to see Tank take him by the arm and lead him away.

Luke headed straight for her. When he reached her, he took her elbow and gestured toward a quieter section of the parking lot.

Once Tank and Emmett disappeared around the front of the garage, and with one last glance at the group gathered around the sedan, she fell into step with Luke.

"What is going on? Is Joey all right?"

"Joey's fine. He's not here; he's home." He took a small notepad from his pocket and flipped it open, then stopped and angled it toward one of the many spotlights set up throughout the lot.

Cass's patience was wearing thin. "Is Emmett okay?"

He frowned as he read over something in his book, then flipped through several pages. "I guess that depends on your definition of okay."

"What's that supposed to mean?" She couldn't help snapping. Even though she'd walked onto what was obviously a crime scene, and had no right to demand answers, Emmett was her friend.

Luke looked up from his notepad. "Sorry. I wasn't being sarcastic, just distracted. He's not hurt or anything, if that's what you're asking, but he might be in some trouble."

"Emmett? What could he have done? And what did he mean when he said he wouldn't have called the police if he'd killed him? Killed whom?"

Luke lifted one brow and stared at her.

Her cheeks heated. "Well, I might have overheard . . ."

There wasn't much sense in finishing the statement, since they both knew full well it was a lie. She hadn't overheard anything; she'd been eavesdropping after he'd told her to stay where she was. In about two seconds, she was going to give up on Luke and go find Bee. He'd have answers quick enough.

"Listen, Cass, I'm not trying to be difficult right now. I was actually heading over to see you as soon as I was done talking to Emmett. You saved me the trip by coming out here."

She stayed quiet, not quite sure how to feel about that.

"Can I ask you a favor, though?"

She bit the inside of her cheek and nodded.

"I'm exhausted, and I'm not getting to bed anytime soon. I need to ask you some questions before I can tell you what's going on. Could you just answer them, and then I'll tell you everything?" Dark circles ringed his eyes, and deep lines bracketed his mouth. He wasn't exaggerating; he looked beyond exhausted.

"Sure, no problem."

"First, what are you doing here?"

Despite his support and his fairly regular attendance at her group readings — before tonight, anyway — Luke didn't believe in the supernatural. But as a detective, he would understand following your instincts. Though she'd never lie to him, it probably wouldn't hurt to leave out the thought that someone or something might have influenced her decision to visit him.

"I've been having a weird feeling all day, like something was wrong. I knew Beast, Bee, and Stephanie were okay, but I thought I'd swing by the hotel and see if your car was there." Heat crept up her cheeks, and she had no doubt her chest and face were probably beet red. "I had a rough night, and I thought maybe you were going to call it quits, you know, between us, and I just wanted to get it over with."

Luke's eyes widened. "What made you think that?"

This wasn't the time or place for that discussion, so she just shook her head. "We can talk about that later."

He held her gaze but let it drop. "Why did you have a rough night? What happened at the reading?"

"Pretty much everything went wrong. The air conditioner isn't working, and Emmett couldn't get a part until tomorrow. I managed to embarrass more than one guest, including an investor Bee was hoping to impress. Some guy heckled me all night, then he and Emmett got into an argument, and it got out of hand, and—" She stopped short. "Oh, no."

"Dirk Brinkman? Was he the guy heckling you?"

Unable to force the words out, Cass simply nodded.

"How were things left between him and Emmett?"

"I . . . uh . . . the police came." She shook her head, but the shock wouldn't dissipate. "They talked to Emmett and Dirk, then sent them both home to cool off."

"Did you talk to Emmett before he left?"

"Yeah. Um . . . After the police questioned me, I started cleaning up. Emmett found me after the police left and apologized. I told him there was no need to be sorry, he was just defending me. I thanked him, and he left."

"That's it?"

"He said he'd be back tomorrow to finish fixing the air-conditioning, but that's it. Is Dirk dead?"

Luke flipped his book closed and stuffed it back into his pocket. "How did Emmett seem when he left? Was he still angry, upset, anything?"

Cass shrugged, still trying to wrap her head around whatever was going on. "He seemed . . . I don't know . . . embarrassed, I guess. Contrite. Sorry he'd let Dirk get the better of him. He wasn't in any kind of homicidal rage, if that's what you're thinking."

"Look, Cass, I really need to speak to as many people as I can before the details of Dirk's murder get out."

"You can't possibly think Emmett killed Dirk? Or anyone, for that matter."

"It's not that I think he killed him. As far as I'm concerned, he's innocent until proven guilty, but if I'm being honest, it doesn't look good. Dirk didn't climb into the trunk of a car in Emmett's lot and beat himself to death."

"There's no way Emmett would e—"

"Stop, Cass." Luke held up a hand. "You don't have to argue for him. I know he's your friend, but I have to look at everything, and the more people I can speak to before their memories get clouded by public opinion, the better it will be. Especially for Emmett."

She nodded. That made sense.

He cradled her cheek and tilted her face toward him. "I guess you already know I'm not going to be able to make our breakfast date?"

"I kind of figured." At that point, all that mattered was clearing Emmett's name.

"Maybe we can get dinner tonight?"

"Sure." Though she wasn't optimistic. He'd already had a full case load, even without the added pressure of a murder investigation, and all of those investigations had to take priority over soothing any insecurities she might harbor. "I'll see you later, maybe. And don't worry, I completely understand."

"For the record . . ." Luke took her shoulders and looked her in the eye. "I was not planning on breaking up with you."

A smile tugged at her, despite the dire circumstances.

"I . . . uh . . . uh . . . I have very strong feelings for you, Cass. If you are willing to be patient with me while I adjust to my new responsibilities, I'd like to see if things can work between us."

When he put it like that . . . "I'd like that."

Luke kissed her cheek, then lingered beside her ear and laid on the thick Southern drawl as he whispered, "I'll see y'all later then."

Cass left him to his work, but she could feel his gaze lingering while she walked to her car and climbed in. She checked the backseat—there was still a killer lurking around somewhere, after all, and despite what anyone thought, it wasn't Emmett—then she waved as she locked the door and pulled away.

She checked the clock on the dashboard. At a little past one in the morning, chances were good Bee was already tucked away in the back room of his shop creating something magical. Since he tended to ignore his phone when he was "in the zone," she'd probably get a reprieve until morning before he subjected her to the third degree. Hopefully, Luke could interview everyone he needed to before then, because once Bee got wind of a murder on Bay Island, the rumor mill would be working double time.

Chapter Five

Cass's imagined reprieve came screeching to a halt as she rounded the last curve before her house and found Bee's black Trans Am idling in her driveway. So much for "the zone." Of course, he could have had trouble working and just stopped by to chat. It wouldn't be the first time he'd done that.

She pulled in and waved as she passed him and followed the driveway around the side of the house to park.

Bee was already standing beside her door by the time she turned off the ignition. So much for hoping he hadn't heard.

Bee yanked the door open. "Where have you been? I've been waiting here half the night."

"What are you talking about, Bee?" She grabbed her purse and her house key as she climbed out of the car. "I only left you like an hour ago."

"Well, it feels like half the night when you're waiting for someone." He stepped back to give her room to shut the door, then fell into step beside her.

"Why didn't you just call my cell phone?"

He ignored the question but stayed glued to her side as she hurried around the back.

She double-checked the gate was closed behind her so she could let Beast out, jogged up the steps to the deck, then unlocked the back door. Once Beast heard the car pull in, the race was on. If he got too excited before she could get him out, she'd be mopping the floor. "And why didn't you just go into the house and wait?"

She barely had the door cracked open before Beast wiggled through and launched himself at her. The giant Leonberger's front paws landed against her shoulders.

Bee caught her as she staggered back. "That's reason number one."

"I know, Beast. I missed you too." Cass tried to pry the big dog off her. "You have to get down now, though. You're supposed to greet me calmly. Remember?"

Bee laughed. "Like that's ever going to happen."

She ignored him. For some reason, Beast behaved much better

for Bee, though he'd still bowled him over a time or two. "Want a cookie, boy?"

Beast dropped down and wagged his whole back end.

"Go potty, and I'll get you a cookie."

Beast ran off to do his thing, and Bee followed Cass into the house.

"What's the second reason?" She hung her keys on the hook by the door, dropped her bag onto the table, and rummaged through the pantry for Beast's snacks.

"Second reason what?" Keeping a wary eye on the back door, Bee pulled a chair out from the table and sat.

Aha. There they are. For a minute, she'd thought she was out of treats. "You said Beast was the first reason you didn't come in to wait, that implies there was a second reason."

"What you said earlier at the diner, about thinking someone was trying to contact you." Twin red patches flared on Bee's cheeks. "Wouldn't want that someone to think it was you coming through the door and make an appearance."

Laughter bubbled out before Cass could censor it.

"Whatever," Bee mumbled.

"I'm sorry, Bee. You just make me happy is all." She leaned over and kissed his cheek before opening the back door to let Beast back in. A quick survey of the kitchen told her Beast hadn't eaten anything. Or, at least if he did, he'd disposed of all the evidence.

"You were a good boy while I was gone, weren't you?" Cass ruffled Beast's mane. "Sit."

Beast plopped right down.

She gave him his treat, and he bounced off to sit beside Bee and chow down. Maybe there was something to this training stuff after all.

"So, to what do I owe the pleasure of your company in the middle of the night?"

Bee pinned her with a glare.

Maybe she could just play dumb. "Do you want coffee or something?"

"No, thanks. I already had two cups—one of them yours, by the way—and a couple of donuts while I was waiting. Are you going to tell me what's going on? Where have you been for the past hour?"

She tried a grin and fluttered her lashes. "Maybe I was visiting Luke."

"Mm-hmm . . ." Bee crossed one leg over the other, hooked his elbow over the chair back, and struck a pose that could rival any Hollywood diva. "From what I hear . . ."

Uh-oh.

"That's exactly where you were. Now spill it, girl, and I want all the juicy details."

"Luke asked me not to say anything." She took a Diet Pepsi out of the fridge, popped the top of the can, and poured it into a glass. She definitely didn't need the caffeine at that time of night, but she had a feeling she wouldn't be sleeping anytime soon, anyway.

"Uh-huh." Bee's eyes narrowed. "And I'm sure he meant don't say anything to anyone else besides me."

Cass choked. She was quite sure Bee was exactly whom Luke had meant by "anyone."

"Very funny." Bee stood and patted her back, a bit harder than necessary. "Now, are you going to give me the dirt, or am I going to have to wait until the deli opens?"

"Ugh . . ." They both knew if Bee had to wait, he would make the next few hours torture for her. "Fine. I'll tell you, but you're not leaving my sight until morning when the news leaks out some other way."

"Yeah, whatever." He waved her off. "I can think of worse ways to spend the night."

"All right, but let's take a walk." She grabbed Beast's leash but didn't bother hooking it to his collar. If it wasn't the middle of tourist season, she wouldn't have even bothered bringing it, but this time of year, you never knew whom you might run into walking along the beach, even at one in the morning. "I can't sit still right now."

Her nerves were strung tight, and even though she'd offered a token protest, truth, she wanted to talk to Bee. Bee knew Emmett as well as she did. He'd know Emmett wouldn't harm anyone. And she needed someone to talk to who would support her faith in Emmett's innocence. "How'd you find out so fast, anyway? I thought you'd be at the shop until morning."

"Pul-eaze, girl . . ." He walked bedside her along the shoreline, just out of reach of the gently lapping waves. "My phone literally blew up a few minutes after I walked into the shop. I never even made it into the back room."

"Let me guess, Emma Nicholls?" Emma worked at the deli and was Bee's closest rival in the gossip department. Since the deli's owner, Rick, was also a volunteer EMT, Emma got info pretty quickly, though not usually as quickly as Bee.

Bee laughed. "She was the first."

"Yeah, I figured." Cass stretched her back and kept an eye on Beast as he bounded down the beach, thrilled to have room to run. "Tell me what you know."

"Just that a body was found."

"It was Dirk Brinkman."

Bee gasped and pressed a hand against his chest. "Are you kidding me?"

"I wish I were." She tried to collect her thoughts. No matter how many times she tried to envision it, she just couldn't see Emmett killing anyone. "He was found in the trunk of a car at Emmett's garage."

Bee stopped walking and turned to face her. "They can't possibly think . . ."

"I don't really know what they think. Luke assured me he was considering Emmett innocent for now, but I just don't know." She warred with the question she wouldn't have dared ask anyone else, then lowered her gaze to the sand and spoke quietly, "You don't think he could have done it, do you, Bee?"

"No." He propped a finger beneath her chin and lifted it until her gaze met his. "Absolutely not, Cass. He didn't do it."

He spoke with the same conviction she'd used while speaking to Luke. Too much conviction, as if trying to convince himself as much as her.

"You said yourself he and Dirk had some kind of falling out in the past, then what went on in the shop during the reading. You don't think he could have just snapped?" A chill raced up her spine, and she shivered, despite the stifling heat.

Bee pulled her close and hugged her. "No. I don't. Emmett doesn't have it in him to kill, Cass. When you look into someone's eyes, you see that."

"He was pretty angry tonight. I've never seen him like that." She pulled back so she could watch his expression for his reaction.

"But he never seemed out of control. Just ticked off." He huffed out a breath, then said softly, "I think Luke could kill someone if he had to in order to save a life. And Tank probably could. But I don't see that same determination, that same . . . hardness, in Emmett's eyes. I just don't. Maybe, if left with no other alternative, he could kill to protect Joey, but I don't even think he could kill to protect himself, Cass. I honestly don't."

"Thanks, Bee." He always seemed to know exactly what she needed to hear. She hugged him tightly, then hooked her arm through his and started walking toward Beast, who'd stopped to sniff at something along the shoreline down the beach. "So, tell me, what else did Emma and whomever else you spoke to have to say?"

Bee winced and stared out over the bay. He was too sensitive to just blurt out whatever was being said. He'd censor it enough to try to spare her feelings, but his hesitation said it all.

Clouds had started to gather, blocking some of the moonlight, but she could see his pained expression well enough. She didn't push him, just waited, watching the clouds drift across the moon. Maybe it would rain and cool things off a bit. That's what they needed, a good thunderstorm to suit her current mood.

He bent and picked up a rock, smoothed his fingers over the flat surface, then let it fly. It skipped four times, rippling what moonlight still reflected off the water's surface, before sinking. "Emma said Ellie's not doing well."

It took a second for Cass to refocus. She'd been expecting to hear rumors about her failed reading. "Ellie Callahan?"

"Yeah."

"But she was doing so much better after Jay disappeared."

Bee shrugged and looked down the beach toward Beast. "Emma said she ran into her at the library, and Ellie was huddled in the far corner engrossed in something on the computer, but when Emma stopped to say hello, she minimized the screen before Emma could see what she was looking at."

No surprise there. Everyone knew better than to let Emma know anything you didn't want shared with all of Bay Island.

"She said Ellie's hair is back to its former mousy brown, stringy, like she hadn't washed it in a couple of days. She's lost weight, got dark circles around her eyes . . ."

"The last time I saw her, she looked great. She'd added highlights to her hair, gained a few pounds, didn't have that stressed look about her that she'd always had before." Cass was going to have to give her a call. She'd fallen out of touch with her recently but hadn't thought much of it. Summer was a busy time for Bay Island's full-time residents. "What do you think is wrong?"

"I don't know. I hope she hasn't gotten mixed up with another abusive man."

"Yeah." Calling Ellie shot to the top of her to-do list. "Me too."

Bee narrowed his eyes as he stared down the beach. "What is he into down there?"

Her gaze shot to Beast. "I don't know. He's been playing there for a while now."

"Well, unless he's chewing something up, his attention span is not that long."

"You're right." She started toward him and yelled, "Beast. Come."

Beast looked up at the sound of his name, then want back to whatever he was doing, which as they got closer appeared to be digging. "Uh-oh."

"Yeah, no kidding." Bee picked up the pace. "Remember what happened last time he was that intent on digging something up on the beach."

"Beast. I said come." They already had one body to deal with. She patted her jeans pocket. How could she have forgotten to bring treats? "Now."

He ignored her and kept digging. Oh, well, at least he didn't run away. Maybe he was starting to listen better.

She crept closer, careful not to spook him and make him run. The instant she was close enough, she hooked the leash to his collar. Feeling triumphant, she turned to Bee. "See, he's starting to listen better."

"I guess." Bee bent over to see what Beast was digging up, then gagged and lurched back. He pulled his shirt collar up to cover his nose. "Ugh . . . what is that smell?"

The odor hit Cass like a ton of bricks, and she staggered back, almost dropping the leash in whatever mess Beast had uncovered. "Smells like rotten fish."

"Someone must have buried it there."

"Why would anyone do that?"

"Who knows? Maybe they buried the remnants after they cleaned their catches, or maybe they buried their bait. All I know is, it's better than what he dug up last time, and that monster needs a bath." Bee allowed his gaze to linger on Beast too long.

Beast took it as an invitation to play and started bouncing around, jumping first toward Bee then the opposite way.

Bee staggered one way then the other in a desperate dance to avoid getting covered in whatever coated Beast's muzzle.

Cass held the leash in a death grip, trying not to laugh, until Beast turned on her. He nuzzled her leg and looked up at her, his big brown eyes filled with innocence. She didn't have the heart not to pet him, so she laid a tentative hand on his head and scratched. "Come on, boy. You need a bath."

Bee's laughter echoed down the empty beach. "You can't be serious."

"What?" Cass had half a mind to let go of the leash. "The groomer doesn't open for hours yet, and there's no guarantee they'll have room for him."

"I'm pretty sure they keep an appointment slot open for you every day, just in case."

"Ha-ha." She glared at him and let the leash slip a little.

Bee stopped short. "You wouldn't dare."

He was right. As much as she'd like to, she'd never do that to Bee. He might be enjoying her misery at the moment, but he'd been there for her enough times to earn him that. "You're right. I wouldn't. But keep it up and I might change my mind."

They resumed their trek back to the house, with Beast at Cass's side as far from Bee as she could keep him. The combination of the night's events, too much coffee and diet soda, and Beast's stench turned her stomach. She couldn't very well bring him to Mystical Musings smelling like that, even if she didn't have any customers left. "Did Emma say anything about the fiasco at the reading?"

"Not too much, and I did feel her out. I told you people would forget all about your blunder as soon as the next good gossip hit.

And what better gossip than a body turning up, especially since that body was fighting with someone in your shop a few hours earlier."

She glanced at him from the corner of her eye.

He held up one finger. "No, for the record, I did not kill Dirk to salvage your reputation. And if I find my name on any kind of suspect list, I'll ruin your reputation myself."

"Oh, come on, Bee. It was one mistake I've apologized for a hundred times."

"And will have to apologize for a hundred more. At least." He nudged her arm and grinned. "Good thing being so forgiving is on my never-ending list of good qualities, huh?"

Chapter Six

Cass tried to hold her breath to stave off the smell as she pulled Beast closer to her side and quickly crossed the kitchen. She was going to need a shower anyway, and keeping him close was better than letting him spread the mess all over the house.

Bee followed a safe distance behind.

She shot a look over her shoulder. "Don't you have work to do or something?"

"And miss this?" he scoffed. "Not a chance. Besides, you made me promise I'd stay with you 'til morning if you told me what went on at Emmett's, remember?"

Great. Just what she needed, an audience. "I don't see what the big deal is. Nicole always says he's good when she grooms him."

He laughed out loud. "That's because Nicole knows what she's doing, but you, my dear, don't have the first clue."

She led Beast to the bathroom. Thankfully, his nose only nudged the hallway wall once. She could clean that later. She'd have to vacuum and mop, anyway, after she scrubbed the bathroom, since she hadn't bothered to brush any of the sand off their feet, but it could have been worse. She guided Beast into the bathroom and scowled at Bee when he stopped in the doorway. "If you're going to stand there, why don't you at least make yourself useful and turn on the tub."

He eyed Beast warily. "You'll hold on to him?"

She smirked but gripped Beast's collar.

With one eye on Cass, Bee reached in and turned the water on full force.

Beast jerked back, jumped up, and practically crawled into Cass's arms.

"It's okay, Beast," she soothed. "It's only the bathtub. Just like at the groomer."

Bee leaned over and adjusted the water, but his shaking shoulders gave his laughter away. Once he was satisfied with the water temperature, he unhooked the handheld showerhead and let it hang so she could reach it easily, then bowed, gestured toward the tub, and retreated to the doorway. "Have at it."

Used to his theatrics, she ignored him and concentrated on calming Beast, who was still cowering against her. "You've lain on the bathroom floor while I showered a million times. How do you even know this time is different?"

He stared at her with those soulful eyes, and she wished she didn't have to disappoint him. Then he snuggled closer, and she got a good whiff of dead fish. "I'm sorry, Beast, but you have to get washed."

Bee rested his forearms against either side of the doorjamb and crossed one leg over the other, settling in for what promised to be a good show.

Smart aleck.

"Come on, boy, let's get this over with so I can shower and get a couple hours of sleep before I have to open the shop." With a firm grip on his collar, Cass started leading him toward the tub.

Beast sat.

Keeping her gaze pointedly focused on anything but Bee, Cass slid around behind him, still holding his collar, and tried to push him across the floor to the tub.

He didn't budge.

Bee snickered.

How hard could it be to move this animal? The floor was tile; he should slide right across the lousy three feet it would take to get him to the tub. Cass put one foot on Beast's behind and a hand on his back and tried to slide him across the floor. When that didn't move him, she put her hip into it, releasing his collar for just an instant to get a better grip.

Beast bolted for the door.

Bee's squeal could probably be heard from town as he jumped back and tried to dance out of Beast's path. He hit the opposite wall of the hallway hard, bounced off, and crashed straight into Beast, who was trying desperately to escape.

Beast rebounded off Bee, twisted himself around, and aimed for the door again.

"Okay, Beast, that's it." Thankfully, Cass was able to grab Beast's collar before he made it all the way through the doorway. She coaxed him around Bee toward the tub. "No more Mr. Nice Guy. You are going in that tub and getting a bath."

Bee stood in the middle of the bathroom, arms out to the side, mouth and eyes open wide, staring down at his shirt.

"Oh, Bee, relax. There's not even anything on your shirt."

"Maybe not, but I can smell fish from here."

Ha! Not laughing now, are you, buddy? "I'm sure whatever was on him is already dry. You just imagine you smell it, or you smell it because the whole bathroom stinks."

He lifted his shirt and took a tentative sniff. "Hmm . . . I guess you might be right."

Cass snatched a rubber chew toy from a small basket in the corner and tossed it into the tub.

Beast dove in after it.

Before he could change his mind, Cass grabbed the showerhead and wet him down, rubbing her free hand over his back, trying to soothe him while soaking the water into his thick fur. "See, boy, that's not so bad, is it?"

Beast shook his whole body, spraying water everywhere.

She sighed, having already resigned herself to scrubbing the bathroom before she could sleep. "Bee, squirt some shampoo on his back. Quick, while he's staying still."

Without a word, Bee complied.

She lathered him up, making sure to get the suds all the way to his skin, especially through his thick mane.

He tried to lick the suds.

"No, Beast." She nudged his mouth away from the soapy water circling around the drain. The last thing she needed was him throwing up that mess. Once he was fully lathered from head to toe, she glanced over her shoulder at Bee. "You can either come hold his collar while I rinse all the soap off or run the risk of him escaping when I let him go. Your choice."

He muttered something about this not being as fun as he'd expected, then tentatively gripped Beast's collar between his thumb and forefinger. "Hurry up, because that's the best you're gonna get."

Beast licked his arm.

"Ugh . . . Can you brush his teeth or something?"

"Now you're pushing it." But she was going to have to do something. The bath was actually going smoother than she'd expected, so maybe she could get his teeth brushed too. Nicole managed all the time.

"It's Raining Men" blared from Bee's pocket.

"Don't you dare let go. I'm almost done."

He reached across his body, using his left hand to fish his phone from his back right pocket. "Hmm . . . that's weird. Hello?"

Cass looked Beast over, rinsing the last of the soap from underneath him, making sure she got it all off. No way was she going through this again. And next time she took him to the groomer, Nicole was getting a massive tip.

"Uh . . . yeah. I'm just helping Cass give Beast a bath . . . Don't ask."

There was no mistaking the deep, rich laughter she could hear from the other end of the line. But why would Luke be calling Bee? Even though they'd become friendly, she didn't think they regularly chatted on the phone in the middle of the night. Maybe he was trying to reach her. Where had she left her cell phone? Probably in her bag in the kitchen. She took Beast's collar from Bee and whispered, "Could you grab a towel, please?"

Bee nodded, retreated to the hallway linen closet, and returned with a towel. He handed it to her while still listening to whatever Luke was saying.

Hoping to keep the water damage to a minimum, she threw the towel over Beast's back before helping him out of the tub. Then she scrubbed him as dry as she could. The instant she took the towel off, he shook himself again, and water sprayed everywhere. Apparently, she hadn't gotten him as dry as she'd thought.

"Uh-huh. Okay. I'll be there." Bee disconnected the call and stood staring at his phone.

"Is something wrong?" Cass scraped the wet dog hair off her arms and untangled it from between her fingers, then dropped it into the garbage pail and washed her hands. As much as she dreaded the thought, she was going to have to get the hair dryer out and try to do something with Beast's sopping wet fur.

"Luke wants to talk to me." Bee frowned.

"Okay, so why do you look like you're about to be handed over to the executioner? I thought you liked Luke."

"Oh, don't get me wrong, I do. As a friend." He stuffed the

phone back into his pocket and went to the sink to wash his hands.

Beast used their momentary distraction to make his escape. He bolted through the doorway, skidded on the hallway floor, scrambled to right himself, and barreled toward the kitchen.

"Then what's the problem?" So much for drying him. At least now he was clean, and she already had to vacuum and mop so, really, what was the difference? Not like he'd be cold, considering their current heat wave and the fact Mystical Musings still had no air-conditioning. But she was going to have to give him a good brushing. If she didn't get to it before she left, she could always take him out on the deck at the shop and brush him.

"He doesn't want to talk to me as a friend; he wants to talk to me in an official capacity, as a detective." Bee swallowed hard.

Even though Bee was prone to theatrics, this was different. Talking to the police wasn't easy for Bee. "It'll be fine, Bee. Do you want me to come with you?"

He shook his head. "Thanks, but he told me to come alone."

"Oh." A roller coaster of emotions rocketed through her, then settled. Luke had already told her he needed to question everyone involved, and Bee had been there the night before. "Don't worry about it. He said he had to question as many people who attended the reading as possible before morning. He knows you're usually up at night, so he probably just wants to get your opinion on what happened."

He offered a shaky smile and kissed her cheek. "I'm sure you're right. Anyway, I have to meet him at Emmett's garage, so I'll see you later."

"Yeah . . . see you later." She watched him go, then looked over the bathroom. Water pooled in big puddles all over the floor, splatter marks covered, well, pretty much everything, and loads of dog hair and dirt covered the tub, clogged the drain, and carpeted the floor. It was going to be a long night, especially until she heard back from Bee.

• • •

By the time she'd finished cleaning the house and showering, there hadn't been much sense in going to bed. Between the fiasco at her reading, the situation at Emmett's, and Bee's nerves about being questioned by Luke, she wouldn't have been able to sleep anyway.

With a couple of hours before she had to go into Mystical Musings, she left Beast sleeping, apparently exhausted from his bathing ordeal, and headed out. If she wasn't mistaken, Ellie usually worked the early shift at the antique shop just outside of town. If she could catch her before they opened, she might be able to talk to her for a few minutes and at least make sure she was okay.

Leaving the boardwalk, quaint shops, and residential areas behind, Cass headed toward the center of Bay Island. Farmhouses nestled amid patchwork quilt fields, and early morning mist hovered over everything. Despite the early hour, farmers had already begun their work, and she crept along the narrow road behind a tractor taking up too much room for her to pass.

She was in no hurry, though, enjoying the scenic view and the change of pace from the hustle and bustle of tourist season in a beach community. She needed time to figure out what to say to Ellie, anyway. She certainly didn't want to admit there had been speculation she'd taken up with another loser.

The tractor turned onto a narrow dirt road, removing any excuse for procrastinating. She rounded a curve, and a line of statues announced she'd arrived. Several life-size cows painted in a variety of colors and patterns lined the road in front of the shop. What anyone would do with a life-size cow covered in a map of Bay Island or blue and black stripes, she had no idea.

At least the dinosaur statues looked real or, at least, how Cass imagined they'd have looked—reptilian, painted in greens and browns, not birdlike with bright colors as some people now theorized. But who knew?

She parked in the small dirt lot and approached the two-story Victorian that housed Auntie V's Closet. Now, if she could just figure out how to get Ellie to confide in her and how best to help her out of whatever mess she might have gotten herself into.

"Cass?"

She barely focused in time to keep from running smack into Ellie. "Oh, Ellie, I'm sorry. I must have been more caught up in my thoughts than I realized. I didn't even see you there."

"No worries." Ellie stood from beside the porch where she was bent over a large barrel filled with potting soil and brushed the dirt off her hands. "Is there something I can help you with?"

Bee wasn't exaggerating about Ellie looking bad. If anything, she looked worse than he'd said. Her cheeks had become sunken, and dark shadows lingered beneath her eyes. Her hair had returned to its natural mousy brown and hung in limp strands over the front of her shoulders and covered her eyes. Even her posture had returned to its former please-don't-notice-me slump.

"Are you okay, Ellie?"

She peered out from beneath her long bangs. "I'm fine, thanks."

When was the last time she'd seen Ellie? She couldn't recall offhand, but not more than a month ago. She'd definitely seen her since the weather had turned warmer. How could so much have changed so quickly? "I . . . um . . . what's that you're doing?"

"We had a barrel of potting soil left over after we did our planting for the season, and we've had this adorable antique tricycle with the little basket in the front hanging around for quite some time . . . Here, let me show you." She looked around then climbed the few steps to the porch and gestured toward a rusted tricycle sitting on a stand beside a stack of paintings partially covered with a canvas. "So, I figured I'd plant some impatiens in the basket and try to sell it as a planter."

"That's such a cute idea." Ellie had found her calling working in the antique shop. The work suited her, and she'd discovered a talent for recycling old things. Cass spun the trike's front wheel. Despite a small squeak, it seemed to be in perfect working order. "You really love what you're doing, don't you?"

She smiled. "I really do."

"I'm happy for you." How could she possibly approach the subject of what was bothering her when she seemed so content?

"So, what can I help you with this morning? Surely you didn't drive all the way out here to discuss my well-being."

Actually, that's exactly what she'd done. "I was thinking of putting a few more rocking chairs out on the porch at Mystical Musings. And maybe a couple of those barrels with the checkerboards on top, you know? So people could sit outside and have something to do while they waited."

Ellie's brow furrowed. "We have a rocking chair or two, but I know we don't have any of the checkerboard tables." She grabbed the rim of the barrel she'd been taking soil from. "Unless you want to take this and maybe have Emmett make a checkerboard for the top."

Since she didn't bat an eye at the mention of Emmett's name, Cass could only assume she hadn't heard what happened. Not surprising, since Ellie generally kept to herself. "That's a good idea. I'll have to talk to him about it when I see him."

"If you want, I can pull out whatever chairs I think you'll like once we open and have Willie drive them over later on today."

"That'd be perfect, thanks, Ellie."

"If I find any more barrels, I'll throw them in the back of the truck too."

"Great, thank you. Just send him with a bill, and I'll pay cash."

"No problem." She pushed her hair back behind her ear, leaving a dirt smudge across her cheek.

"How's everything else going?"

She narrowed her eyes. "What do you mean?"

So much for being discreet. "Oh, I don't know. You seem happy with your career choice, so I just wondered how things are going in your personal life."

"Fine." She carried the small bucket she'd filled with dirt onto the porch, then glanced around, suspicion darkening her eyes.

"Do you want to come in for a reading later?" Ellie wasn't one to open up about what was going on in her life, but if Cass could get her into the shop for a reading, she might be able to figure out what was wrong.

Ellie swallowed hard and looked over her shoulder, then down the road, before settling her gaze on Cass's feet. "That's okay. Thank you, but I'm fine."

"You know if you change your mind, you can just come in, right? Anytime."

She shrugged and used the small gardening shovel to fill the tricycle's basket with soil, her attention fully focused on the task. "Sure, thanks."

"I mean it, Ellie." No matter how hard Cass tried to make eye contact, Ellie's gaze lingered on the basket. "I'll always make time for you."

Ellie finally looked up and focused on something over Cass's shoulder. "I know, Cass, and I appreciate it. I have to get this done now, though. It's almost time to open. It was good seeing you."

"You too, Ellie. Thanks." With no idea what else she could say to her, Cass turned and walked to her car. Before climbing in, she stopped and watched Ellie work.

Every couple of seconds, Ellie lifted her head long enough to look around, then returned her full focus to the ground in front of her. She hadn't acted like that since her domineering mother had been killed. Or since her abusive ex-husband had fled Bay Island to avoid prosecution and disappear . . . ed . . . Oh, no. The thought Jay Callahan might have resurfaced and contacted Ellie sent a skitter of sheer terror up her spine.

But what were the chances? Jay knew he'd be arrested the moment he showed his face anywhere on Bay Island. He could have called Ellie. But would a phone call warrant such a drastic change in the woman's behavior and appearance, make her fully revert to her former self? Maybe. Cass just hoped Ellie hadn't gotten involved with someone new. When you were as used to submitting to someone as completely as Ellie had to her mother and then Jay, it was a difficult cycle to break.

Cass made a mental note to get in touch with her and push to find out what was going on.

Her phone rang, and she checked the caller ID. "Hey, Bee, what's going on?"

"Can you meet me at the deli?"

"Sure thing." She climbed into the car. "I'm on my way. Did everything go okay with Luke?"

"I'll tell you when you get here."

Chapter Seven

Cass circled the block for the third time, then crept past the deli, hoping a parking spot would open up. None did.

Sunlight glinted off the hood of Bee's Trans Am where it was parked against the curb directly out front, almost like it was mocking her. She wondered how long he'd had to wait for such a prime spot.

Who was she kidding? Bee was not only the king of gossip, he'd been questioned by the police regarding the murder. Heck, Emma had probably stood out front holding the spot open for him.

She'd try one more time. Surely someone had gotten their breakfast and was ready to leave. She rounded the corner again, passing several people walking along the sidewalk toward the deli. Apparently they'd given up on getting a close parking spot. The cool air blowing full force on her face from the vents burned her eyes. If there was nowhere to park this time, she'd have to give up and walk. If she didn't get a dose of caffeine soon, she ran the risk of falling over.

Still no open spots.

With no hope of getting closer, Cass drove three blocks down and parked. The walk would do her good, anyway, maybe wake her up a little.

She locked the car and started toward the deli. Despite her eagerness to find out how things had gone with Luke and Tank, since Bee had refused to share any of the details over the phone, she took her time strolling down the block. Already the sun beat down on her. It would be another hot, still day on Bay Island. If this heat wave didn't break soon, she was going to have to give in and call a repairman for the air conditioner, though even the thought brought a wave of anxiety. Emmett had handled Cass's repairs since she'd opened the shop. How could she call in someone else? Especially after he'd stuck up for her the night before.

The closer she got to the gossip hot spot, the more she regretted letting Bee talk her into meeting him there. Despite having a new topic to draw attention from her blunder the night before, that dirt was still new enough to earn some gossip time, especially since it was somehow connected to the murder at Emmett's.

Then again, it was the middle of the summer tourist season, and the deli would be packed at that time of the morning regardless of whether or not there was good gossip. Locals were heading off to work, and tourists often grabbed breakfast before heading to the beaches or to browse the boardwalk shops or to ascend one of Bay Island's lighthouses.

She only hesitated a moment before bracing herself and walking in. To say the place was packed would be an understatement. People were crammed in everywhere, forcing her to turn sideways and finagle her way through to try to find Bee. She couldn't even get to the small area that held a few tables for dining, never mind sit down and eat.

Murmurs followed her as she passed, the undercurrent sizzling like a live wire as she moved deeper through the crowd. Stares weighed heavily. A headache started at her temples, pounding a steady rhythm through her brain.

A woman she didn't recognize leaned closer to the man she was with and whispered something in his ear, all the while staring directly at Cass. The man's gaze shot to her as well, then lingered as Cass passed.

A few people said hello, but more than a few either studied her openly or turned away when her gaze met theirs. Heat blazed in her cheeks.

Crossing the small shop seemed to take forever before she finally found Bee holding court beside the coffee counter, the crowd gathered around him hanging on his every word. When he spotted her, he held up a finger for her to wait and pointed toward the kitchen doorway behind the counter, indicating he'd already ordered their breakfast. Thankful she didn't have to wait on the line that wound through most of the shop, she found a quiet corner beside the front door and leaned against the wall, willing herself invisible.

At least they'd be out of there soon. As much as Bee loved being the center of attention and trading good dirt, he wouldn't try to eat in the middle of that crowd. When he sat down to a meal, he wanted peace. So much so that he'd bribed the four Talbot boys to behave more than once so he could eat his meal without them acting up in the diner. He considered it four dollars well spent.

Cass's vision blurred. She rubbed her eyes. For just a minute, she entertained the idea of closing Mystical Musings for the day. If her welcome in the deli was any indication, she doubted she'd have any customers anyway, and she really needed some sleep.

She tried to listen to what people were talking about, but her mind drifted in a fog of confusion. Sleep deprivation?

"Help him." The words came to her softly, barely loud enough to hear.

She jerked away from the wall and looked around. Everything was the same as it had been a moment ago. She didn't even think the line had moved. She shook her head and tried to dispel the fog. Had she dozed off?

"He needs you." A woman's voice, soft, melodic.

Cass sagged back against the wall and closed her eyes. She tried to focus on where the sound had come from. As terrified as she was, she tried to clear her mind and open herself.

Until recently, she'd always thought her "psychic" skills were a combination of good instincts and years of psychiatric training. But that wouldn't explain how she'd been able to "read" people so accurately as a teenager, before she'd received any of that training, when she'd spent her summers on the beach, swimming, sunbathing, playing volleyball, and "reading" tourists. And she'd been accurate, very accurate.

It hadn't scared her then. She'd simply open herself and things would come to her, information she shouldn't have any knowledge of but somehow did. That had been before she'd left Bay Island, before she'd gone to school, before she'd met and married Donald Larson, before . . . her world had crumbled.

She opened her eyes and shook off the haze. It was no use. Her mind was too closed, too chaotic. Whatever, or whoever, was trying to contact her wouldn't be able to get through.

"Well, well . . ." A man she didn't recognize had started to walk out, then stopped short when he'd spotted her. "If it isn't Cassandra Donovan."

Cass shivered, not because she recognized him, but because she didn't. No one had called her Cassandra since she was a kid, which meant he knew her from way back, and if his stone-cold expression was any indication, he wasn't a fan. "I'm sorry. Do I know you?"

"Why am I not surprised?" His paunchy features twisted into a sneer. "What kind of woman doesn't even remember the man whose life she ruined?"

Her heart rate kicked up, and she straightened from the wall. What was he talking about? She tried to imagine what he'd look like younger, slimmer, with a full head of hair rather than the thinning combover he currently sported.

"Don't worry." He leaned closer and pitched his voice low. "I'll give you time to figure it out for yourself before I return the favor."

"Is there a problem here?" A big hand landed on the stranger's shoulder.

He whirled around straight into Bee's solid chest, then jerked back. His head moved down as he took in the more than six feet of red-faced, well-built Bee, paused when he reached the platform shoes Bee always wore with his skinny jeans, then inched back up until he faced him. "Nope. No problem."

Bee stepped back and gestured toward the door.

"Not yet, anyway," he mumbled as he nudged Bee with his shoulder on his way by.

When Bee started to turn, Cass grabbed his arm. "It's okay, Bee, but thank you."

Bee looked after him but, thankfully, let it go. "What's his deal, anyway?"

Cass shook her head, no closer to remembering who the man was than when he'd first confronted her. "I have no idea, but I have a strong feeling I should figure it out sooner rather than later."

"Define feeling." Bee looked out the window in the direction the man had gone. "Like a gut instinct or an 'I should go find myself a cross and some garlic' feeling?"

The tension eased out of her and she laughed. "Just a feeling, Bee. And for the record, crosses and garlic fend off vampires, not ghosts."

"Yeah, well, you can never be too careful." He picked up his bag and a cup holder with three coffee cups from the wide front window ledge. "We can leave your car here if you want, and I'll drop you off to get it later."

She nodded. She probably shouldn't drive. If whatever had happened to her before happened again while she was driving, she might lose control. And if whatever it was came back, she wanted to be able to open herself completely. Or at least try.

"Hey." Bee frowned. "You okay?"

"I'm fine." She pulled the door open for him, then followed him out.

He hit the button to unlock the door, then stopped beside the car and studied her. "Are you sure he didn't do anything to you?"

"I'm sure."

"You look a little pale." Like Beast with a bone, Bee was not going to let this go.

"I'm fine, Bee. I just . . . something happened in there . . . and I need some time to wrap my head around it. I'll explain while we eat." She reached for the door handle.

The door locks popped back down. Bee stood, lower lip caught between his teeth, staring at her.

She lowered her hand. "What's wrong?"

"Give me your keys." He tucked the paper bag beneath is arm, stuffed his keys back into his pocket, and held out a hand.

"What?" She didn't need this right now.

"I said, give me your keys." He didn't budge.

"But I'm parked three blocks down."

"It's a nice day for a walk, and dieting is turning out to be harder than expected, so I need the exercise." Patting his flat belly, Bee studied her, his eyes filled with hope.

She pinned him with a glare. "Bee . . ."

"Oh, all right, fine. Last time I took you to the cemetery, my baby's engine was wonky for months. And now you're acting all weird and voodoo-y, and I don't want anything . . ." He looked around her, as if searching for a spirit hanging over her, then gazed lovingly at his Trans Am. "I don't want anything . . . you know."

"No, what?" She bit back a smile and feigned innocence. She knew exactly what he was talking about, but she was going to make him say it.

He huffed out a breath and held his hand back out for the key. "Fine. I don't want you bringing anything in my car with you."

"That's okay, Bee, I want to swing by the house and pick up Beast, anyway." And there was no way Bee was putting Beast in his car. She laughed and started walking down the sidewalk with Bee beside her. She was too used to him to be offended, and who knew? This time he might actually be right. Though she'd never admit it to him. "So, what happened with Luke and Tank? You never said."

He shrugged. "It was fine, they just questioned me about what happened and that was it."

"Did it seem as if they thought Emmett was guilty?" She still couldn't wrap her head around Emmett as a killer.

"I couldn't tell. They're completely stone-faced, those two."

"Yeah, tell me about it."

Bee stared off for a moment, his thick eyebrows furrowed into a deep V. "They did ask one strange question, though."

"Oh? What was that?"

"They asked me if I knew if Emmett played baseball."

Chapter Eight

Cass went through her morning routine, preparing to open Mystical Musings while Bee stuck their breakfast sandwiches in the microwave. Most everything was already done, since they'd stayed late the night before to organize it all. She considered propping the doors open to ease some of the crushing heat, but that could wait until after they ate. She didn't want anyone to walk in while she, Bee, and Stephanie were having breakfast.

Stephanie, who was not only one of her best friends but also her bookkeeper, skimmed through the sales book for the week. "Your sales have practically doubled since last summer."

The news brought a burst of pride in how much she'd accomplished in such a short time, a dash of relief she might have enough savings to make it through next winter, and then sadness that all her dreams might collapse because of one bad night.

"Don't worry, Cass. It'll all work out." Stephanie closed the ledger and returned it to the shelf beneath the register. "Come on, let's eat."

"Go ahead. I'll be right there." Cass took a small stack of bills from the safe. She hadn't left cash in the register overnight since someone had broken in — not that they'd stolen anything, but the knowledge of how easily they could have had spooked her.

She counted out singles for change, then hit the button to open the register drawer and paused. Two crystals sat in one of the compartments. She lifted the first stone. Black tourmaline. Its protective powers were well known, its ability to repel negative energy quite strong. She'd given one to Bee at a time in his life when he'd needed the aid. "Bee?"

"Yeah?" He put one sandwich on the table and popped another in the microwave without looking at her.

"Did you leave this here?"

"Leave what where?" he asked without turning around. "And knowing how OCD you are, probably not."

"This." She held up the black tourmaline. Sunlight reflected off the black crystal, and it warmed in her hand.

He told Beast to sit, tossed him a piece of bacon from the

container he'd gotten for him, then turned to Cass. "What is it?"

"A black tourmaline."

He frowned and patted his pocket. "Nope. Mine's right here."

Warmth surged through Cass. Bee didn't believe in her hocus-pocus, and yet he'd kept the stone she'd given him. Tears welled in her eyes.

"What?" His cheeks turned red. "It was a gift from a friend."

Not wanting to embarrass him, she let it drop. "When I opened the register, there were two stones in the drawer."

Bee frowned. "Who put the cash away last night?"

"I did," Stephanie said. "There was nothing in the drawer when I emptied it and put the money in the safe."

Cass vaguely remembered Stephanie saying she'd put the money in the safe sometime during the night. "When did you put it away?"

"I took what was there out of the register when I first came in, before I went up for the reading. When the reading . . . uh . . . got interrupted, I never bothered putting it back in the drawer."

"So, anyone could have opened the drawer while we were upstairs." Cass loved the old-fashioned register, loved the way it looked sitting atop the driftwood counter, and since she had no other employees, she'd never worried about needing codes or a key to open it. Now that she'd added the upstairs room and wasn't always in view of the register, she might have to consider getting a newer model.

"What's the big deal, anyway? It's not like it's going to hurt you. I thought black tourmaline was supposed to protect against negative energy?" Bee blushed an even deeper shade of red. "Or some such nonsense."

"It is. But how did it get there?"

He shrugged. "Maybe you dropped it out of the basket when you pulled it out from beneath the counter."

"Maybe . . ." Though they all knew that wasn't likely, especially since she hadn't sorted any stones or crystals since Stephanie emptied the drawer and moved the money to the safe. "Except, this was sitting in the drawer next to it."

She held up the stone. The instant the sunlight hit the layers of iridescent minerals, the crystal ignited with the illusion of flames flickering within it. Swirls of brownish red, orange, and green danced beneath its surface, gripping, hypnotic. Cass stared deeper into the flames, losing herself in the kaleidoscope of colors. A spot of black filled its center.

A chill gripped her.

The black churned among the flames, teasing, disappearing only to resurface somewhere else an instant later.

"He needs you." The voice came not from within the stone but from inside her own mind. It filled her, consumed her with the need to help—

"Cass!" Bee shook her arm.

"Huh?"

"I said, are you all right? You zoned out there for a minute."

Cass glanced at the fire agate again, but whatever trance had gripped her had vanished. "Yeah, yeah. I'm okay."

"What is that thing?" Bee pointed to the crystal still held out in her hand. "And what did it do to you?"

Cass laughed, laid her hand over Bee's, which was still resting on her arm, and squeezed. "It's okay, Bee. It didn't do anything to me."

He lifted a brow, released her, and took a step back. "I don't know about that. You took one look at it and went . . . somewhere else."

Stephanie, who didn't hold Bee's reservations about the supernatural, stared into the translucent bands, her eyes wide, mesmerized, but not as caught up as Cass had been. "It's beautiful."

"It's fire agate, a stone used for protection since ancient times. Some say it adorned the armor of warriors going into battle, was used by magicians to ward off storms, used by kings to protect their kingdoms."

"So, someone put two stones used for protection in the register drawer where you would be sure to find them, but why?" Bee studied the stone over Stephanie's shoulder but made no move to touch it or take it from her.

"Fire agate is not only used for protection. Aside from creating a shield to protect you from negative energy, it brings a sense of calm, peace, and security. It soothes and calms you, directs your focus, clears your mind . . ." She hesitated, knowing Bee would immediately grasp the implication if she continued.

"And?" Bee asked.

"It also brings strength, enhances your analytical ability, improves perceptiveness, and gives you the courage and confidence to take action—"

"Nope." Bee held up his hands. "You can stop right there. You will not be taking any kind of action."

"Bee—"

He covered his ears and retreated toward the table. "Not hearing you. La la la la."

"Ignore him." Stephanie frowned. "So, what do you think it means? And how did it get in the register drawer?"

"As for how it got there, I have no idea." Agate worked best if worn in the area below the heart, so she put both stones into her shorts pocket. "But I think it means I need to help someone."

"Oh, puh-leaze." Bee pulled out one of the velvet chairs at the round table in the back corner of the shop and sat. "Don't you think that's a bit of a stretch? Assuming someone needs your help because there were two rocks in the register drawer?"

Cass and Stephanie joined him at the table. Knowing he'd gotten all the food he was going to get from Bee, Beast settled at Cass's side with a chew toy.

Cass unwrapped her sandwich and sipped her lukewarm coffee. "Actually, there's a little more to it than just the stones."

"Of course there is," Bee muttered and took a big bite of his bacon, egg, and cheese.

Cass ignored her sandwich in favor of the much-needed caffeine. "A couple of times now, I thought I heard a woman's voice."

Stephanie perched on the edge or her chair, her breakfast still wrapped in front of her. "What did she say?"

"Once, I'm pretty sure I heard the words 'help him.' But a couple of times, I'm certain she said 'he needs you.'"

"Who do you think she meant?" Stephanie asked.

Bee swallowed and wiped his mouth. "Would you two please stop talking about some disembodied voice like it's a person. It creeps me out."

"Sorry, Bee." Stephanie offered her sweetest smile, but they all knew she wasn't the least bit sorry.

"So, what?" He set his sandwich down. "All this time, you've been telling me you're not actually psychic, that you are just extremely intuitive and well-trained at figuring out what people are hiding, even from themselves. Were you lying?"

"Of course not." The insinuation hurt. "I would never lie to you or take advantage of anyone."

He folded his arms on the table and tilted his head. "So, what's different now?"

Relief came with the realization he wasn't accusing her, just trying to get to the bottom of what was going on. And he did have a point. What was different now? Were latent psychic abilities coming to the surface with her return to Bay Island? Had she somehow unlocked a talent she'd always possessed? Or had something happened since she returned?

"When I was a kid, things just came to me, things I shouldn't know but somehow did, and I didn't question it." Perhaps the innocence of childhood had allowed her mind to accept what she couldn't justify as an adult. "When I was a teenager, I used to talk to tourists on the beach, tell them things that often, but not always, turned out to be true. It's how I earned extra money during the summers."

She took a bite of her sandwich, chewed, and swallowed, more to buy herself a few minutes to think than from hunger. The salt and grease sat in her stomach like a lump. The roll, rubbery from its time in the microwave, didn't help matters.

"When I went to college and then to medical school, my life became more grounded in reality. I started searching for explanations for everything. It wasn't good enough to accept things were just because they were; I needed answers for why things were that way. When I married Donald, the need for order became an obsession. I think, on some level, I always knew he was cheating on me." Actually, that wasn't true. He hadn't always cheated on her. But she'd always known he was going to, deep in her gut, and she'd ignored that instinct, couldn't accept the knowledge she should have had no way of possessing.

"Anyway, when I lost my patient, a patient I saw just before he died, a patient I might have been able to save if I'd listened to my instincts . . . I think something inside of me broke. Then when I went home and found Donald, well . . . I couldn't take any more. And then my parents passed away. I came back to Bay Island a mess." All that remained of Dr. Donovan had shattered during that year, leaving only a shell. Cass, a woman who needed to be strong enough to leave her past behind her and create a future, had emerged from the pieces.

Bee got up and rounded the table. He crouched at her side and took both of her hands in his. "I am so sorry for the pain you've suffered, sweetie. But look what you've accomplished since your return. You're an amazing woman, Cass. A good woman, who only wants to help people. And you know what? You do. Every day. If you say you can talk to g-ghosts, then I believe you think you can. Whether or not it's real, I have no idea, but however you receive your information, I say you should follow your instincts, because they seem to be spot-on most of the time."

"Thank you, Bee." She forced the words past the lump in her throat. Bee always had a way of knowing just what she needed.

"Of course." He smiled. "And let's face it, even the best of us make a mistake once in a while."

Cass laughed and threw her arms around Bee's neck. "Thank you, Bee. I needed that."

The pep talk and the laugh.

He hugged her back, then returned to his breakfast. "So, where does that leave us?"

"Well, I was thinking about it on the way over here. Whatever is happening, it's coming to me in the form of a woman's voice."

"Like last time, when you saw a woman?" Stephanie asked.

Bee rolled his eyes.

"Not exactly. I haven't seen anything." Except for that black swirl in the center of the fire agate, a swirl that shouldn't have been there, was foreign to the stone. "I just hear a distant voice. But just like when it started last time, it only seems to happen when I'm sleep-deprived. When my mind is completely clear, open, drifting, often in the moments just before I would doze off."

"So, maybe you're blocking it the rest of the time," Stephanie suggested.

She'd thought of that, while Bee was driving and she had allowed her mind to drift, and it did make the most sense. "I think that's exactly what's happening. I think I need to accept—sorry, Bee—that ghosts are real, and I am somehow able to hear messages if they are directed at me. I just need to learn how to open myself up more to receiving them."

After everything that had happened since her return to Bay Island, there was no denying their existence.

"Is that possible?" Stephanie finally unwrapped her sandwich and started eating.

"I'm not sure." But she was going to have to figure it out, and quickly.

Bee groaned. As much as he didn't want to accept anything related to the paranormal, there was no way he'd be left out of the discussion. "Are you having dreams again?"

"No, not this time." At least, not yet, anyway.

"Okay, all of that aside." Bee waved his hand around, dismissing what he couldn't deal with.

Cass didn't mind, though. Actually, she understood. "Yeah?"

"I want to ask you a question, and I want you to answer immediately. Don't think about your answer at all, just blurt out your first gut instinct. Okay?"

"Okay." Cass settled, facing him.

"I'm serious, Cass."

Cass took a moment to try to clear her mind. She closed her eyes and imagined the black swirl in the center of the agate's flames, brought the image up in her mind, focused fully, keeping her mind blank. "Go ahead."

"Where does that leave you right now? What do you think you're supposed to do?"

"I have to help Emmett."

Chapter Nine

"And how do you propose we help Emmett?" Bee stood and started to clear the table without finishing his breakfast, a sure sign he was agitated.

Cass wrapped the paper around her nearly full sandwich and handed it to him to throw out. "I didn't say *we* had to help; I said *I* had to help."

"Yeah, well, *I, we,* what's the difference?"

"Thanks, Bee. You're the best."

"Hey!" Stephanie folded her arms across her chest in feigned outrage. "What am I, chopped liver?"

"You're the best too, Stephanie."

Stephanie grinned at Bee.

He stuck his tongue out at her and walked toward the front of the shop. "Sorry, Cass, but I have got to open a door. I'm roasting in here."

"Go ahead, I have to open in a few minutes anyway." Cass hauled herself out of the chair and went to open the back door as well. Hopefully she'd get some kind of cross-breeze.

"Do you want me to call someone in to fix it?" Stephanie asked.

"Nah. I'll wait and see what happens with Emmett later on."

"Are you sure? This heat is supposed to stick around for at least the next few days."

"I'm sure." Especially considering Emmett probably wouldn't be in half as much trouble if he hadn't come to her aid during the reading. "It feels like too much of a betrayal, you know? Especially after he stuck up for me last night."

"Yeah, I get it." Stephanie fiddled with the thermostat but let the matter drop. "Anyway, the question remains, what can we do to help?"

Cass pulled her hair back and tied it up with a band she kept on her wrist. "Did you see Tank yet?"

"He came home for a little while early this morning, but he couldn't stay long."

"Did he have anything to say?" Bee asked.

She stared pointedly at him. "You mean the kind of anything I'm not supposed to tell anyone, especially you two?"

"Yup, that's the kind." Bee grinned from ear to ear, the prospect of good dirt making him forget all about the stifling heat. "I'll tell you what, why don't you just tell us the stuff you're allowed to tell us? Then, afterward, we'll coax you into telling us the good stuff. This way you can say it wasn't your fault you spilled the beans."

She scowled and leaned back against the counter. "He didn't actually say too much, just that it didn't look good for Emmett. Apparently, Emmett found Dirk in the trunk of a car on his lot late last night and called the police."

"Why would he have called the police if he'd killed him?" Bee beat Cass to the argument she'd have made in Emmett's defense.

Stephanie shrugged. "That's what I said, and apparently Emmett posed that same argument, but Tank said it could have been a lot of things: guilt, remorse, fear Joey would somehow stumble across the body. Who knows why people do things when they're not thinking clearly?"

Cass couldn't really argue that. Plenty of people, even innocent people, had been known to react inappropriately or out of character to unexpected situations. "Did he say what Emmett was doing at the garage so late?"

Stephanie was already shaking her head before Cass finished the question. "All he said was Emmett insists Dirk was alive last he saw him."

"I heard him say that last night, said Dirk came to the garage looking for a fight, but Emmett didn't engage. He says he went back inside, and I believe him. There's no way Emmett would have risked leaving Joey alone, not for anyone, especially someone like Dirk Brinkman, who's clearly nothing but a bully."

At the mention of bullies, an image of the stranger who'd accosted her in the deli popped into her head. She still had to figure out who he was and why he had a problem with her. Could he have had something to do with Dirk's behavior at the reading? Had the stranger put Dirk up to heckling her? Had the two been in cahoots somehow? The man *had* threatened to ruin her life.

Bee had come to Bay Island after Cass had left for college, and they'd met and become fast friends since her return. But Stephanie had grown up on Bay Island, had gone to school with Cass. "Stephanie, do you remember someone having a major grudge against me?"

She frowned. "What do you mean?"

"I ran into a man in the deli today who said I ruined his life and threatened to return the favor. Do you know of anyone who'd be that angry with me?" How could she not remember someone who harbored such a grudge against her? Someone she'd obviously hurt in some way?

"What did he look like?"

"Heavy-set, sallow complexion, graying combover, maybe ten or fifteen years older than us." When would she have even interacted with someone so much older than her?

Stephanie shook her head. "No one I can think of, but I can get some yearbooks out later if you want. I'm pretty sure the school keeps a copy from every year, and the receptionists are still in for half a day, even during the summer."

"Do you think he could have something to do with this?" As usual, Bee's thoughts ran along the same line as Cass's.

"I don't know, but what better way to ruin my life than to destroy my reputation? And even worse, to hurt one of my friends in the process."

Stephanie stared hard at her. "You do know you're going to have to tell Tank and Luke about this guy, right?"

Cass shifted uncomfortably. The instant she mentioned it to them, any hope of her investigating would be shot down.

"Cass . . . ?"

"Yeah, yeah, I know. I'll tell them."

The tinkle of the wind chimes announced her first customer of the day, bringing their conversation grinding to a halt before she could mention seeing Ellie.

"When are you going to call them, Cass?" Stephanie persisted.

"As soon as I get a break from work." Cass smiled and slid from beneath Stephanie's glare to greet her customer, but stopped short when she recognized the woman from the night before—Aiden Hargrove's date.

And she didn't look like she'd gotten any more sleep than Cass had. Dark circles ringed her bloodshot eyes, made worse by the tear tracks running through the black eye makeup that had smudged beneath them.

What could she say to this woman? She'd embarrassed her

publicly, hurt her in a terrible way. Problem was, she'd told her the truth. What was she supposed to do now? Lie to her? Try to soothe her feelings? At what expense?

Bee crossed behind her and nudged her in the back discreetly with his elbow.

"I . . . uh . . . I'm sorry about last night." That sounded completely lame.

"Is it true?" The woman rushed toward her, wringing a wad of tissues in her hands. "Is what you said true? Please, whatever the truth is, I have to know. Aiden swears you're a fraud, but what you said . . . and the way he reacted . . . well . . . I just have to know."

Cass relaxed. She didn't have to tell this woman anything. She already knew the truth. "What's your name?"

"Nanette. Nanette Coldwater."

Cass shot a quick glance at Bee, who stood talking quietly to Stephanie at the register.

He nodded and pointed up.

Confident he'd stay and watch the shop until she returned, Cass led Nanette upstairs. She usually conducted individual readings at the round table in the back corner of the shop, and that's where she kept the aids she sometimes used, like her colored pencils and her crystal ball, but she had a feeling she wouldn't be needing those for this reading. Nanette only wanted one answer, and she already knew it, Cass just had to help her realize that.

"Can I get you anything before we start? Tea, coffee, water?" She gestured toward a table by the window, far from the table where she'd sat with Aiden the night before. "I know it's not enough, but I am truly sorry about what happened last night. It shouldn't have happened, and I have no excuse for it."

Nanette shook her head and wiped her eyes with the wad of tissues, then pulled more from her purse and mopped the sweat beading on her forehead. She yanked her long, limp red hair back and tied it into a knot at the back of her head.

"I'm sorry, it's so hot in here." Cass jumped up and opened the windows. "I still haven't gotten the air-conditioning fixed. Are you sure I can't get you some water?"

"No, I'm fine, thank you. I just want answers."

With all of the windows open, and Nanette refusing any kind of refreshment, Cass couldn't procrastinate any longer. She joined Nanette at the table, choosing a seat next to her rather than across the table. "What do you want to know?"

"Is what you said true? That Aiden's in love with someone else?"

Cass blew out a breath. She wouldn't lie to this woman, but she would search her memory to be sure she was right. She owed Nanette that much.

The weird feeling that something was wrong had nagged at her all day. That, combined with the heat, the heckler, so many things could have caused her to be mistaken. She thought back to the night before, Aiden's shocked expression when she said he was in love, his immediate reaction to look at the other woman. She wasn't wrong. She might have been wrong about a lot of things last night, but that wasn't one of them. "I believe so, but there's always a chance I could be wrong."

She spread her hands wide. "So, what am I supposed to do?"

"Have you tried talking to him?"

"Of course," she scoffed. "But he was so angry, so bent on revenge against you, that he wouldn't even listen. He told me if I didn't believe him, I could just go home."

Just what she needed, Aiden Hargrove out to get her. "And what did you do?"

"I left. What else could I do?" She sobbed and blew her nose.

It was time to lead her around to the inevitable truth. "You've come into the shop before, seeking a love potion, if I remember correctly."

"A lot of good it did." She snorted and yanked the small velvet bag of crystals Cass had sold her from her purse, then slammed it onto the table.

If Nanette had believed Aiden was in love with her, she wouldn't have needed the love potion, but Nanette needed to figure that out for herself. "Before the reading last night, did you suspect Aiden was interested in anyone else?"

Tears streamed down her cheeks, and she swiped them roughly with the heels of her hands. "That woman. The one he looked at when you said that? I've seen him with her before."

Cass remained quiet, waiting Nanette out, letting her draw her own conclusions. She knew the instant realization came.

The flow of tears dried up, and her eyes went cold, hard. Her mouth firmed into a thin line. This was the woman Bee had told her insulted several guests before coming upstairs to the group reading. "I asked him about her more than once, and he swore there was nothing going on between them. But he was lying, wasn't he?"

Cass schooled her features, careful not to lead her in any way.

"I should have known, did know, I think, on some level, but how much easier to stick your head in the sand than to accept the truth?" She stuffed the tissues into her bag, stood, and paced back and forth in front of the window. "I should have known something was up when he agreed to go to the reading. I'd been asking him, begging him, really, to take me for months, and he laughed at me. Said stuff like that was nothing but nonsense for weak-minded people."

Cass didn't flinch, too used to the sentiment to let it bother her. "What made him change his mind?"

"I don't know. I was sitting in the waiting room outside his office, and I overheard him on the phone with someone." She peered from beneath her lashes, studying Cass.

Nannette hadn't overheard anything; she'd been eavesdropping. Apparently, her suspicions had run deep.

"He sounded agitated, not really angry, but annoyed, you know what I mean?"

Cass nodded.

"He was saying he didn't want to do something, didn't understand what difference it would make. Next thing you know, he comes out of the office and tells me we're going to the reading."

Who could have wanted Aiden at the reading? His lover? It's not like anyone could have known what Cass would say. What reason would anyone have for wanting him there? "When was that, if you don't mind me asking?"

"Friday afternoon. Two days before the reading."

"Do you know who he was talking to?"

"No, but I think I have a pretty good idea." She stopped abruptly and slung her purse over her shoulder.

"Why don't you sit for a while longer, have a cup of tea, let me do a proper reading for you?" Going off half-cocked and angry wasn't going to solve anything.

"I don't need time to think." She strode toward the stairs. "What

I need are answers. I was foolish to come here, to think you could tell me what's going on between him and that woman. There are only two people who can answer that question, and I assure you, before the day is out, one of them is going to."

Cass hurried after her, but it was no use.

Nanette stormed out without another word.

Bee stared after her. "I take it that didn't go very well."

Cass tilted her head back and forth, stretching her neck where exhaustion and stress had coiled, leaving her stiff and sore. There was nothing more she could do for Nanette Coldwater. Maybe she should just close the shop and go home. But she couldn't. She had to stay just in case Ellie showed up. "I saw Ellie today. You were right. She doesn't look good."

Stephanie grabbed her bag from beneath the register. "I saw her the other day, and she didn't even say hello, just walked past me with her head down."

"I'm worried about her. Have you heard anything, Bee?"

"Nothing more than what I told you already. But I can ask around."

Stephanie kissed her cheek. "I've got to run. Calvin Morris is sending a courier with the books he wants me to look over."

"And I have to go home and get some shut-eye. I want to make sure I get up early enough to hit the deli again before they close." He winked and blew Cass a kiss, then turned to Stephanie. "Hey, can you drop me off at the deli to pick up my car?"

"Sure, come on."

"Thanks." He started out with Stephanie. "A courier? Hasn't he ever heard of email?"

"Apparently he doesn't believe in digital records."

"Seriously? Isn't that unusual?"

The screen door banged shut behind them, and Cass was left alone with her thoughts.

As if reading her mind, Beast barked once.

"I'm sorry, boy." She pulled out a chair, sat next to him, and smoothed a hand over his sleek fur, then kissed his head. "I'm never alone when you're around."

He nuzzled his head against her leg and stared up at her, his big brown eyes filled with love. No matter what was going wrong in her life, she need only look into his eyes to bring serenity. If only the sense of doom would give up its grip on her and allow that contentment to last.

Chapter Ten

The minute hand ticked another minute past opening time, and still no customers. Not that it was unusual to go as long as an hour past opening with no one coming in, but still, she wouldn't start to feel better until she could gauge how people were reacting. And she couldn't do that until people started coming in.

She started the coffeepot, despite the hundred-degree weather. If the fact she had no air-conditioning had gotten around, she might never get a customer.

The wind chimes above the door rang out, startling her. She whirled around, and her elbow caught the handle of her favorite mug and sent it crashing to the floor.

Beast scrambled to his feet and barked.

"I guess you should have seen that coming, huh?" A man she'd never seen before smirked as he swaggered into the shop through the back door from the beach. If she had to guess, based on the multicolor jungle-print shorts, polo shirt, and Sperry boat shoes, she'd say tourist, but something seemed off. The sunglasses he wore backward on his shaved head with the arms hooked over the front of his ears didn't help matters. Nor did the two buddies he had in tow, both dressed similarly—except their sunglasses hung folded from the front of their shirt collars—and both laughing at his lame attempt at humor.

Just what she needed, another heckler. Best to get them out of the shop as soon as possible without causing a scene. At least there were no customers around to witness whatever happened.

"You're probably right." She smiled, leaving the shards of glass where they were but keeping a close watch on Beast so he wouldn't step on any. Not too hard, since he'd glued himself to her side, head tilted, keeping a watchful eye on the strangers.

She lay a hand on his head. "What can I help you gentlemen with today?"

Their leader strolled through the shop, ran a finger along an expensive crystal decanter, then turned and pinned her with a glare.

His compatriots wandered through the shop without straying too far from him.

"I'm looking for a love potion. Rumor has it, at least from the friend who recommended you, that you specialize in those." He folded his arms across his puffed-up chest, giving her a good view of the tan line on his left ring finger.

"Are you looking to make someone fall in love with you?" Because she had a feeling it was going to take a whole lot more than a potion. And not a woo-woo feeling — as Bee would put it — either. He would be a hard man to love if he was always this obnoxious. "Or is it a gift for a friend?"

"Does it matter?"

She folded her arms, matching his stance. No way she'd let this crew intimidate her. "Oh, I don't know, but I bet it would matter to your wife."

He jerked back as if she'd slapped him. "Is that a threat?"

She hadn't meant it that way, just an observation, but if his own guilt made him feel threatened, that wasn't on her.

"Besides . . ." His face turned red as he regained some of his composure. "Who even says I'm married?"

Too late. His reaction had already confirmed her suspicion. She tapped a finger against her temple. "Psychic, remember?"

That and the white line circling his finger where he must have recently removed his wedding band. Of course, there was always the possibility he was newly divorced, but she'd trusted her gut, taken the chance, and his reaction had proved her right.

"Anyway . . ." She relaxed her stance, lowered her arms. She wasn't about to stand there and argue with him. "I'm sorry, but I don't carry love potions."

"Really?" He cocked his head and lifted a brow. "Because rumor has it you try to make people fall in love, even if they don't want to. What are you? A witch?"

Cass's mind raced. Whom could he have spoken to that would have said that? Sure, she often put together bags of crystals that were supposed to aid in romance. That was a routine request from people visiting her shop. But she'd never sold anything she proclaimed to be a love potion. And yet . . . hadn't someone come in looking for the same thing recently? "Nothing can make someone fall in love. You either love someone or you don't."

Usually, at that point, she would have offered a selection of crystals that might help. Instead, she simply waited him out. They both knew he wasn't there seeking love, or anything else she had to offer.

"If you really believe that, then why do you sell this junk?" He gestured toward the glass cases filled with a variety of colorful stones and crystals.

How could she explain to him without destroying her reputation or hurting the people who depended on such things? "It's not that I'm saying a rock can make someone love you, though certain stones definitely seem to aid in that area. A lot of the time, all my customers need is the confidence to act on their feelings. If wearing a crystal offers that confidence, offers the reminder that they love someone enough to seek assistance, offers the boost they need to trust their instincts, then so be it. Who is it hurting?"

The man swiped a hand over his crew cut, knocking the perched glasses askew. He ripped them off, folded them, and tucked one arm into his shirt collar. "Why don't you ask yourself that question? Who did you hurt with your stupid love potion nonsense last night?"

Aiden Hargrove. The thought came unbidden, but she knew it was right, even though she'd hurt Nanette as well. And probably the dark-haired woman she'd fingered as the object of Aiden's affection.

The question remained, who was this guy, and what did he have to do with Aiden? "Last night was unusual, and I've apologized to everyone involved."

At least she'd tried. Aiden hadn't given her the chance before he'd stormed out.

"But you can't take it back, can you?" he pressed.

She lowered her gaze to the floor and spoke quietly. "No, I can't."

He stepped closer and pointed a finger at her an inch from her face.

Beast stiffened and growled a warning.

The man ignored him. "I just came to tell you that you may as well close your doors now, you fraud, because there's no way my brother's going to allow you to keep selling this nonsense to unsuspecting victims. And he's already started making sure any potential customers know what a scammer you are."

He whirled away from her without waiting for a response, shoved one of her freestanding display cases on his way past, and sent it crashing down. The glass shattered, and crystals spilled across the floor.

Beast backpedaled, barking frantically.

The man strode across the shop and out the back door with his two companions on his heels.

Cass grabbed Beast's collar to keep him from stepping on any of the glass shards. She crouched beside him, still holding tight, and weaved the fingers of her other hand through his thick mane. "It's okay, Beast. It's all right. Shh . . . now."

He whined and tried to squirm free of her grip.

She held firm and continued to soothe him. "Shhh . . . easy, boy. Everything's okay now."

He looked up at her, his tail tucked close to his body.

"Come on, let's get you in the back room so you don't get hurt." She used her foot to push away the few glass pieces that had skittered in her direction and led Beast toward the back room, which was actually a room on the side of the shop, separated from the sales floor by a long red curtain. She guided him through the doorway, then put the gate up behind them. "There you go, boy. Want a cookie?"

Beast looked back and forth between the treat she held out and the shop. Finally, his desire for the treat won out, and he bounded toward her.

"Sit." He plopped down, suddenly feigning obedience because he knew a treat was forthcoming. Had she been standing there empty-handed, he would probably have made a different choice. She gave him the treat and petted his head. "Good boy, honey, I'll be back in a little bit."

She filled his water bowl, then left him where he'd be safe while she cleaned up the mess.

Tears spilled down her cheeks as she gathered what she needed to clean up, not because of the broken case, but because she couldn't help but feel like the man had been right. What was she doing? Obviously, not helping people, which had been her intention all along.

Careful to avoid the shards of glass still clinging to the case, Cass righted the wooden base. She shook the garbage bag open, set a big basket just out of the mess, and started picking up the larger chunks of glass from the floor, careful to separate the crystals, wipe them off, and put them into the basket.

When she'd first decided to remain on Bay Island, after her parents' funeral, she'd dreamed of opening the small shop on the boardwalk, a comfortable walk down the beach from her childhood home. She'd dreamed of using her skills to help people, of connecting with them on a more personal level than a doctor-patient relationship would allow for.

The wind chimes tinkled, and Cass's gaze shot to the door. "Hold on."

"Oh, my." Grace Collins stopped short and stared at the mess. "What happened, dear?"

Cass stood and brushed off her hands. "Good morning, Grace, it's so good to see you."

That statement couldn't have been truer. The elderly woman had come to Cass not long after she'd first opened seeking, of all things, a love potion. "Where's Rudy today?"

"He's visiting a friend on the mainland, but . . ." She hesitated.

"Is everything all right?" Cass didn't think she could bear to hear something had gone wrong. Not this morning, not after everything else that had happened, not when that feeling of impending doom sat in her gut like it had over the past few days. "Is Rudy okay? Sadie? The baby?"

Cass had "helped" Grace's granddaughter when she'd been depressed over not being able to conceive, and Grace had come into the shop seeking something to make her feel better. Grace and Sadie both credited Cass's mix of crystals and essential oils for her luck in getting pregnant soon after. And it could be true, if the assistance Cass had offered had helped Sadie relax enough to let nature take its course.

"Sadie and the baby are both fine." Grace took one of Cass's hands in both of hers and laughed. "I took Sadie shopping for maternity clothes last weekend, if you can imagine. Just between us, she barely has more than a bump."

Cass laughed with her, relieved everything was going well. "Can I get you something? Tea? A cold water?"

"No, no, dear, thank you, though. What happened here?" She gestured to the mess as Cass led her to a small seating section.

"Oh, it's fine." She left Grace sitting on the couch for a moment, turned both signs to *Closed,* and locked the doors. She rarely locked up in the middle of the day, but she couldn't have people traipsing through broken glass, and she was going to take a few moments to sit with Grace, who'd become a good friend since she'd first come in. Cass settled in an armchair across from Grace. "So, tell me, what brings you in this morning?"

"Well, dear, I, uh . . ." She smoothed a hand over her tight blue-gray curls. "I heard about what happened last night, and I just wanted to come in and see how you were doing."

Tears pooled in Cass's eyes, and she tried to blink them away before Grace could notice.

Although Grace was too sharp to miss them, she simply waited while Cass got a grip on herself.

"Thank you, Grace, I'm doing okay."

Turbulence danced in Grace's gray eyes. "Are you sure?"

Cass shrugged. What could she say? That she was second-guessing her entire life, wondering if she'd made the right choice staying on Bay Island?

"I met with the ladies from the senior club this morning, and they were discussing the fight and, of course, the murder, and I just wanted to make sure you weren't feeling responsible." Just like Grace to cut to the chase.

Though Cass was sort of relieved the gossip had been about the murder and not her screwup with Aiden, Nanette, and the other couple she'd inadvertently embarrassed, her heart ached for Emmett. And even worse, for Joey, whose father had become the newest gossip fodder. "Emmett is a good man. There's no way he could have had anything to do with what happened to Dirk."

"Actually, that does seem to be the general consensus."

"Really?" Why did that surprise her? Emmett was a local and well-liked. But even she had to admit, the evidence she'd heard about so far didn't bode well.

"Yes. The feud between those two goes way back, and if he didn't kill Dirk way back when, chances are, he wouldn't bother now." Grace dug through her bag, pulled out a handkerchief, and mopped the back of her neck.

"Are you okay? I'm sorry it's so hot in here. The air conditioner broke, and I haven't had a chance to get it repaired." Cass jumped up and grabbed a bottle of water from the fridge, then handed it to Grace.

"Thank you." She took a few sips, then put the cap back on and set it on the coffee table.

"We could sit out on the back deck if you'd like." Not that there was much of a breeze, but it might be better than the sweltering heat in the shop with the doors closed.

"No, no, that's fine." Grace waved her off with a laugh. "I'm not that fragile."

Though delicate, Grace was far from fragile.

"So, what were you saying about Emmett?"

Grace crossed one slim ankle over the other, adjusting her long, flowing print skirt to hang neatly. "I hadn't given those two any thought in years, but Eleanor Cunningham was going on this morning about the scenes they used to cause on a regular basis. That was back before Joey was born, you know, when Emmett and Tanya were still dating."

"Tanya? Is that Emmett's wife?" Emmett had never mentioned her name, hadn't spoken about her at all that Cass could remember.

"Yes, bless her soul." Grace made the sign of the cross before continuing. "Very sad she passed so young, and with a little one at home too."

"What happened?" Although Cass knew she'd passed away when Joey was little, she didn't know many details.

"Emmett was a rough boy, played all kinds of sports, but he was never very outgoing, kind of socially awkward, if you know what I mean."

There was no arguing that. Emmett usually stuck to one-word answers, was not much on small talk, though he'd gotten a bit better since Cass had gotten to know him.

"Anyway," Grace continued, "Tanya, she was more outgoing, a cheerleader, captain of the debate team, a real go-getter. Dirk had a thing for her, and Dirk was very used to getting what he wanted, but Tanya's heart belonged to Emmett."

A pretty classic story from what Cass could see. "So, they fought? Emmett and Dirk?"

Grace's blue eyes sparkled. "Often."

That made sense. Emmett had never struck her as violent, but the way he took care of Joey, jumped wholeheartedly into the things Joey enjoyed—which did not include any kind of sports—Cass could see where he would have been protective. Funny, Cass didn't remember any of that from before she'd left Bay Island. Then again, Emmett was older than her and would have been ahead of her in school.

"It didn't really get bad until they were older, a few years after they'd graduated and Dirk's persistence didn't wane. From what Eleanor, who was friends with Emmett's mother's sister, said, Emmett started to get concerned that Dirk was stalking her, even tried to talk her into reporting him to the police, but Tanya didn't want to cause a fuss."

That timing made more sense. Cass had probably already been gone by the time their conflicts had escalated.

Grace fanned herself with her hand. "By the time Joey was born, Tanya had become an obsession to Dirk."

She'd have to hurry if she was going to get any more information before she'd need to open the doors again. "Had they ever dated? Tanya and Dirk, I mean?"

"Not from what I've heard. Dirk was a spoiled boy, and not a very nice one—not to speak ill of the dead, mind you. General consensus at the senior club is Dirk didn't love Tanya; he just obsessed over her because he couldn't have her. Ironically, if she had dated him, he probably would have gotten bored and moved on. When Tanya got sick, Emmett had his hands full between caring for her and taking care of a young boy. He started ignoring Dirk's taunts, which just irritated Dirk even more."

Cass wasn't surprised. If Dirk was as spoiled as Grace said, he wouldn't have taken well to being ignored.

"Once Tanya was gone, Dirk seemed to let things go. He and Emmett settled into a sort of peaceful but strained co-existence because they lived in the same small town and couldn't always avoid each other. But by then, after Emmett kept refusing to engage, they tended to just ignore each other."

"From what you've heard, people don't think Emmett killed him, though?" No one knew gossip like the members of the senior center, especially gossip rooted in Bay Island history. Except, of course, Bee. And possibly Emma.

"Nah, trust me, Emmett wasn't the only one with a grudge against Dirk."

"Did Dirk ever date other women or get married?"

"He married once, but it didn't last long. Dirk's temper wasn't conducive to marriage." Grace took another drink of her water, then stood. "On that note, I'm going to go and let you get back to cleaning up so you can open the doors again."

"Thank you, Grace. For visiting and for making me feel better."

"Of course, dear." Grace reached for Cass's hand and clasped it in both of hers. "And don't you let the rumors Aiden Hargrove is spreading get you down, either."

Cass resisted groaning out loud. If Aiden's ire had already spread to the senior center, there was no stopping it. Spreading like wildfire, it would consume her.

"I know how genuine you are, how much you care about people, and I'll make sure everyone else knows too," Grace promised.

"Thank you, Grace." Cass walked her to the door and watched her leave, then turned and surveyed the mess. It wasn't going to clean itself up, and she couldn't very well run the shop with glass all over. And she was going to keep it open, fight to restore her reputation, if need be. Customers like Grace, those who returned to her over and over again, happy that she'd helped them in some way, who believed in her, made it all worthwhile. Aiden Hargrove wasn't going to take that from her.

Chapter Eleven

"I hope your wife enjoys her gift." Cass pushed the register drawer shut, dropped a business card into the bag atop the customer's purchases, and handed it to the gentleman. "Enjoy the rest of your day."

She checked the clock for the third time in the past five minutes. Still crawling toward three o'clock. Exhaustion burned her eyes, and she headed for the coffeepot, then paused. No way could she drink another cup of coffee in this stifling heat. What she needed was a diet soda, still loaded with caffeine but at least it would be cold.

She grabbed her cell phone and dialed Bee's number.

It only rang once before he picked it up. "Hey, beautiful, what's happening?"

"I guess you weren't still sleeping." She'd have called anyway, but he was always more agreeable when she didn't wake him.

"No, but what if I was? Were you calling to wake me?"

She paused, too exhausted to tell if his tone held humor or accusation.

"Lighten up, Cass, I'm just kidding. You know I'm usually up earlier during the summer."

"Yeah, I know. I'm sorry, Bee, I'm just tired." And the slow trickle of customers all day had left her bored, as well; it was a bad combination.

"I imagine you must be, considering you didn't get any sleep last night, you poor thing. Maybe it's time for you to think about hiring some help." Ever since Bee had hired an intern, he constantly harassed her about hiring help. Although she suspected it had something to do with him wanting her to hang out at the beach with him, she couldn't say for certain. "At least then you could get a day off, maybe relax a little."

"We'll see." But they both knew she wouldn't. Mystical Musings was her baby, and she preferred to run it alone. She'd set up seating arrangements throughout the shop and offered free refreshments if customers wanted to wait. Most did. At least, they had before she'd messed up. Now, who knew?

It would probably depend on how far Aiden was willing to go to destroy her. Plus, the man who'd threatened her in the deli had his eye set toward revenge. Of the two, Aiden certainly had more influence on Bay Island, but the other man was an unknown, which made him scarier in a way.

"If not for Tim doing an internship with me this summer, I'd have had to go into the shop already too." Bee's shop, Dreamweaver Designs, sat just down the boardwalk from Mystical Musings. During the winter months, he didn't often open during the day unless a client scheduled an appointment. A good part of his inventory went to buyers, and a large portion of his business was done by appointment only. Bee was used to staying up all night, working in the back room of his shop until the wee hours of the morning, escaping to "the zone" so he didn't have to deal with interruptions to his creativity, so he liked to sleep in.

"I saw Tim the other day. He loves it. That was really nice of you to let him work with you." Tim Daughtry had just finished his first year of school and was majoring in fashion design, a program Bee had helped him get into. "I'm glad he's working out so well."

"He's working out wonderfully. I've helped him with a few of his designs for his summer classes, and the boy is very talented. Anyway, I'm on my way into the shop. Would you like me to bring you coffee?"

Her stomach rolled over. "If I drink another cup of coffee, I think I'll be sick."

"Diet soda." He knew her too well.

"Perfect. Thanks, Bee."

"Did you eat lunch?" he asked.

Her stomach growled. She hadn't even thought of eating after most of her breakfast went in the garbage. "No, I didn't have time."

"So, you've been busy then?"

"Not exactly." Unless you count cleaning up slivers of glass from pretty much everywhere. "At least not in the way you mean."

"Is something going on?"

"I'll explain when you get here." No need to get into it all before she got her caffeine.

"Fine. I'm on my way. Do you want me to bring something to eat, or do you want to see if Stephanie wants to meet up at Island Grill?"

The barbeque place sat at the end of the boardwalk and only opened for the summers, despite repeated requests from the locals for it to stay open all year. The comfortable, homey atmosphere, dim lighting, soft music, and good food might be just the thing to help her relax, especially when shared with good friends. If she fed Beast at the shop, she could leave him there until they ate, then pick him up and go straight home and drop into bed. "Island Grill sounds great."

The wind chimes behind her signaled a customer coming in from the beach. "Gotta run, Bee. See ya in a few."

She turned to greet the older gentleman who'd walked in and held out her hand. "Good afternoon. I'm Cass."

"John Hicks." The man smiled and shook her hand. "Nice to meet you."

"Can I help you with anything special today, or would you just like to browse?"

"Well, I don't know exactly." His deeply tanned cheeks reddened, and the gold flecks in his brown eyes sparkled. He turned his wedding band around his finger, then pulled it up and down. "But I sure hope you can get me out of the mess I've gotten myself into."

Since he didn't seem too distressed, she didn't get the impression he was in any kind of real danger. She smiled. "In trouble with your wife?"

"Ha!" He laughed. "You really are good. Cayden said you were a miracle worker. I just hope he's right."

An ironworker in New York, Cayden suffered with rheumatoid arthritis. When he'd come to her out of desperation, she'd given him crystals to aid in healing, and he swore they worked. He and his wife, Sophie, had been loyal customers ever since. "How do you know Cayden?"

"He's a good friend. Actually, he's the reason my wife and I are here on Bay Island. He and Sophie are always going on about it, so we figured we'd give it a try."

"I haven't seen Cayden and Sophie in a while. How are they doing? How's the baby?"

"Oh, they're great. And Cayden Junior is getting so big already, looks more and more like his mama every day."

"I'm so happy to hear that." Though she wanted to ask about Estelle, Sophie's mother, whom Cass had helped with some problems a few months earlier, Estelle's problems were personal and had required more counseling than Cass could offer, so she let it drop. Maybe she'd give Sophie a call later and see how things were going. She should have remembered to do so sooner, but she'd been so swamped all summer, time had gotten away from her. Maybe Bee was right. Maybe she did need to hire someone. She shook off the thoughts and refocused on the man standing in front of her. Her mind tended to wander when she got overtired. "So, how do you like Bay Island so far? Is it living up to your expectations?"

"We've only been here a few days, but so far we love it." He lowered his gaze to his wedding ring. "Except, somehow, with the excitement of getting away for a couple of weeks, which we haven't done in years, I forgot our anniversary."

She laughed. "That certainly explains the mess you're in."

He looked at her eagerly. "Do you think you can help?"

"I'm certainly going to try." This was the kind of customer Cass loved. Someone she'd send home happy, someone she could help.

"Oh, thank you."

"Does your wife believe in psychics?"

"Yes, despite me trying to convince her that no one can actually speak to the dea . . . uh . . . I mean . . ." His eyes went wide, and his cheeks blazed a purplish shade of red. "Sorry. I didn't mean—"

She grinned. "Don't worry about it. A lot of people don't believe, and that's okay. It's your wife's beliefs that matter."

He nodded, but the horrified expression remained glued to his face.

"Do you think she'd be interested in a reading?" Normally, Cass would have told him about her group readings. They were more like a show, entertaining for couples to attend together, socialize, enjoy refreshments afterward. But with what had gone on at the last reading, she wasn't even sure she'd have any more.

"What is that exactly?" he asked.

"Individual readings are very personal. She'd come sit with me, and we'd see what I could tell her."

"Sophie has talked about having readings before, and Marilyn always seems fascinated."

"How long will you be on Bay Island?"

"Two weeks." His posture finally relaxed.

"If you'd like, I can set up a reading during that time, then we can put together a basket of crystals and stones, with maybe a Bay Island souvenir of some sort to remind her of your time here? That way you'd have a gift to give her as well."

"That would be perfect."

Cass led him toward the counter, pulled out a basket, then looked around. "Can you tell me a bit about Marilyn? What she enjoys? Does she work? Does she tend to stress?"

"Hmm . . . let's see." He concentrated hard, and in that moment, all the love John Hicks had for his wife showed on his face. "She loves the beach, and she'd never seen a lighthouse before, so she was very excited about that. Made me climb to the top three times already; my legs are killing me. I told her I needed a break today, mostly so I could get away to come here, so she went to check out the lighthouse on the other side of the island by herself."

It struck her this man would do anything for his wife. What a lucky woman she was. Cass hoped to share that kind of relationship with Luke . . . or with someone . . . someday.

"And she's delicate, my Marilyn. She likes dainty things, pretty things. You know what I mean? She loves to read, especially fantasy books. She does tend to stress, though. Even since we've been here, she's worried about everything back home. I keep telling her to relax, but it's hard for her to just let go."

"That's perfect, thank you." Leaving the basket on the counter, Cass crossed the shop, then stopped at a row of glass shelves along the back wall. She scanned the row of lighthouse figures, searching for the one that felt just right for Marilyn Hicks, then lifted an etched glass replica of the Bay Island Lighthouse and returned to the counter. "Do you think she'd like this?"

John took the lighthouse from her and turned it over in his hands, studying every detail, running a rough finger over the etchings in the glass and the delicate seagull soaring along its side. "It's beautiful, perfect. I think she'll love it."

"How many years have you been married?"

"Twenty-four years," he said with no hesitation.

"Ah, you need something with a stone theme then."

"A stone theme?"

"Sure. Each year has a certain theme, and twenty-four is the stone theme." Not that she had them all memorized, but since last-minute anniversary gifts often brought men to her shop, she kept a cheat sheet beside the register.

Cass sifted through the baskets of crystals she kept in a glass case beneath the counter, but the pouch of crystals she usually offered didn't feel quite right for this occasion. Instead, she put them away and went to an octagonal glass case in the middle of the shop. She removed a velvet box, lifted a beautiful necklace from its cushion, then held it up for him to see. "This is a moonstone."

Sunlight glinted from the opalescent stone, sending shimmers of pink, blue, and green skittering across its surface. But when you looked deeper into the stone, billowy blue clouds appeared to be surrounded by white light. The oval stone sat in the center of a hand-woven antiqued silver design and hung from a silver chain. She laid the necklace in John's hand. "Moonstone is said to bring calm, peace, and balance. It's also known as the 'traveler's stone' and is reputed to offer protection against the dangers of travel, especially over water."

"Oh, wow. That's incredible. It's just so perfect. It looks like something out of a fairy tale. She would love it, but . . ." His gaze shifted for a moment, then returned longingly to the necklace. "Not that I wouldn't do anything for Marilyn, but how much is it?"

"Don't worry. Moonstones are not particularly rare, so it's not expensive." She turned the box over for him to see the price.

He looked up, his eyes wide. "Seriously?"

"Yup."

"I'll take it." He gently cradled the necklace and laid it in its box. "And the lighthouse."

"Perfect." She collected a few more things. "I'll even wrap it all up for you."

"I can't thank you enough. I just know she's going to love it."

"So, when's your anniversary?" She returned to the small basket on the counter and filled it with light blue tissue paper.

"Today."

"Nothing like waiting 'til the last minute." She laughed and put a few candles in the basket, then added bath salts. She held one of the candles out for him to smell.

"Wow, that smells good, like peaches."

"I've been getting really nice feedback on these. They're supposed to help you relax." Hmm . . . maybe she'd take some home with her. A candlelit bath sounded amazing, and she could definitely use some relaxation.

Cass placed the lighthouse in the center, set the box with the moonstone necklace at its base, added the gift certificate for her individual reading, then wrapped the basket in blue cellophane and tied it closed with white and silver ribbon. She rang up his purchase. "Do you have dinner plans for tonight?"

He counted out the bills and handed them to Cass. "Not yet, but I'd like to take her somewhere special."

"Might I make a suggestion?"

"Absolutely."

She handed him his change. "Does Marilyn like barbeque?"

"She loves it. We both do, but I was hoping to do something a little more special tonight."

"In keeping with the stone anniversary tradition, you might check out Island Grill. They offer a picnic basket to-go. You can order dinner and a nice bottle of wine. They pack it in a picnic basket for you with plates, utensils, silverware. Most people take them out to the beach for a romantic dinner, especially when the moon is near full, which it will be tonight. But if you go out past the lighthouse, the shore is lined with huge boulders."

"We saw those from the top of the lighthouse." He grinned. "All three times."

"There are picnic tables scattered around out there, or you can spread a blanket on the beach beside the stones, and it makes for a beautiful, romantic dinner spot." Not that she knew from firsthand experience, since she and Luke hadn't had time to give it a try, but she often heard about the picnics from newlyweds and couples looking to get married at the lighthouse. And she always tried to support local businesses when she could. "Then you just drop the basket back off after you're done."

A shadow flitted across the floor as someone passed the window on the back deck. Whoever it was disappeared from view before she could identify them. Maybe Bee had arrived with her soda and didn't want to interrupt, though he usually came right in and made himself comfortable while he waited. Maybe he'd decided to sit on the deck by the beach until she was done. She wouldn't blame him with how hot the shop was.

John studied her. "You know, I was a little worried about coming in here today. I always like to do something special for Marilyn on our anniversary, and I was kicking myself for forgetting. It's been a long time since we got away together, just the two of us, and it totally slipped my mind. When I called Cayden and asked for suggestions, I never expected to end up with such an amazing day for her. Thank you."

Warmth rushed through Cass, and not because the air conditioner didn't work. "You're very welcome. I hope she loves it."

"I'm sure she will." He shook her hand and took his basket, leaving much happier than when he'd come in.

Customers like John were the reason she'd gone into business in the first place, and also the reason she wouldn't walk away. She might have a lot of work to do to restore her reputation, but it would be well worth it.

As soon as he left, she crossed to the back of the shop and opened the screen door.

A woman sat in one of the rocking chairs, staring out at the water, a big floppy straw hat covering her head, casting a shadow across her face. She turned to Cass and lifted the brim enough for Cass to see her face. "Can I talk to you? In private?"

Chapter Twelve

"Ellie?" What in the world? "Are you okay?"

"Yes, but I can't sit out here." She kept her voice low. "Could I please come in?"

"Of course, but Bee will be dropping by soon." Actually, he should have been there already.

"That's okay, I guess, but I don't want anyone else to see me." She peered in all directions from beneath her hat's wide brim. "When you came by this morning, you said it was okay if I came in."

"Of course it is. Come on inside." Cass held the screen door open for Ellie to precede her. "But be warned, the air conditioner is on the fritz."

"The heat doesn't bother me." Ellie took another quick look around the beach from beneath the brim of her hat before Cass shut the door.

Cass had spent the better part of an hour with John Hicks, and she'd been contemplating closing early, anyway, since she was so exhausted. Plus, it wasn't like there'd been a mad rush of customers. It had been her quietest day all summer. She turned the *Closed* sign over, then locked up the front door as well.

Ellie chewed on her bottom lip and stared out the window. "Would you mind closing the curtains?"

Alarm bells screamed in Cass's head. "We could sit upstairs if you'd prefer."

"No, thanks." She glanced back and forth between both doors before perching on the edge of a chair at the back table Cass usually used for readings, taking care to choose a seat facing the front door. "This is fine."

While Ellie had always been a bit high-strung, this behavior was extreme, even for her.

Cass pulled the curtains across the back window. Though she kept curtains on the back window to avoid direct sunlight streaming in and blinding her customers during readings, she didn't bother to keep them on the front window, so there was nothing she could do to block the view into the shop from the front deck. "Would you like something, Ellie? Tea, water?"

"No, thanks, I'm fine." She motioned for Cass to sit. "Please, I don't have much time, and I need you to do a reading."

"Sure thing, Ellie." Ellie always left calmer after a color reading, so Cass grabbed the basket of colored pencils and a stack of white paper she kept on the back shelf. She lit a few candles and set them on the side of the table, then sat and tried to calm her nerves enough to focus. "Okay, what's got you so spooked?"

"Don't worry about it, Cass. That's not important."

Respecting Ellie's wishes, Cass let it drop. For now. She'd get to it in time. She centered a sheet of blank paper in front of her and laid a row of colored pencils on the table within easy reach. She rolled the pencils back and forth a few times while discreetly studying Ellie.

Ellie knew Cass's routine, and they usually chatted while Cass tried to tune in to her feelings, but today she remained quiet, her right knee bouncing up and down beneath the table. At least she finally took her hat off and set it on the table within easy reach.

Without looking, Cass took a pencil from the row and started scribbling a swatch of color on the paper. Red. The color of fire and blood. While red could definitely symbolize danger, it could also have many other meanings. It was sometimes associated with power, though that didn't feel right, not in connection with Ellie, who was as meek as they came. At least, she always had been before her husband had disappeared. Once Jay was gone, she'd become more independent, stronger. Strength; another of red's possibilities. Could the choice show the strength Ellie had gained since losing both Jay and her mother? Maybe. She'd have to see what came next.

Ellie leaned forward. "Is something wrong?"

Usually, Cass explained her thoughts while doing a reading, but she didn't know what to say to Ellie yet, so better not to say anything. "Oh, no. I'm sorry, Ellie, I was just caught up trying to determine why I chose red as your first color."

She lurched forward, sitting even closer to the edge than she'd been, like a skittish animal ready to bolt at the slightest provocation. "Is that unusual? I don't remember you ever using red for my color readings before. Does it mean something bad?"

"No, not necessarily. I just have to figure out what it's trying to tell me. It may take another color or two before it becomes clear." A fleeting memory resurfaced. Earlier in the day, she'd been concerned Ellie had met someone new, another man just as abusive as Jay had been. Red could also symbolize love.

"You'll tell me even if you see something bad, right?"

Probably not, unless it could help save her. "Of course, but you know I only let good spirits in."

"Oh, that's right." Ellie slumped back a little.

Though Cass couldn't see her hands beneath the table, her arms kept moving, and she could envision Ellie weaving her fingers together, then pulling them apart, a nervous habit Cass had come to recognize from past readings.

Cass set the red pencil aside, then chose another. Black. Her tension level ratcheted up a bit, though whether it was an empathetic feeling brought on by Ellie nervously twisting her fingers or a feeling in her own gut, she had no idea. She began to color, moving the pencil back and forth, slightly overlapping the blotch of red she'd already colored.

"Black is bad, isn't it?"

"Not always. It can be, but it can also symbolize a lot of other things." She needed to settle her own nerves or she'd never be able to help calm Ellie.

Ellie glanced nervously from the front door to the back and back to the front, tears shimmering in her eyes, then leaned closer across the table and whispered, "It doesn't mean I'm going to die, does it?"

"What? No! Of course not."

"You'd tell me?"

"Yes. I would absolutely warn you if I saw something like that. I promise." Not only would she warn her, she'd stick to her side like glue until whatever threat hovered over her had passed. "Black can symbolize a lot of other things, mystery, for instance, or fear."

Heat spread through Cass, burning through her veins. Her heart pumped harder, faster, thudding almost painfully. In that instant, the certainty slammed through her. Fear. Ellie was terrified. But Cass could already tell that from her behavior. So, was she *feeling* Ellie's fear in some psychic capacity, or had she simply chosen the color because she could tell how afraid Ellie was? Though she always tried not to look at the pencils, she could have inadvertently noticed where in the line the black pencil had been. "What are you so afraid of, Ellie?"

"What?" She jerked as if Cass had slapped her. "I don't know what you're talking about."

Ellie had never been one to open up or share her feelings. She'd thought she'd hidden her husband's abusive behavior from the world, though it was common knowledge that Jay Callahan had treated his wife horribly. She'd refused to see his philandering ways, even though he thought nothing of parading around Bay Island with other women. If she'd gotten herself into another relationship like that, Cass needed to figure it out, and fast. But she was going to have to approach it a different way. "I started with the color red, which can symbolize strength. Then moved to the color of mystery and fear."

She could interpret that two ways. Either Ellie had been strong and was now afraid, or Ellie would show great strength against her fears. The latter seemed right. "I think the combination of red and black is showing that you will remain strong even though you are frightened."

Ellie scoffed, then caught herself. "I'm sorry. I didn't mean that the way it came out. I guess I just don't view myself as strong."

"How can you say that?" Ellie didn't need a reading, she needed a friend. Cass set the paper and pencils aside. "You showed incredible strength when Jay left, leaving you to answer a million questions from the police. You seemed confident, determined to make a life for yourself. What's changed?"

Tears shimmered in Ellie's brown eyes, and she jumped to her feet. "I have to go."

"What are you talking about?" Cass had to keep her there, couldn't let her run out in the condition she was obviously in. "We didn't finish your reading."

"I have to get out of here." Her head swiveled in every direction at once. "I shouldn't have even come. If he catches me here . . ."

"If who catches you, Ellie? What is going on?"

Ellie slung her bag over her shoulder, smashed the straw hat back on her head, and whispered, "He's back."

Despite the heat in the shop, Cass's insides went cold. "Who's back?"

Ellie looked around and leaned even closer, even though the shop was clearly empty. "Jay. He's back."

"What!" The burning through her body intensified, nudging out the cold. "Has he contacted you?"

Ellie caught her bottom lip between her teeth and shook her head. "But I saw him."

"Where?"

"All different places. It's like he's everywhere, watching me, stalking me. I'll be walking along, minding my own business, and all of a sudden, I get this feeling like I'm being watched. If I turn around quick enough, I catch just a glimpse of him as he disappears around a corner or behind something. It's driving me crazy." Ellie slouched against the table, deflated, as if telling her story had taken everything out of her.

"Are you sure it's him?" Had Ellie become paranoid? Because that made more sense than Jay actually returning to Bay Island. Cass moved closer, wanting to put an arm around her, comfort her.

Ellie stiffened, and Cass froze and remained where she was.

"Positive," Ellie sobbed.

"All right." What could she do? Ask around and see if anyone else had seen him, for sure. "Have you called the police?"

Ellie's eyes went wide and she stared at Cass as if she'd gone crazy.

"Ellie, if he's back on Bay Island, you have to contact the police." They'd arrest him the instant anyone laid eyes on him, but first they had to find him.

Ellie's head whipped back and forth before Cass had even finished her sentence. "Not happening."

"Okay. Just let me think for a minute."

"Sorry, Cass. I shouldn't have involved you. I have to get out of here. As much a Jay hates you, if he finds me here, well . . . it wouldn't be good." She hurried across the shop and paused at the back door, then sobbed. "Of course, you're not the only Bay Island resident Jay has a major grudge against. So, I pretty much can't talk to anyone."

She had to stall, had to gain control of the situation, had to calm Ellie. And she had about two seconds to accomplish it all. "When did you start seeing him?"

"I don't remember. Maybe a few weeks ago?"

"Where?" She had to get answers quickly, before Ellie bolted.

"All over."

"And what did you do?"

"What do you think I did? I ran home, called out sick for the rest of the week, and dyed my hair back to its original color. Then, this morning, I went back to work. I thought maybe I overreacted, you know?"

Cass nodded, afraid Ellie would clam up if she interrupted.

"But then, I saw him at the shop, or rather, outside the shop, right after you left."

Cass's heart broke for her. It hadn't been easy for Ellie to come out of her shell, to go to work full-time, to put her life back together after losing everything she knew. "Please, Ellie. Just sit down and give me a few minutes to figure this out."

"I'm sorry, Cass. I can't. If he catches me here, it won't go well for either of us. Don't forget, he hates you even more than he hates me. Anyway, mostly I guess I just wanted to warn you." She shook her head then unlocked the door and rushed out the way she'd come in.

Cass looked after her, helpless to stop her, not sure what she could do to help. She grabbed her cell phone and started to dial Luke's number. If Ellie wouldn't contact the police, then Cass would have to do it herself. But what if Ellie was wrong? Cass hadn't seen Jay or anyone else hanging around when she'd visited Ellie at the shop. The entire area had been pretty much deserted, except for the farmer driving the tractor.

She put the cell phone down atop the stack of paper on the table. Leaving the paper and pencils where they were, Cass got her crystal ball from the side counter. While the color readings seemed to relax her clients, and even her, the crystal ball allowed her to focus better. She put it on the table, grabbed a bottle of water from the fridge, and chugged down half of it. She locked the back door and gave a quick look around to make sure Jay wasn't lurking outside somewhere.

Tourists packed the beach as far as she could see, their scattered beach tents and umbrellas impeding her view. Where on earth was Bee?

Beast scrambled to his feet and trotted to her side. He tilted his head and watched her. Was he tuned in to her change of mood? Or did he think they were going for a walk because she'd stood at the back door so long? Probably the latter, but you never knew. Dogs followed their instincts more readily than humans.

She checked the front door lock, scanned the boardwalk for any sign of Jay, then returned to the table and centered the crystal ball in front of her.

Her mind reeled, jumping around from thoughts of Ellie to Jay. The art thefts Luke and Tank were investigating made so much more sense now. She would definitely have to call them sooner rather than later, but there was one thing she had to try first.

The sense of impending doom that had been plaguing her all week returned with a vengeance. Instead of ignoring it, though, Cass latched on to it, embraced it, searching her heart for what was troubling her so badly. If Ellie was right, and Jay really had returned to Bay Island, it was more important than ever that she figure out what was going on.

The thought of seeking guidance from a spirit brought both terror and awe. She gazed into the crystal ball, her focus fully absorbed in its distorted depths. She concentrated, bringing the woman's voice she'd been hearing into her mind.

Blackness filled the orb's center, only a small swirl at first, as it had been within the fire agate, then the dark patch expanded. The churning mass solidified into a shape, a silhouette of a woman. No discernible features marked the blackness.

"Help him."

Cass tried to latch on to the voice, to the woman's image, but both eluded her, slipping away every time she tried to grasp them like sand pouring through her fingers. *"I will help, if you tell me what I need to do."*

"He needs you."

"Who does? Emmett?"

"Help him."

Features started to emerge within the ball, colors. Blond hair billowed and whipped behind the woman, as if caught in a ferocious windstorm. Blue eyes, magnified by the crystal's distortion, pleaded for help.

Cass tried to connect, tried to reach out. *"I don't know what to do."*

"Find him."

Find whom? Jay? There didn't seem to be much sense in asking the vision. Their communication seemed to be totally one-sided.

"Find him."

The blackness started to fade, returning to its former abstract, contorting form. Cass tried to hold on, concentrated harder. Drops of blood splattered against the table. Still, she held on. The flow of blood from her nose increased.

"Find him. Help him," the shape repeated in Cass's mind as it receded.

"No. Wait. Please. I don't know – "

Pounding on the front door ripped her from the vision.

Chapter Thirteen

Beast's deep bark echoed through the shop.

Cass shook her head. Her eyes fluttered open and closed. Had she fallen asleep? Dozed off while looking into the crystal ball? Dreamed of the woman? Would she recognize the unfamiliar face if she saw the woman somewhere? Probably, though she couldn't be sure.

Something hammered against the front door.

She jumped up and grabbed a handful of tissues to stop the flow of blood from her nose.

Beast scrambled toward the door, his paws slipping on the hard wood as he throttled himself forward.

Bee's face filled the front window, his hands cupped around his eyes as he tried to see inside.

Pinching her nose with the wad of tissues, Cass opened the door for him.

He barreled through the door like a hurricane. "You'll never guess who's back on Bay Island!"

When Beast started to pounce, a warning glare from Bee stopped him dead in his tracks, and he settled for bouncing up and down until Bee petted his head.

"Good boy, Beast. See, all you have to do is say hello nicely, and you get pet. Sorry, I didn't bring any food today. Maybe I'll bring you something special later."

Beast barked once, then dropped his tongue out the side of his mouth.

"Now, back to the matter at hand. You'll never guess who's back on Bay Island." Bee resumed his trek across the shop but stopped short next to the base of the case Aiden's thugs had knocked over, then whirled toward her as he started to speak. "What happened to the ca— Oh, dear, what happened to you?"

"I'm fine, Bee."

He rushed toward her. As soon as he reached her, he smoothed her hair away from her face and studied her eyes. "Are you hurt?"

"It's nothing." She waved it off. "Just a nosebleed."

Bee stared at her from the corner of his eyes. "Cass?"

"I'll explain later, and as for who's back on Bay Island, I already heard."

"What? Seriously?" Bee grabbed a bottle of water from the fridge and slumped into the chair. "I didn't even wait in line for the sodas after I heard, just rushed right over to tell you. How'd you hear already?"

Cass felt a little bad. Bee loved being the first to share gossip, and she hadn't meant to steal his thunder. She'd just been overwhelmed by everything. The suffocating heat wasn't helping. "I'm sorry, Bee. Ellie came in for a reading, and she told me."

"What does Ellie have to do with it?" Bee frowned. "And how in the world did Ellie find out before me?"

"She said she's seen him on and off for a while now, that he's been stalking her." Although Cass hated to admit it, she'd been leaning toward the theory Ellie hadn't actually seen Jay. She was kind of relieved Bee had corroborated her story.

"Wait." Bee sat up straighter and set his water aside. "Why would he be stalking Ellie? What are you talking about?"

"Jay."

Bee's mouth dropped open. "What! Jay Callahan's back on Bay Island?"

Uh-oh. She hadn't meant to let the cat out of the bag, had been sure Bee already knew or she never would have betrayed Ellie's confidence. "Isn't that who you were talking about?"

"No!" He paused and studied his hands for a moment. "But that would explain the drastic change in Ellie over the past week or so."

"Bee, you can't say anything, please. She told me that in confidence during a reading."

"Of course, I won't repeat it." An instant of hurt flashed across his face but then disappeared just as quickly, and he held his hand up. "Scout's honor."

"Thanks, Bee."

As much as Bee loved to gossip, he'd never betray her trust. If she specifically asked him, or if he knew it would come back to haunt her in some way, he usually kept his mouth shut. But speaking of gossip . . . "If not Jay Callahan, who were you talking about being back?"

"Oh, right." He settled more comfortably in his seat with all the drama he could muster now that he once again had a captive audience.

Used to his theatrics, and knowing interrupting would only prolong the drama, Cass waited. She didn't bother to unlock the back door—she'd be closing soon anyway—she just took a seat at the table across from Bee.

"So . . ." He cleared his throat and took another sip of water. For Bee, gossip was an art form. "I walked into the deli to pick up our sodas."

Cass nodded. "Thank you."

"Well, don't thank me, because I never did get the soda. But, anyway, Emma was waiting by the door when I walked in. She must have seen me pull up out front and hurried to meet me. According to her, Bruce Brinkman showed up to get lunch earlier today on his way to see Stanley Roth, the attorney handling Dirk's will."

"Sooo? Who's Bruce Brinkman?" She could only assume he was some relation to Dirk.

"Seriously, Cass?" Bee massaged the bridge of his nose. "What am I going to do with you? Bruce Brinkman is Dirk's son. The two haven't spoken in years, supposedly had some kind of falling out a while back, a huge battle, by all accounts. The two hated each other. Bruce left Bay Island after a massive blowout and hasn't been back since."

"That's not unusual, Bee. His father passed away, and fight or not, he would have been notified and asked to see to the final arrangements and all that." Just as she'd returned to see to her parents' final wishes not that long ago. The memory still brought a pang of grief. No matter how many years passed, it probably always would.

"Well, you see, that's the thing." He paused, watching her to be sure he had her full attention. Apparently satisfied that he did, he continued. "He didn't come in on this morning's ferry. He came in last night. Hours *before* Dirk was killed."

Cass's mind raced. While she had to admit his appearance was quite a coincidence, she didn't know what it had to do with the current situation. If Bruce Brinkman had shown up to bury the hatchet and reconcile with his father, she could only hope he'd had the chance before Dirk had been killed.

Bee watched her expectantly, obviously waiting for some reaction.

"I don't understand. Did he and Dirk fight again?"

"Ugh . . . Really, Cass?" He blew out a breath and shoved his chair back. "Clearly you aren't thinking rationally. I guess you needed that caffeine more than I realized."

"What are you talking about, Bee?"

He started the coffeepot, then returned to the table and plopped down. He rolled his hand, urging her to put together the pieces he'd obviously already connected.

She curbed her impatience. Everyone knew Bee had a flare for the dramatic. Besides, he was making her coffee, so, at the end of the day, let him have his fun. "Look, Bee, I realize there's something you think I'm missing, but I've had a long day, and I'm exhausted, so you're going to have to at least give me a hint."

"Oh, fine." He slid forward and folded his arms on the table. "I'll give you a little nudge. Think about it. Don't you find it just a little odd that Bruce Brinkman, who according to all accounts hated his old man with a passion, just happened to show up on Bay Island after a years-long hiatus just hours before Dirk was found dead?"

"Oh, come on, Bee." As much as she'd like to cling to the idea Bruce had come to Bay Island and killed Dirk, clearing Emmett of any suspicion, she couldn't make it work in her mind. Of course, there was always the possibility his rage had festered over the years, but still . . . "What reason could Bruce have had to come back here after so many years and kill his father? If he was going to kill Dirk, it makes more sense he'd have done it in the heat of passion during the blowout you were talking about, not years later."

Bee leaned back in the chair with his arms folded across his chest and pouted. "Well, I still find it suspicious."

"I guess. I'm not completely disagreeing; I just think he'd have needed new motivation to return." Since he clearly wasn't going to get up and get the coffee, and she was running on fumes, she got up, grabbed two mugs, and started to fill them. "What would he have to gain by killing him?"

"Millions."

"Huh?" Cass whirled toward Bee, spilling coffee across the counter.

"I said millions. Turns out Dirk Brinkman was worth a fortune."

He settled in with a smug look on his face and fanned himself with the stack of papers she'd left on the table from Ellie's reading. "You really do need to get this a/c fixed."

"Yeah, no kidding." Now he was starting to get on her nerves. She set the coffeepot back on the burner, grabbed a couple of dishrags, and started mopping up the spill.

He lifted a brow.

She finished cleaning up, wiped the mugs, then filled them, determined to wait him out. They both knew how badly he was aching to dish. She set his mug in front of him, sat across from him, and pinned him with a glare.

Bee crossed one leg over the other, lifted his mug, and blew delicately on his coffee.

Oh, fine! "Please, elaborate."

"Truth be told, I can't believe I've missed this until now," he blurted. Setting the mug on the table without taking a sip, he scooted forward to the edge of his seat. "Supposedly, Dirk Brinkman was worth millions when he died. Family money, which everyone says was a lot more before he squandered it, spoiling himself after he gained ten times that amount when his parents were killed."

Though that was probably an inflated estimate, Cass had a hard time wrapping her head around Brinkman being wealthy. He just didn't come across that way. But hadn't Grace said the same thing about Dirk being spoiled? "Killed, how?"

Bee waved his hand. "A car accident. Tragic, but definitely an accident. They slid off an icy mountain road while on vacation, leaving their only son their vast fortune. He was an adult at the time but had no interest in taking over his father's business or adding to the family wealth, so he sold it, all of it, everything the old man owned except for a small rental house. He lived in that."

A flicker of sympathy Cass wouldn't have thought possible for the man who'd ridiculed and embarrassed her in public and possibly helped destroy her reputation tugged at her. Dirk had spent his whole life spoiled and indulged to the point of being unable to accept he couldn't have everything he wanted. No wonder he'd obsessed over Tanya. She was probably the first person to ever say no to him.

"So . . ." Bee waggled his bushy eyebrows, giving the impression of two caterpillars jumping up and down on his forehead. "I showed you mine, now you show me yours."

"I'll tell you what; let me take care of Beast and lock up. We'll talk over dinner."

Bee sulked. "Okay, I can totally see how annoying that is now."

Despite her exhaustion, she laughed. "I'm not being difficult, Bee. I promise. I'm just exhausted, I've had a rough day, and I want to go sit somewhere, have a good meal, and spend some time with friends. We'll talk about everything. Cross my heart. I'll tell you about Jay and Aiden's brother and his thugs. Everything."

That tidbit prodded him into motion, and he jumped out of the chair. "Oh, fine. I told Stephanie I'd pick her up for dinner. Do you want me to swing back and get you, or do you want to meet us there?"

Either way, she'd have to come back to the shop for Beast. May as well let Bee drive. "Pick me up. I'll be ready by the time you get back."

"Sure thing." He shot her a two-finger salute and hurried out the door.

She shook her head and locked the door behind him. No matter how much of a character Bee was, she could always count on him. "Come on, Beast, want to eat?"

Beast ran to the spot in the back room where she always fed him and started spinning in circles, the *click, click, click* of his nails against the wood floors echoing through the shop.

She laughed as she started to fill his food and water bowls.

The closer it got to her putting the bowls down, the faster Beast spun.

"You're so silly. I've never seen anyone get so excited about food. Well . . . except maybe Bee. Hmm . . . I wonder how his diet's going. He hasn't mentioned it lately." She stopped beside him and waited, as Herb Cox had taught her to do during one of the many training sessions Beast mostly ignored. Herb had also told her she could make him stop turning in circles before every meal, but she didn't have the heart to curb his enthusiasm. "Sit."

Beast plopped down, his whole back end wagging frantically against the floor. Getting him to sit before she put his bowls down was one of the few training exercises she'd been able to manage.

That one had been easy, since he didn't get fed if he didn't sit.

"Stay." She put the bowls down.

Though Beast stared at the bowls, head down, ready to pounce, to his credit, he didn't budge until she released him. Then he shot forward like a cannonball and practically inhaled his food.

Leaving him to devour his dinner, she dumped the remainder of the coffee in Bee's mug down the sink, washed the mugs and the coffeepot, dropped the used filter in the garbage, and put in a new one. She tied up all the garbage, including the glass from the damaged case, and set the bags beside the front door. She'd throw them in her trunk on the way out and take them home with her. Since there was no food in the bags, it would be easier than lugging them down the beach to the Dumpster she shared with several other stores.

By the time she was done, Beast had finished eating, and she washed his bowls, put the food bowl away, and left the water bowl on the floor. She bent and slid her fingers into Beast's thick mane. How she'd ever lived without the giant Leonberger, she had no idea. "Come on, boy. We'll go for a walk, and then you have to be good for a bit while Mommy goes out to dinner, okay?"

Beast whined as if he'd understood every word she said. Who knew? He probably did. She spent enough time talking out loud to him all day long. She wondered briefly if other people talked to their pets like they were people, then decided it didn't matter. Beast was one of the best friends she'd ever had, and he seemed to enjoy their conversations as much as she did.

She grabbed the leash and a small garbage bag from beneath the counter in the back room. As much as she'd love to walk along the beach, this time of year brought too many people, even in the evenings, for her to walk him on the public beach. Maybe after dinner she'd take him out to the stretch of beach by her house, where there would be few if any tourists.

She started to clip the leash to his collar, but the tinkle of wind chimes stopped her. She'd been certain she'd locked the door after Bee left, and it was too soon for him to be back.

Beast barked once and lurched toward the doorway.

Thankfully, Cass was still holding his collar. Keeping him against her side, she poked her head between the curtains into the shop.

Chapter Fourteen

Emmett stopped short when he spotted her and held up a cardboard box. "Sorry. The door was locked. Figured you were gone, so I used my key. Wanted to get the a/c up and running."

"No problem, Emmett." Since Emmett did all her handy work, including the renovations to the upstairs, it had made sense to give him his own key. That way he could work after she closed and after he'd finished working at the garage. "Come in. How are you?"

Beast ran for Emmett the instant she let go of his collar. Since he was naturally wary of strangers, she was able to keep him at the shop all day without him harassing the customers too much, though there were times she had to put him in the back room, but when friends came in, all bets were off.

Since she already knew Emmett didn't mind, loved Beast, actually, she didn't bother apologizing. She simply waited until they were done saying hello, then approached Emmett and gave him a hug.

He squeezed her tight with one arm for just a moment, then stepped back and looked down at the box in his hand. Emmett was a sweetheart but not the most affectionate person, nor the most open.

Getting information out of him was going to be like pulling teeth, but she was definitely going to give it her best shot. "Are you okay?"

He blushed all the way to his hairline. "Fine, thanks."

"Are you really?"

"I don't know, Cass." He crossed to the counter and set the box beside the register, then pulled off his red baseball cap and smoothed his long graying hair. "I didn't do anything wrong."

"I know, Emmett."

"Really?"

It broke her heart that he'd have thought anything different. "It was never a question in my mind."

He blew out a breath and fitted the cap back on. "Thank you."

"Of course." As much as she wanted to offer him reassurance, she couldn't repeat Luke's statement about believing he was innocent. That wasn't her sentiment to share, and she'd never betray his trust. "I'm sure Luke and Tank will figure that out too."

"Then why'd they arrest me? I had to be arraigned and post bail and everything." For Emmett, that was pretty much akin to rambling.

"I'm sorry, Emmett. I know you're going through something awful right now, and I wish there was something I could do to help, but you'll—"

"Actually, I wanted to ask you about that."

"About what?"

"You know . . ." He gestured toward the back table. "That stuff you do."

"Readings?"

He shrugged. "Whatever they are. I thought maybe . . . you know . . . you could maybe . . . get in touch with someone that could help. Maybe tell me who the real killer is?"

"Oh, Emmett." What could she say? She'd never turn him away, but she really wasn't sure what she could do for him. Unless he had some knowledge of who the killer was, it was unlikely she'd be able to figure it out. "Come on in and sit down. Do you want anything? A drink? Something to eat?"

"Nah, thanks. Sara's making dinner."

"How are things going with you two?" She didn't want to ask outright if Sara was being supportive. She was one of the kindest women Cass knew, but she also had a teenaged daughter to think of.

Emmett sat in the chair Bee had vacated. "We're good. She says I'll beat this."

"And she's right. You will."

Emmett took his hat off and fidgeted with the brim, running his finger along its edge.

Thinking Emmett might need a little space, knowing how hard this must be for him, Cass sat opposite him rather than next to him. "How's Joey doing? Does he know what's going on?"

Emmett nodded and folded his hands together on the table. "That's why I'm here. I'd never ask you to do this for myself, but there's nothing I wouldn't do for my son, and he needs me."

"Of course he does, Emmett, and you can ask me anything. You're my friend, and I would do anything in my power to help you."

He nodded and lowered his gaze. "I know. It's just . . ."

"Just what, Emmett?"

"I'm scared," he whispered. Tears shimmered in his pale blue eyes, then spilled over and ran down his cheeks. He swiped them away. "Not for me; I deal with what I have to. Very few things could be as bad as what I went through with . . . Anyway, not much can bring me down, but I'm scared for Joey. We don't have any family. It's been the two of us forever. All of this, everything that's going on now, well, it made me wonder what would happen to him if I wasn't here to take care of him."

"Where's Joey now?"

"With Sara. She's amazing, but I couldn't ask her to support him if I had to go to prison. It's not like there'd even be life insurance or anything. Any savings we ever had got eaten up when Tanya was sick." He paused and fitted his hat back on. Pain creased his features, carving deep lines into his forehead and around his mouth.

Emmett had never spoken to Cass about his wife, and she waited silently, giving him a moment to collect himself and decide what direction to take the conversation.

"Anyway, Sara barely supports herself and Jessica. I can't ask her to take on the burden of another mouth to feed."

The logistics of what he was saying ran through her mind, and she turned them over and over trying to figure out what he could do, but Emmett was right. She didn't know his financial situation, if he owned his house and business outright or had loans and mortgages to pay. It seemed the latter, based on the number of odd jobs he took on in addition to his work at the garage, but the situation with Dirk had reminded her things weren't always as they appeared. Then again, if he owned anything of value, he wouldn't be so upset.

"Don't worry about it right now, Emmett. Nothing's going to happen to you. You hear me?"

"You can't know that." He paused and met her gaze, then frowned. "Can you?"

She ignored the question. Though Emmett showed up to all of her group readings, she honestly didn't know what his beliefs were. He might just enjoy socializing, especially since he'd gotten close to Sara Ryan while at the readings. The fact he was asking her for help might indicate some level of acceptance. Or it might only show his level of desperation.

"You are not going to jail for this, Emmett, but just so you know . . ." She reached across the table and laid a hand over his clasped ones. "If anything ever happened to you, I'd take care of Joey. I promise you that."

He looked into her eyes. "You'd do that?"

"Absolutely, and I don't even have to ask to know Bee and Stephanie would help me. It wouldn't be you, but I can promise you he'd be surrounded by love and have all the support he needed. Always."

Emmett sobbed, his broad shoulder shaking.

Knowing he wouldn't want to be coddled, Cass got a box of tissues from the shelf and put them on the table, then waited.

After a few minutes, Emmett wiped his face, blew his nose, and met Cass's gaze. "I don't know how I can ever thank you."

"You just did. Now, let's see what we can figure out." She set the colored pencils and a stack of paper back on the table, then changed her mind and pulled the crystal ball closer to her. "I can't help if I don't know what happened, though."

"I'm not gonna lie; I was angry when I left here last night, really angry."

Could it really have only been last night that Dirk was found? It seemed like ages ago. Probably lack of sleep. "How'd you get arraigned and post bail so quickly?"

"I'm pretty sure Tank and Luke had a hand in that."

"See, even though they can't say it, they must believe in you too." That was the best she could do to offer reassurance on that front.

Emmett nodded and looked down at his clasped hands.

Cass hadn't realized just how alone he'd been since his wife's death. "So, what happened last night? How'd you end up at the garage in the middle of the night?"

"I stopped home, but I couldn't relax. I knew I wouldn't be able to sleep, and I was getting on Joey's nerves." He smiled affectionately at the mention of his son, a man clearly comfortable with his role in his son's life, both good and bad. "He was supposed to have a big math test today. He didn't do so well in math this year, so it was either summer school or repeat calculus next year, so he opted for summer school. It's been a lot of work to cram into two months, and he's been stressed about it."

"He's a good boy and a good student. He'll get through it."

"Yeah. Well, me pacing around the house agitating the dogs wasn't helping matters, so I took the dogs and went to the garage. Figured I'd get some work done, work off some of the tension, ya know?"

She knew exactly what he meant. She'd come into the shop more than once in the middle of the night when she couldn't sleep. And Bee did his best work overnight when there were no interruptions. Plus, she could see where Emmett's two huge mutts pacing the floors would probably have made studying impossible for Joey.

"Anyway, I hadn't been there more than ten minutes when the dogs started fidgeting and then barking. I heard someone yelling and went out to see what was going on. Dirk was out there, madder than I've ever seen him. Just lookin' for someone to take it out on. And I wanted to punch him so bad it hurt. But I thought of Joey, heard Tanya's voice in my head, telling me Dirk Brinkman wasn't worth leaving my son for."

"Help him."

Cass jumped, startled by the woman's voice.

Emmett continued without interruption, so she could only assume he hadn't heard anything, but a niggle of an idea started to form.

". . . went back inside and that was it. My head wasn't in it anymore so I decided to leave. It took about ten minutes for me to clean up the stuff I'd taken out to work on."

Cass recalled the meticulous way Emmett kept his garage. Not only did everything have its place—tools neatly arranged, hanging from hooks or tucked away in boxes—but Emmett's was the only garage she'd ever been in with clean floors. No stains, no grease, nothing. Maybe Emmett's need for order came from a more difficult time in his life, not unlike Cass's own.

"The minute I opened the door, those hounds bolted for that car, howling like crazy. I looked inside, then opened the trunk, worried Dirk did something to the car, and there he was."

"How would Dirk have gotten the trunk open?"

"Lock on that thing's been busted forever."

Convenient? Maybe, but she believed him.

"And that's it. I called the police, and Tank and Luke showed up." Emmett flopped back in his chair, defeated. "So, are you gonna help me?"

Help him. The same words the imaginary woman had been repeating all day.

Luke and Tank's voices protested in stereo in her mind. She ignored them, much as she would have in real life.

"Of course I'll try to help, though I don't honestly know what I can do." The thought that had begun to surface earlier came screaming back. "Can I ask you something?"

"Yeah." Apparently he was back to his abrupt answers.

"Do you know a woman with long blond hair and big blue eyes. And a small crescent-shaped scar right here?" She pointed to the outside corner of her left eye, not that she'd seen the scar on the woman, but the sudden knowledge of its existence filled her as if she had.

Emmett paled. "Why do you ask?"

"Just humor me. Please?"

He shrugged, pulled out his wallet and opened it, then laid it on the table and turned it toward her and tapped the woman's picture staring out at her. "That's my Tanya."

Ice cold gripped her as she stared into the smiling features of the woman from her vision.

Chapter Fifteen

Cass rested her head against the booth's seat back and closed her eyes, thankful for a moment of peace before she'd have to recap her day for Bee and Stephanie. The rhythm of the pop music pulsed through her. She'd left Beast at Mystical Musings with Emmett to fix the air-conditioning and prayed it would be fixed tonight and cooled off by morning. She didn't have it in her to suffer another day in the sweltering heat.

"Do we get to hear what's going on now?" Bee looked at her over the top of his open menu.

"Yes. Let's order, and I'll tell you everything while we wait for our food."

Stephanie closed her menu and laid it on the table. "Sounds like you had an eventful day."

"You don't know the half of it."

"That's right, we don't," Bee whined. "Because you haven't told us anything."

The waitress approached and pulled a pad from her pocket. "Good evening. What can I get for you?"

The woman wasn't familiar to Cass, and for one fleeting moment she wished they'd gone to the diner instead. James Ingram, the owner of Island Grill, didn't live on Bay Island, and instead of hiring locals he mostly hired people who enjoyed spending the summers on Bay Island but couldn't afford the astronomical prices many of the inns charged during the height of tourist season. Then again, going to the diner would have given her the comfort of familiarity, but it wouldn't have offered the same anonymity the grill did.

Stephanie ordered a Caesar salad.

In need of something more substantial than greens, Cass ordered a steak and shrimp combo with mashed potatoes with a side of garlicky string beans. And a Caesar side salad.

Bee lowered his menu a little. "Are you done now?"

"Ha-ha."

He grinned and pointed to something on the menu. "I'll take today's special."

They handed their menus to the waitress and she hurried off.

Cass was pretty sure the special of the day consisted of a variety of fried seafoods with rich creamy sauces. "What happened to your diet, Bee?"

"What do you mean? I ordered seafood. That's good for you."

"Not when it's fried."

"Yeah, well, I don't see what difference it makes. Seafood is seafood. Right?"

Cass let it drop. Bee was in no dire need of a diet, though a lifestyle change probably wouldn't hurt. His cholesterol levels had to be through the roof with all the junk he ate.

"Thank you for waiting outside for me when you got back to the shop. I'm sorry I held you up." If he'd have come in while she was speaking to Emmett, she might still not be aware the woman trying to contact her was Emmett's wife.

"No worries. When you didn't come right out, I peeked in the window and saw you with Emmett. I figured you were trying to help—he made air quotes around the word *help*—then wiggled his fingers. "I didn't want to get in the way of any of your hocus-pocus."

"I appreciate it." Her connection to Emmett had been tenuous at best. The slightest interruption would probably have made him clam right up.

"Yeah, well, wouldn't want to get whammied or anything," Bee mumbled.

"Very funny." Cass sat up straighter before she risked dozing off. She'd already tried Bee's patience making him wait so long. But where to start?

"I know you won't go into specifics, but how's Emmett holding up?" Bee asked.

"He's doing okay, all things considered. Mostly, he's worried about Joey, about what would happen to him if Emmett went to jail."

"That's got to be a scary thought." Stephanie leaned back to allow the waitress to set their drinks on the table.

Cass waited for her to finish before continuing. "I told him if anything ever happened to him, I'd take care of Joey. I also told him you two would help."

"Of course we would." Typical Bee, no hesitation whatsoever, just jump right in to help a friend in need. "Did that make him feel better?"

"I don't really know. It seemed to." She couldn't imagine a scenario where Emmett actually went to prison for a crime he didn't commit, but it had been known to happen. "Did Tank say anything to you, Steph? Do they really think he did it?"

Stephanie twirled the straw around in her water, seemingly mesmerized by the small whirlpool and the clacking of the ice cubes.

"Stephanie?"

She sighed and let go of the straw without taking a drink. "He said they don't know. All evidence points to him, and yet, he knows Emmett. He doesn't want to believe he killed him, but Dirk had a way of getting under your skin."

"Ain't that the truth," Bee said a little too loudly.

Cass looked around to make sure no one could overhear their conversation. Their booth sat in a corner and no one on either side of them seemed to be paying them any mind. Stephanie had said all evidence pointed to Emmett, but how could there be evidence if he didn't commit the crime he was accused of? "Did he tell you what kind of evidence they have?"

Stephanie looked around and lowered her voice. "Witnesses from the reading, timing, opportunity, motive . . ."

Bee waved it off. "All circumstantial. I heard that much in the deli, the bakery, and the diner today."

Stephanie stared at him and lifted a brow.

"What? Did you expect anything else? Now . . ." He took a sip of his Diet Coke then sat back. "Skip all that and get to the good stuff. You know, the stuff you're not supposed to share with us, but Tank knows full well you will."

Stephanie eyed him for a moment, then leaned across the table a bit.

Cass and Bee leaned in closer.

"Supposedly, they found a bat with Emmett's fingerprints on it by the back of the car where Dirk was found."

"Aha . . ." Bee pointed a finger at Cass. "That's why they asked me if Emmett played baseball. Now it makes sense."

"Was it, you know . . . ?" Cass couldn't bring herself to ask if it had been the murder weapon. As much as she wanted to believe Emmett, having his fingerprints all over the murder weapon found at the scene would not bode well.

Stephanie nodded.

Bee sank back and rubbed a hand over his face. "Is there any other physical evidence?"

"Not that he told me, and to be honest, I think he only told me that much so we wouldn't get involved."

She was probably right, not that it was going to stop Cass. "Is that all he said?"

"No, he also said, and I quote, 'I don't want you and your buddies getting involved in this. Stay out of it, and let us handle it.'"

Bee looked Cass in the eye. "Are you going to stay out of it and let the police handle it?"

She tried to gauge Stephanie's reaction, but Stephanie kept her expression blank as she studied Cass and waited for her answer.

"I can't. I'm sorry, Stephanie, and you don't have to help, but Emmett asked for my help, and I can't say no."

Stephanie smiled. "I figured as much. You can count me in, if there's anything you need help with."

"Me too," Bee groaned.

"Unless it involves breaking and entering." Stephanie shot her a warning glare. "Then you can leave me out."

"Thanks, guys, and no breaking and entering. I promise." *Probably.* Cass relaxed a little, comforted now that she knew she'd have help, though it had never really been a question.

A familiar-looking man waved to her from the to-go counter.

She waved back and squinted to bring his face into focus in the dim lighting.

He put his arm around the woman he was with and gave Cass a thumbs-up, then lifted a picnic basket and headed out the door.

Thrilled he'd taken her advice, Cass watched them go, Marilyn tucked beneath John's arm, snuggling close to him. After twenty-four years of marriage, they still looked like newlyweds. She hoped Marilyn would come in for her reading so Cass could see how their date had gone.

Stephanie returned to swirling her straw. "Did you ever mention the guy in the deli to Luke?"

"Not yet." She wasn't about to bother him with that nonsense while he was in the middle of the art theft investigation, which had been consuming every minute of his time, and now a murder investigation on top of it. "I haven't had a chance to talk to him."

"Well, good thing I mentioned it to Tank then." Stephanie fidgeted with a sugar packet, tapping it up and down against the tabletop, spinning it between her fingers, then tapping it some more.

"And?"

"He's going to look into it, but without knowing what the guy looks like or anything, he wasn't optimistic. He was going to check if the deli has security cameras, so we'll see."

"Hey, does anyone know if Emmett has security cameras at the garage?" She couldn't recall ever seeing any out there, but she'd never specifically looked for them either.

Stephanie shook her head. "Tank already said he didn't. And the garage is pretty secluded out there, other than the hotel—"

"What about—"

"And before you ask, I don't know. He didn't say if the hotel's security cameras showed any of Emmett's lot or caught anything else." She tossed the sugar packet back into its box.

Even if they didn't show the lot, they might have caught someone coming or going down the street. Cass added a trip to the Bay Side Hotel to her mental to-do list. If Henry, who owned the hotel, wouldn't tell her anything, she could always grab Elaina Stevens, Henry's niece, who worked as a maid at the hotel. Since she also worked as a waitress at the diner, Cass would have to be careful what she said to her, but it couldn't hurt to ask if the cameras had picked up anything or if any of the guests had seen anything.

"Why are you so fidgety today?" Bee pointed at the cardboard coaster Stephanie was bouncing on the table.

She put it down and folded her hands.

Bee studied her another minute before turning to Cass. "Anyway, enough of this. I've been waiting all day to hear what happened with Aiden's date."

"Or is it confidential because it was a reading?" Stephanie asked.

Bee glared daggers.

"I never ended up doing the reading. She was pretty upset, not only with Aiden but with me too, because the crystals I'd given her to aid in her love life didn't work out."

Bee tilted his head. "How do you figure?"

"Seriously?"

"Oh, I don't know," Bee said. "Seems to me the crystals worked just fine."

Seemed to Cass Bee's definition of *fine* needed work. "How can you even say that?"

He shrugged. "Well, now that she's rid of the loser who was cheating on her, she can move on and find someone else. Sounds like a win to me."

Leave it to Bee, who didn't even believe in the power of crystals, to find a way to defend Cass. "If you weren't sitting across the table from me, I'd give you a great big kiss right now."

He waggled his eyebrows. "I'll take a raincheck, sugar."

The waitress returned and set their food in front of them. "Can I get you anything else?"

Cass ordered another water with lemon. Sitting in the sweltering heat all day had made her unbearably thirsty. The aroma of melted butter, garlic, and herbs made saliva pool beneath her tongue.

"You were saying?" Bee dug into his fried calamari, dipping a piece into the lemon-garlic aioli sauce.

"Um . . ." The scent of the food and intense hunger had distracted her, and she'd lost track of the conversation.

"Aiden's date . . ." Bee rolled the hand holding his fork for her to continue.

"Oh, right." She cut a piece of steak. It melted like butter beneath her knife, and her stomach growled. "She said she overheard him on the phone, and it was someone else's idea for him to attend the reading."

Bee chewed and swallowed. "Now, that makes more sense. I found it odd he'd attend a reading in the first place but even more so after I saw his attitude there. He definitely doesn't believe in the occult. At least, it doesn't seem like he does."

"No, I got the same impression."

"Did she say who talked him into going?" Stephanie pushed lettuce around her plate, then finally speared a piece of grilled chicken.

"No, but she seemed to think it might have been the brunette Aiden was staring at, though I don't know what led her to that conclusion." She took another bite of the juicy meat. She hadn't done a reading, and Nanette was certainly not a patient, so sharing information didn't seem a betrayal of trust. "I was a bit concerned when she left."

Bee's fork halted partway to his mouth. "Why?"

"She basically threatened to confront Aiden and the brunette. Seems the two had a history of some sort, and Nanette wanted answers."

Bee shrugged. "Maybe she needs the closure before she can move on."

"Maybe." But Cass wasn't so sure. Her eyes had turned cold, calculating, filled more with anger than sadness. "I'll probably never know. It's not like she left a business card or anything, though she did say her name, so I guess I could look her up. Maybe she'll post something on social media."

"Maybe." Bee ate a piece of coconut shrimp. "Now, do you want to share whatever went on in the shop today that you've avoided talking about?"

Cass paused when a familiar duo walked in and zeroed in on Cass's booth. Great, just what she needed, those two showing up right when Bee was demanding answers to questions she'd rather not discuss.

Chapter Sixteen

Tank approached the booth. "Got room for two more?"

Bee slid out of the booth and let Luke and Cass slide into his side, leaving Stephanie and Tank sitting together across from them. While they took a few minutes to rearrange their food and let Tank and Luke place their orders, Cass tried to decide how much to tell them. She didn't want to worry them with things that weren't important, but at the same time, she had no clue what was going on or what might be important, and past experience had taught her she may as well just tell them everything and let them sort it out.

Bee returned to his meal. "Now, if that's all settled, you guys are just in time. Cass was about to get to the good stuff."

"What are you talking about, Bee?" She didn't need their curiosity piqued any more than it already was.

"You know, the stuff you've avoided talking about until now, like how the glass case got broken and why you had blood gushing from your nose when I got to the shop."

Thanks, Bee.

Luke snapped his head toward her, pinning her with those incredible blue eyes framed by thick, dark lashes.

For just a few moments, Cass wanted to lose herself in their depths.

His arm across the seat back behind her head caged her in, making her feel safe, protected.

Bee cleared his throat.

If she could have glared holes through him, she would have.

"What?" He feigned innocence. "Did you think you were going to get away without telling me what happened?"

No, she really hadn't. Bee was like Beast with a bone when it came to information gathering. She sighed, accepting the moment with Luke had passed. "Aiden Hargrove's brother came into the shop with a couple of his buddies."

Luke's expression hardened. Obviously, someone, probably Emmett, had told him about the fiasco with Aiden at the reading. "Did they do something to you?"

"No, not at all. He just warned me that Aiden wasn't going to let the matter drop, that he would see to it the shop got shut down."

Bee leaned forward around Luke so he could see her. "So that makes twice in one day someone threatened you."

"Wait." Luke held up a hand. "What do you mean twice, and did the bloody nose have anything to do with Hargrove and his goons?"

"No, the bloody nose came later." She gave him a quick recap of what had gone on in the deli that morning.

"And you don't know who the man was?"

"I have no idea."

"All right. How'd you get the bloody nose?" Cass knew Luke well enough to know he'd never let the matter drop that easily. He'd look into it the minute he walked out the door.

Now came the tricky part. If Luke and Tank knew she was looking into the situation with Emmett, they'd want her to back off. "I was just doing a reading, sort of, using the crystal ball, when my nose started to bleed."

"What do you mean, sort of?" Leave it to Tank to pick up on that one little phrase.

"My customer had just left when I got a weird feeling and heard a voice in my head."

Bee sighed. "The same woman?"

"Yes."

"Explain." Luke was down to one-word sentences. That was never good.

"I've been hearing a woman's voice in my head. She always says pretty much the same thing. 'Help him. He needs you.' Like that. So, when Ellie left, I heard the voice again, and it said 'Find him,' which was different. I thought it might be talking about Jay, and I still had the crystal ball on the table, so I tried to focus on seeing the woman."

Luke twisted to face her more directly. "And did you? See her, I mean?"

Cass couldn't tell if he was honestly interested or just humoring her. She answered anyway. "Yes."

"And?"

"I don't know who she was telling me to find, but later on, when Emmett came in, I heard the voice again. I described the image I'd seen in the crystal ball and asked him if she sounded familiar. He showed me a picture of his wife. It's the same woman."

Bee choked and jumped out of the booth, bent at the waist and wheezing.

Luke scooted out of the booth. "Are you all right?"

Bee nodded and held up a finger. He sucked in a couple of deep breaths, then took a sip of his soda. "I'm . . . okay. Thanks."

Luke returned to his seat, and Bee excused himself to the men's room, most likely to avoid the conversation he knew was coming. Oh, well, served him right. If he didn't want to hear the answer, he shouldn't have asked the question.

The waitress arrived with Luke and Tank's dinners and set them on the table.

Once they started eating, Luke continued their discussion, interrogation, whatever. "So, what do you think it means?"

"I have no idea. I thought she meant to help Emmett, which makes sense, but why would she say find him? Emmett wasn't with me at the time, but I knew he was in police custody, so it's not like he was lost. Unless Tanya didn't realize that, but I have no way to know that."

"You have no way to know anything about her, and yet, somehow you did," Luke pointed out. Could it be he was starting to believe in her abilities? Though they'd never discussed it outright, she'd always gotten the impression he was skeptical.

Heck, she couldn't blame him. Until recently, she'd been skeptical herself. "I guess, but I still don't know who she wants me to find. It doesn't make sense."

"Why did you think she meant Jay Callahan?" Tank had been uncharacteristically quiet until then.

"Ellie said she's seen him, that he's back on Bay Island."

Tank's gaze met Luke's and held. Something there . . .

"Listen, Cass . . ." Luke put down his fork and took one of her hands. "Please, leave this to us. I know Emmett's your friend, and I know you want to help, but there's a lot going on here, and I don't want you to end up in trouble . . ."

Though he stopped just short of saying *again*, the implication was still there.

He leaned close, the musky scent of his aftershave enveloping her, and kept his voice low. "I can't talk here, but please trust me. Let this go. We'll handle it."

Cass leaned against him and nodded. What could she really do anyway? Other than talk to Elaina in the morning, but technically, anything she said was just gossip anyway, so that didn't count. Maybe she'd talk Bee into going to the diner for breakfast. She couldn't help it if Elaina just happened to be there.

"And if you get any more visions, or whatever . . ." Luke shifted in his seat and avoided eye contact, clearly uncomfortable with the prospect. "Would you mind letting me know?"

"Sure thing."

Coincidentally, Bee returned right after everyone started eating again. "Did I miss anything important?"

"Just Cass telling us about the ghost woman talking to her, and Luke telling her to stay out of it." Stephanie grinned. "Nothing new."

"In case you didn't realize, that was a rhetorical question, dear. Now, on another note." Apparently, conversations with ghosts weren't gossip-worthy enough for Bee. "What time do you think I need to open the shop on Saturday for the festival?"

The Bay Island Mid-Summer Festival was one of the rare occasions when Bee got up and opened the shop early. Every year, Bay Island celebrated the peak of tourist season with a giant festival. Thousands of tourists flocked to the island for the weekend to watch both semi-famous and local bands play on the beach bandstand, and to enjoy the carnival games and rides that would line the boardwalk, great food, drinks, music, and a host of beach-themed tournaments.

"I'm planning to open at eight. There's not a lot of traffic that early, but I enjoy getting to spend some less-hectic time with customers before things get crazy." At least she hoped they'd get crazy. Once the Mid-Summer Festival passed, they'd be headed toward fall, and the rush of tourists flocking to Bay Island would slow to a trickle. She needed to get some savings put away before that happened, or it was going to be a very long winter.

"Are you playing in the volleyball tournament this year, Cass?" Stephanie nudged her half-empty plate away. She'd been pushing her salad around for the better part of the meal but hadn't actually eaten much.

"Sure, count me in."

"Yes." Bee pumped his fist in the air. "What about you, Luke? Want to join our team?"

Luke shrugged. "Sure, why not, but I warn you, I haven't played beach volleyball since high school."

"Don't worry about it. I'm sure you'll do great, like riding a bike, you know?"

On Sunday evening at sunset, to mark the end of the festival, all of the shop owners along the boardwalk closed their shops and challenged the shop owners on Main Street to a tournament. They could include as many of their family and friends as they wanted. Afterward, Island Grill catered a huge barbeque, paid for by the losing team. They ended the festival with an enormous bonfire on the beach, complete with s'mores.

Bee gestured toward Tank. "What about you? Are you going to actually participate this year instead of just watching?"

"I guess," Tank hedged.

"Look, buddy." Luke pointed at him with his fork. "If I'm playing, you're playing too."

Tank laughed. "Oh, all right, fine, I'll play."

"Woo-hoo!" Bee yelled a little too loudly, drawing stares from several customers. He lowered his voice. "We are so gonna kick butt this year."

Stephanie excused herself and headed toward the restroom. She'd been quiet through most of dinner and hadn't eaten well.

"Excuse me, too. I'll be right back." As soon as Bee and Luke moved to let Cass out of the booth, she hurried after Stephanie. She didn't want to mention her unease in front of anyone, didn't want to put Stephanie on the spot.

The ladies' room door opened just as Cass was about to enter. She stepped back to allow the woman to pass her and found herself face-to-face with Tami Mills. After their last run-in, when Tami accused her of being a murderer, Cass simply stepped aside to allow her room to pass.

Tami started by her, then stopped and turned back. "Listen, Cass, I owe you an apology."

Startled, Cass didn't know what to say.

"I'm sorry about the things I said the last time I ran into you. I felt bad afterward, and I've wanted to come into Mystical Musings and apologize, but quite honestly, I couldn't work up the courage."

"Don't worry about it, Tami." Though her words had stung at

the time, Cass hadn't given it much thought since. "It's fine."

"No, it's not fine. My behavior was unacceptable. There was a killer on the loose, and I was terrified, but that was no excuse to treat you the way I did. I'm truly sorry."

The apology couldn't have been easy for Tami, and Cass appreciated she'd taken the time to say it. "Thank you."

Tami's breath shot out as if she'd been holding it, then she lowered her gaze and smoothed her sundress. "Anyway, if you wouldn't mind, I'd love to come in for a reading one of these days. A few of my friends rave about how accurate you are. Most of them attend all of your group readings."

"I'd like that, Tami." While Cass wanted to believe the apology had been heartfelt, she didn't need to be psychic to realize Tami was probably tired of being left out of the group once a week. She patted her shorts pocket but only found a dog treat, no business cards. "I don't have a business card on me, but give me a call and we can set up an individual reading, or you can just come on in for a group reading."

"Will you be having a reading this week? After . . . you know . . . what happened?"

No way was Cass about to stand there and gossip with Tami about anything related to the murder investigation. "Of course, but it's scheduled for Friday night, so as not to interfere with the festival activities."

"Sounds great." She offered her hand, and Cass took it. "Oh, and I can't believe I almost forgot. If anything, I should be thanking you."

Cass released Tami's hand and stepped back. "Thanking me for what?"

Her features twisted into a sneer. "Twenty years without Malcolm King living across the street from me."

The name slammed through Cass like a sledgehammer, driving the air from her lungs.

"Now, if you could just put him away for twenty more, my life would be complete," she mumbled as she walked away.

Chapter Seventeen

Cass stood rooted to the spot, unable to move. Malcolm King. She hadn't heard that name in twenty years, but she supposed he would think she'd ruined his life. Could he have been the man who'd accosted her in the deli? Yes, though the years hadn't been kind to him. That's probably why she hadn't recognized him; she'd pegged him for well into his fifties, when in reality he was only a few years older than her.

She had to think. Unfortunately, she had to take his threat more seriously now that she knew who he was. Exhaustion burned her eyes. A little cold water should remedy that and, hopefully, clear her head enough for her to figure out what to do.

Cass pulled open the ladies' room door and almost ran into Stephanie. "Whoa, sorry. Are you okay?"

"Yeah, yeah, no problem." Stephanie moved aside but continued typing into her phone.

"Is something wrong?" Try as she might, she couldn't read who Stephanie was texting.

"No." She finished her text and dropped the phone into her shorts pocket. "I was just making an appointment with Calvin Morris. My new client?"

"Oh, right. Another meeting?"

"Yeah, well, he doesn't like to discuss business on the phone, so . . ."

"Isn't he the one you were telling Bee earlier doesn't believe in digital documents?"

She rolled her eyes. "One and the same."

"Weird."

"No kidding." She frowned. "And that's not the only thing that's weird."

"What do you mean?"

"Bernard Schaffer, Mr. Morris's former bookkeeper, worked on his own and apparently left a list of acceptable replacements if something should ever happen to him. My name was on the list, and Mr. Morris and several other clients got in touch after Bernie passed away. But some of Morris's ledgers seem off to me, and I wanted to discuss them. Probably just me having to get used to Bernie's methods, but we'll see. In the meantime, I've scheduled a meeting for Friday morning on the mainland."

"You have to go to the mainland to speak with him?"

"Most likely, but I have to confirm the night before. He might possibly have business on Bay Island this week, in which case he'd meet with me here."

"Hopefully he'll come here. I wouldn't even want to think about having to squeeze onto that packed ferry the Friday night before the Mid-Summer Festival." Cass started toward the sink to splash some cold water on her face and freshen up, then turned back. The thought of having to face all of her customers without Stephanie at her side, after how badly she'd screwed up last time, terrified her, especially now that she knew Malcolm King was back in town. "You'll be back in time for my reading Friday night?"

"Wouldn't miss it." Stephanie studied Cass. "Are you okay? You look a little pale."

"I'm all right, but I ran into Tami Mills outside the door."

"That witch, what'd she have to say this time?" Stephanie's resentment and indignation was more for Cass than herself.

"Actually, she apologized for the things she said to me last time we met."

Stephanie snorted, sounding surprisingly like Bee.

"And she thanked me for giving her twenty years without Malcolm King living across the street and wished I'd give her twenty more."

Stephanie froze. "Malcolm's out of prison?"

"Apparently."

It didn't take long for Stephanie to connect the dots, and her mouth dropped open. "The man in the deli?"

Cass nodded. "I think so, but he looks so much older I can't be positive."

Stephanie grabbed both her arms. "You know you have to tell Luke and Tank, right?"

"Yeah, just give me a minute to freshen up."

"Now, Cass." Stephanie still held tight. "Right now. I'm not kidding."

She pried herself from Stephanie's hold as gently as possible. "I will, Stephanie, I promise. The minute we sit down. But I've been up since yesterday morning, and I can barely function at this point. Just let me get some cold water on my face and wash my hands."

Stephanie nodded but watched her like a hawk, standing just behind her while she freshened up, as if afraid Cass would bolt the instant she was left unattended.

The cold water helped, but not much. Only a good night's sleep would cure her sleep deprivation. After she spoke to Luke and Tank.

Stephanie stayed close on her heels all the way back to the table.

Bee slid out of the booth then stopped and stared at her. "Are you okay? You look like you've seen a gh— uh— You didn't, did you?"

"No, Bee. At least, not unless you count a ghost from the past."

"What are you talking about?"

"Nothing. Just let me sit down and I'll explain."

He moved aside enough for Luke to stand.

Cass slid into the corner of the booth, comforted to have the wall against one side, and Luke, Tank, and Bee on her other side. Malcolm would have to get through those three if he wanted to reach her, and even if he was still in his prime, there's no way that was happening. And Malcolm King, if he was the man who'd accosted her in the deli, was well past prime.

"Okay, you're sitting," Bee said the instant his butt hit the seat. "Now, spill it, girlfriend."

"Cass thinks she knows who the man in the deli was," Stephanie blurted.

So much for giving her a minute to get herself together.

Tank studied Stephanie for a moment, then switched his gaze to Cass. "Who is it?"

"I'm not positive, but I think it might be a man named Malcolm King."

Bee leaned around Luke to see her. "Who's Malcolm King? And why have I never heard of him?"

"He's been out of town for the past twenty years."

"So, he was someone you knew when you were kids?"

"Not exactly, but sort of."

Bee's rapid-fire questions made it hard to think. Though it certainly wasn't her fault Malcolm had gone to prison, she'd had a hand in the length of his sentence. Of course, if he hadn't been robbing the mansions along the beach, there would have been nothing for her to testify about. If the same scenario happened at this point in her life, she had to wonder if she'd handle it the same way. It took all of thirty seconds for her to know she would. She'd been right at the time. She'd done the right thing. Despite the fact it might well be coming back to haunt her now. She'd always understood that risk.

"Cass!" Bee huffed out a breath and shook his head. "Wake up. What is wrong with you?"

Luke held up a hand. "Let her have a minute, Bee. I know you're worried about her, but she's obviously got something on her mind. Just give her a couple of minutes to get her thoughts together."

As much as she appreciated Luke running interference, she didn't miss the reminder that Bee was only getting aggravated because he was worried about her, and she loved Luke even more for it. Wait! What? Where had that come from? Though she liked Luke—a lot—she didn't love him. At least she didn't think she did. Did she?

Yikes, she really did need some sleep.

"When I was in high school, I used to spend all of my free time down at the beach. Not only during the summer, but all year long, really." With each change of season, the beach was a whole new place. From the summer months, which brought mobs of tourists, nonstop music blasting at all hours, the aromas of barbeque all day long, and gently lapping waves that caressed the shoreline, to the dead of winter, when she could walk along the shore for hours without seeing another soul, and storms often sent rough seas crashing against the shore and the strongest scents were those of salt and brine. "One day, I was walking down the beach and it got stormy, really stormy, with lightning and everything. The last place I wanted to be during a thunderstorm was walking along the beach by myself."

It had been a windy autumn day, and the sand had whipped into her face while she walked. She hadn't realized it was going to storm when she'd left school and decided to walk along the beach after Jimmy Watkins had broken up with her. Funny, it had seemed so tragic at the time but was nothing more than a barely remembered bump in the road at this point in her life. She might not have remembered at all if not for what had happened after.

"The wind was blowing the sand into my face, burning my eyes, so I decided to hurry home along the boardwalk rather than the beach. I cut between buildings, and just as I started out of the dunes between the shops, Malcolm King ran out from an alley across the boardwalk." At first, she hadn't been sure who it was. He'd worn a black sweatshirt, the hood pulled over his head and tight around his face. No surprise really, considering the cool temperatures and the driving rain. He kept glancing back over his shoulder, as if afraid he was being followed.

Cass had stood where she was, keeping close to the side of a shop—a candy and ice cream parlor that had been gone by the time she'd returned to Bay Island—using it to shelter herself against the worst of the storm.

"I saw Malcolm, clear as day, pull a gun out of his sweatshirt pocket, look over his shoulder, then drop it into a trash can."

Bee gasped and put a hand over his mouth. "Oh, my."

"As soon as the weapon hit the trash can, Malcolm looked around one last time, ripped the hood off his head, stuffed his hands into his pockets, and walked away as if nothing unusual had happened." Who knew? Maybe for him dropping a gun in the garbage was the norm.

"Did you notify the authorities?" Luke slid his arm off the seat back and wrapped her in his protective embrace, pulling her close.

"Yeah. My father was friends with a detective at the time. I told my dad, and he called his friend. He came over and questioned me."

Tank surveyed the restaurant, then pulled Stephanie closer. "What ended up happening?"

"Malcolm went to prison."

Bee snorted. "I fail to see how he could even possibly think you ruined his life. Isn't that what you said he told you this morning?"

"Yes, and he's right."

"How do you figure? If he hadn't had a gun, he wouldn't have gone to prison."

"Exactly." And he'd almost gotten away with it. Back in the day, the idea of cameras on every corner was reserved for fiction. "Malcolm robbed one of the mansions along the beach. It was off season, and he'd expected the house to be empty. Apparently, he'd done the same before. Often. Only this time, there was someone home. The owner's teenage son had come out to Bay Island to spend the weekend with a friend. He and the girl were home when Malcolm went in. They'd said he had a gun, but no one could find it."

"Except you."

She looked into Luke's eyes, swirls of darker blue swimming in their depths. "Without the gun, he'd have probably done a few years. It was his first offense. Or at least the first time he'd been caught."

"The weapon was a game changer."

"Yeah, he either hadn't been smart enough or he was too scared to think straight. Either way, he forgot to wipe the prints before he dumped it. He ended up doing twenty years."

"And now he's back," Stephanie said.

"And looking to even the score," Bee added.

Luke frowned. "How long has he been back? Do you know?"

"No. Today was the first time I saw him, but I didn't even recognize him. He was only a few years ahead of me in school, but he looks much older. I honestly wouldn't have known who he was if he'd just kept walking. I could have passed him a hundred times and I wouldn't have recognized him."

Tank pulled a pad and pen from his pocket and scribbled something down. "I'll look into it. In the meantime, you be careful, you understand?"

"I will."

He paused for a minute, pen poised above the paper, and stared at her. "I'm not kidding, Cass. If this guy has a vendetta against you, there's no telling what he might do."

She nodded her agreement. She knew all too well what could happen when someone had twenty years to nurture a grudge. "I'll be careful. I promise."

"Um . . . Tank?" Even though Bee and Tank had developed a tentative friendship, Bee still seemed a bit uncomfortable in his presence at times, especially when he was feeling unsure of himself. "You don't think Malcolm King could have had anything to do with Dirk's murder, do you? I mean, what better way to get back at Cass than to ruin her reputation?"

Tank didn't immediately discount Bee's suggestion, which surprised Cass. "Why would he do something like that? And then pin it on Emmett?"

"I don't know." Bee shrugged. "Unless Malcolm had a grudge against Emmett, too."

Chapter Eighteen

Cass carried her shoes as she walked down the beach beside Bee, listening to his argument in favor of Malcolm King as Dirk's killer for the umpteen millionth time. Her feet sank into the damp sand, already warm even so early in the morning. Every few minutes, a gentle wave managed to reach her feet, the cool water sucking the sand from beneath her. "I don't know, Bee . . ."

She'd spent all night tossing and turning. Despite her exhaustion when she'd finally fallen into bed, she hadn't been able to fall asleep. And the few times she had, dreams had plagued her, the fractured remnants of which she'd been unable to piece together upon waking, though Malcolm had made an appearance during at least one. "It seems far-fetched to think Malcolm would return after all these years and kill someone basically unrelated to me. Someone who'd just ridiculed and embarrassed me publicly. Seems he'd have been more likely to pat him on the back and buy him a beer. Don't you think?"

"I think you oughta give Tank and Luke a chance to look into what Malcolm's been up to for the past twenty years. They were supposed to talk to prison officials upstate this morning." He nudged her arm with his as they walked side by side. "Why don't you try not to think about it for now?"

Easier said than done. "Sure thing."

Cass kept a close watch on Beast as he frolicked in the dunes. She'd have to leash him once they reached the more populated section of beach closer to Mystical Musings, even this early in the morning, but for now he was content to scamper along the beach. Seagulls screeched and dove in a boat's wake, and the gentle ripple of waves caressed the shore.

Beast stopped and sniffed at a horseshoe crab lying on its back near the water.

"Beast, no," Bee yelled before Cass could get the words out.

Beast jerked his head up and ran toward Bee.

Bee yanked Cass in front of him and held tight to both her arms, using her like a shield as he cowered behind her.

She glared at him over her shoulder. "Really, Bee?"

"Sorry, honey, been there done that, not interested in doing it again."

Cass couldn't help but smile at the reminder of Bee flat on his back, flailing on the beach with Beast on top of him.

Instead of pouncing when he reached them, Beast skidded to a stop, spraying sand everywhere, then stared running in circles.

Cass laughed. "Okay, Beast, sit."

He plopped down.

"Good boy." She handed him one of the small bacon-flavored training treats she kept in her pocket. "You don't want to mess with those things."

She leashed Beast since they were getting close to Mystical Musings, slipped into her sandals, and they resumed walking. When Cass came to the horseshoe crab Beast had been sniffing at, it still lay on its back, clawing at the air. She handed Beast's leash to Bee. "Hold him a sec?"

Careful to avoid the horseshoe crab's long tail, she grabbed the edges of the helmet-like shell and turned the creature over, then placed him gently in the water. "Thank you for walking to work with me this morning, Bee."

He hooked his arm through hers. "No problem, dear. But you don't leave there without me, you understand?"

"I won't."

He rolled his eyes.

"I mean it, Bee. I won't leave alone."

"Yeah, well, you're just lucky it's the height of tourist season and the shop is busy all day long. Otherwise, you would have had some fight on your hands about opening today. And I don't just mean with me."

As it was, Luke had suggested last night she stay closed today. She still had half a mind to skip opening, go back home, and crawl under the covers. If she walked in and the air conditioner wasn't working, she might just do it. "I can't believe it's this hot already. I hope Emmett was able to fix the air conditioner."

Bee watched her for a minute, then dropped the subject and nodded. "You didn't hear from him last night?"

"No."

"Should you have?"

"Not really. You know Emmett's not the most social creature in the world. He just fixes what needs fixing and locks up after himself." Emmett was one of the very few people Cass had trusted with a key to Mystical Musings, and she was always careful to leave everything else done when he was going to be working in the shop after hours. Emmett was almost as meticulous as she was and always cleaned up after himself, then he just had to turn the lights off and lock the door behind him.

Thoughts of Emmett reminded her she'd wanted to go out to the Bay Side Hotel later and see if she could catch Elaina. Darn, she should have driven. That's what she got for two nights without sleep. She couldn't even think straight. "What are you doing later, Bee?"

He shrugged. "I don't know. Why? What do you have in mind?"

"I was thinking of taking a ride out to the hotel and seeing if Elaina heard any good dirt."

"Ha-ha, Cass." Bee laughed. "Did you really think that would work on me? Luke and Tank specifically told you to stay out of the investigation."

"I'm not investigating."

He pinned her with a stare.

"Technically." She grinned, hoping to win him over. "I'm just hunting up some good gossip, and since Elaina works at the hotel right across the street from Emmett's garage, she'd have all the good dirt about whom the police might have questioned, what they'd seen . . ."

Bee chewed on his lower lip and peered at her from beneath long, thick lashes any woman would envy.

Hooked him. Now to reel him in. "Who knows? The security cameras may have even caught whomever put Dirk in that trunk walking onto Emmett's lot."

"I'll pick you up around four, if you can close a little early."

She laughed as she unlocked the back door and pushed it open. A blast of cool air hit her, and she did a little happy dance in her head. "Sure. As long as I'm not too busy, and if yesterday was any indication, I shouldn't be."

"Maybe you should put a sign on the window that Emmett fixed the air-conditioning."

"Couldn't hurt."

Bee walked her into the shop and looked around to make sure she was safe, then kissed her on the cheek, patted Beast's head, and headed home to go to bed.

Lucky.

Cass set about her morning routine, comforted by the familiarity of it. She'd already fed Beast at home, and having enjoyed a nice long walk on the beach, he settled right down with a chew toy.

She walked through the shop and made sure everything was in its proper place, which of course it was, because she'd left it that way the night before. She started a pot of coffee. She'd certainly need it if she was going to get through the day. Next came the cash for change, which she'd put in the safe before leaving. She pulled it out of the safe, then paused before opening the register and patted her shorts pocket where she'd tucked the crystals she'd found yesterday. What if there was something in there again? What if it was something less innocent than the crystals?

She sighed and set the stack of cash on the counter, then pushed the button to open the register and jumped back. The empty drawer slid open, and she laughed at herself.

Beast looked up from his spot by her feet and barked once.

"Don't worry about it, Beast. I'm fine. Or at least I don't think I'm completely crazy. But I could be wrong about that." She separated the bills into their slots in the register drawer and pushed it closed.

She tried to ignore the heaviness of the crystals in her pocket, calling out to her, begging her to understand. Who could have put them there? Anyone, really. She unlocked both doors and turned the signs from *Closed* to *Open*. She grabbed the glass cleaner and wiped down the already spotless cases, ordered a new case to replace the one Aiden's brother had damaged, pulled out a few boxes of inventory from the back room to restock the shelves, then gave up.

No way she wasn't going to surrender to the urge to look into the fire agate again. Leaving the boxes on a shelf beneath the register, Cass filled her coffee mug and left it on the counter.

As she twirled the fire agate in her hand, it began to heat. Warmth spread through her palm. She lifted it and stared into its center, seeking whatever might be hidden deep within the brown stone. Bright morning sunlight poured through the back window, setting the stone ablaze. She concentrated harder, willing the agate to reveal its secrets, to share hidden confidences, to unlock its mysteries.

"Excuse me?"

"Ahh . . ." Cass jumped and jerked her arm back. Her hand hit the mugful of coffee and sent it tumbling off the counter. The glass shattered, spilling coffee across the hardwood floor.

The brunette from the reading, the apparent object of Aiden Hargrove's affections, smirked. "Oh, uh, sorry about that."

"Don't worry about it. It was my own fault." Bee's voice read her the riot act in her head, as real as if he'd actually walked into the shop and found her so oblivious to her surroundings that she hadn't even heard the wind chimes above the door announce the arrival of a customer, never mind the woman's four-inch heels clacking across the hardwood floor.

Cass stuffed the crystal into her pocket. No more losing herself while she was alone and vulnerable. She should have known better. "Just give me a minute to clean this up and I'll be right with you."

"Sure, no problem." The woman meandered through the shop, stopping now and then to browse through crystals and stones.

After wiping up the last of the mess, Cass approached the woman and held out a hand. "I'm sorry about that. What can I help you with?"

The woman ignored her hand, folded her arms, and cocked a hip. "For starters, you can tell me why you told Aiden's date he was in love with me."

O-kay . . . Looks like today is going to pick up where yesterday left off. I guess I should have stayed in bed after all. "I apologize. I shouldn't have said that."

The woman tilted her head, and streaks of red shimmered through her dark hair. "You shouldn't have said it because it wasn't true?"

"No, I shouldn't have said it because it embarrassed everyone involved."

Her cat-like green eyes danced with mischief. "Are you saying you believe it's true?"

"I'm not saying anything except I'm sorry if I embarrassed you."

She wasn't going to get into an argument with this woman, but the cocky attitude was beginning to grate on her nerves. Cass waited her out. Whatever the woman had come in for, she'd get to it eventually. In the meantime, Cass studied her.

The woman kept her arms folded tight across her chest. The beam of sunlight she stood in should have kept her warm, even with the air-conditioning fixed, so she shouldn't be cold. Closed off, then. Keeping secrets? Or just stand-offish? Distrustful of Cass? "Can you really tell that? If someone's in love with someone else? Just by looking at them?"

Of course you could. Most of the time. The way lovers gazed at one another, or even more in the way someone looked at a lover when the person wasn't aware and their expression was open, unguarded, as Aiden's had been that night. Thanks to Cass surprising him with her pronouncement. "Usually."

"So, tell me then, does Aiden really love me?" Some of her attitude slipped, just for an instant, and a touch of vulnerability peeked through the smug façade.

"Why don't you come sit, and I'll do a reading for you, and we'll see what we can tell?" And, with any luck at all, she'd be able to figure out why this woman had talked Aiden into attending Cass's reading. If Nanette Coldwater was right.

The woman only pondered her proposal for a moment before nodding her agreement, making Cass wonder if that had been her purpose all along. Manipulative? Maybe. That would jive with what Nanette had told her.

"Take a seat." She gestured toward the large round table by the back window. "What's your name?"

"Olivia." She sauntered toward the table, pulled out a velvet-covered chair, sat and crossed her legs, the movements deliberate, a woman used to commanding attention. "Olivia Wells."

"It's nice to meet you, Olivia." Cass paused before sitting. A color reading might be a good way to go. It might help relax Olivia. Or she could use the crystal ball? No. She tended to lose herself in the crystal's depths, as she had in the fire agate. Not that Olivia had done anything to threaten her, but Cass had no intention of turning her back on the woman or being caught unawares again if someone else walked into the shop.

She grabbed the colored pencils and paper, lit a white candle and set it aside, then sat. She tapped the stack of paper against the table to line all the sheets up and set out a row of pencils, careful not to pay attention to the order of the colors.

Olivia held her hands out to the sides. "What do I have to do?"

"Nothing. Unless there's something specific you want to know, we can just chat and see what we come up with."

She shrugged and folded her arms on the table. "Okay."

Cass lifted a pencil and started to color, the *scratch, scratch, scratch* of the pencil against the paper soothing, hypnotic. "Interesting that orange would be your first color, a color that can mean enthusiasm and energy, determination even."

But Cass had chosen her darkest orange, the color of insincerity and deceit. She scribbled a wide swatch along the top of the paper, then laid the pencil aside and chose another.

One corner of Olivia's mouth turned up in a slight smirk. She sat up straighter and clasped her hands in front of her on the table.

Cass watched Olivia as she scribbled back and forth, searching for each reaction so she'd know if she was on the right track. "Hmm . . . red. A color of power and passion."

Her eyes widened a bit, barely noticeable, and Cass would have missed it if she hadn't been looking right at her in that moment.

Olivia fluttered her lashes and peered from beneath them, accentuating the feline tilt. A confident woman, well accustomed to using her beauty to get her way. "Is that all red means?"

"Not at all. Each color can mean a lot of different things."

"So, how do you determine which things the colors you choose mean? Could red mean that Aiden Hargrove actually loves me?" Her laughter didn't reach her cold, stormy eyes.

"Different shades tend to have different meanings. A darker shade of red might signify anger, while a lighter shade might indicate joy. An orange with more red in it would have a different meaning than one that leaned more toward yellow. Some of it is interpretation of the colors as they come together. The combinations I choose begin to tell a story, to paint a picture of the individual I'm reading." As did the reactions of said individual. That's why Cass always tried to study her clients while coloring, trying to appear casual, yet watching carefully for any sort of reaction. The swatches of color would form whatever random design they formed, but the person's reactions to each and every statement would bring the story to life.

"So does that dark red you're using mean I'm angry?" She tilted her head; a small smile flickered and disappeared. She was interested in the mechanics of it all, but she clearly didn't believe.

Maybe Cass could change that. "Not necessarily. It can indicate willpower and strength as well. A determined, strong-willed person will often evoke red early in a reading."

But orange and red together early on weren't quite as common. The combination piqued Cass's interest. Now, if she could just figure out how to use the information to determine an accurate portrayal of this woman without outright calling her a liar or sneak.

Chapter Nineteen

Black. Cass wasn't surprised she'd chosen the black pencil next. A color of mystery and elegance, both of which suited Olivia Wells. But when combined with red or orange, a symbol of aggression.

Wind chimes tinkled, interrupting Cass's focus. A young man held the door open for his companion to enter, then placed a hand on her back and guided her toward one of the display cases.

"Excuse me for one minute?" She didn't like to interrupt a reading, hated losing the flow, but she wanted a moment to collect herself and decide how to proceed with Olivia. Plus, she always tried to greet new customers.

"Sure thing." Olivia nodded.

Cass held out a hand as she approached her new guests. "Good morning."

They shook her hand in turn.

At the table, Olivia pulled her cell phone out of her purse and frowned down at it.

Cass couldn't risk losing her. While she couldn't quite peg Olivia Wells, the certainty she had something to do with this whole mess churned in her gut. "I'm in the middle of a reading right now, but you are welcome to look around and help yourselves to coffee, water, or snacks if you'd like to wait."

"Thank you," the young woman answered.

As Cass returned to the table, Olivia set her cell phone aside, but not before Cass caught the letters JC on the screen. JC? A common enough nickname. Or could it be initials? Jay Callahan sprang immediately to mind. "I'm sorry for the interruption."

"No problem." Olivia weaved her fingers together and propped them beneath her chin. "Do you need to tend to your customers?"

"No. I always finish my readings first. My customers understand that since I will give them the same time and attention when it's their turn."

"Okay, then." Olivia sat back in the chair, smoothed her skirt, and folded her hands on her knee. "Read away."

She picked up where she'd left off, scribbling a swatch of black beneath the red blob. "Black is a color of strength and power."

"And death," Olivia added.

"It can be. It's also a color of mystery." Cass watched closely. "And secrets."

Olivia's eyes flickered away, barely an instant, but long enough for Cass to recognize she was on the right track, then immediately back to Cass. "He told me not to come in here, you know."

"Who did?"

Olivia pursed her lips.

"Aiden?"

She smiled sweetly. "Why don't *you* tell *me*?"

What kind of game was this woman playing?

"She came to see me after she left here, you know, demanded answers about Aiden and me, about our relationship."

Nanette Coldwater. So, she had confronted Olivia. Cass had suspected she'd follow through on the threat. "And what did you tell her?"

"The truth, of course."

Cass waited. It really was none of her business, so she wouldn't ask, but she had a strong feeling Olivia wanted to tell her, and it had nothing to do with being psychic.

Her eyes narrowed, a predator on the hunt. "You almost blew everything the other night with your stupid declaration."

"I've already apologized for the other night."

"Indeed." Olivia clammed up, her lips pressed into a tight line.

Cass rolled the line of pencils back and forth, searching for calm. She needed to focus. She lifted another pencil. Green. The color of greed. And envy. "Green is the color of nature. It can be a color of healing and peace."

Olivia leaned toward her and lowered her voice to a whisper. "So, what? I'm supposed to be at peace? What do I need to heal from? Convenient, if you ask me, that you should first cause me grief and then tell me I'm supposed to heal and be at peace. Is it also a color of forgiveness? Perhaps you think I should forgive you for humiliating me in public?"

Heat flared in Cass's face, burned her cheeks. Sweat popped out on her forehead and chest. Darkness crept into her peripheral vision, narrowing her focus to just Olivia. "Look, I—"

"No, you look." Olivia stood and rounded the table. She leaned over Cass's shoulder and whispered in her ear, "You're falling right into his master plan, following along like a puppet, as if you'd read the script. He's right, you know? He does know you. He should have come back to Bay Island to deal with you long ago."

Cass sucked hard to get air into her lungs, despite the crushing pressure. Come back? Who was she talking about? Malcolm? Jay? Bruce Brinkman? Darkness descended, slid across her vision, dark, oily, evil. "Be careful."

"Of what?" Olivia laughed. "You?"

Cass didn't know, and even if she did, she wouldn't have been able to get the words out to warn her. She couldn't get enough air. "I'm afraid you're in danger."

"Want a piece of advice?" She laughed, a cold, devious sound, meant to intimidate. "You're the one who needs to be careful."

Cass jerked to her feet, tipping the chair back.

Olivia caught it before it could hit the floor. She smiled, pulled a wad of bills from her purse, and threw a few on the table. Then she grabbed the paper Cass had colored on, folded it, and stuffed it into her purse. "Thanks for the reading."

The *click-clack* of her high heels against the wood floor followed her to the door. The wind chimes tinkled as the door opened. "Why, thank you, handsome."

"Any time, ma'am."

Luke's slow drawl ripped Cass from the trance, and she whirled around.

He crossed the shop, gripped both of her arms and gave her a quick peck on the cheek. "Hello, beautiful."

"I . . . uh . . ." She had to get a grip.

Luke stared into her eyes and frowned. "Are you okay?"

She nodded, though she had no idea if she was. She resisted the urge to tell Luke to run after Olivia. What had she really done? Nothing illegal, for sure. She hadn't made any outright threats. What could Luke do? He couldn't arrest her. He might be able to detain her for questioning, but on what grounds?

What had she said? It's all part of his master plan? Whose? Aiden's? If so, it had been Cass's own fault for embarrassing him. And her. But Aiden had never left Bay Island, as far as Cass knew. Who had come back? Malcolm King, who blamed her for his incarceration? Jay Callahan? Though it wasn't her fault either of them had chosen a life of crime, they definitely blamed her for bringing it to the attention of the police. What about Bruce Brinkman, who by all accounts had come back to Bay Island before his father was killed? What grudge could he have against Cass?

Either way, the shadow that had crossed her vision had been real, and every other time a shadow had appeared during a reading, a death had soon followed. Someone close to Olivia Wells was going to die. Cass had to warn her. She'd tried, but she'd been caught too off-guard by the whole incident. She'd have to try harder. Later. When she and Bee went to the hotel, she'd ask Elaina to check and see if Ms. Wells was a guest. If she was, Cass would give it one more shot. She wouldn't be able to live with the guilt if she didn't and something happened to her or someone close to her.

"Cass?" Luke shook her gently, and she realized he was still holding her arms and staring at her. "Are you all right? You're shaking and you look pale."

Cass summoned a smile. She barely got to see Luke, she certainly wasn't about to ruin their time together with this nonsense. "I'm sorry, just distracted."

"Cass?" His tone held a note of warning.

"It's fine, Luke. Can you give me a few minutes to take care of my customers?"

"Go ahead." He released her and stepped back. "But don't think this conversation is over."

She grinned at him. "My dear, you sound suspiciously like Bee."

Luke laughed out loud, a deep rich baritone that slid through Cass like warm honey.

"I'll be right back." She crossed the shop and approached the young couple. "I'm sorry for taking so long."

"Oh, don't worry about it," the woman answered. "I love browsing in your shop. You have so many fun things."

"Thank you." She held out a hand and introduced herself properly.

"It's nice to meet you, Cass. I'm Kyleigh, and this is my boyfriend, Wade." She gestured toward her companion and giggled.

A new romance, still in the fireworks stage, not quite completely comfortable with each other yet.

"Nice to meet you both. How can I help you today?"

"I already chose a few things I just have to have and put them on the counter by the register. I hope that's okay?"

"Of course."

"Also, I was wondering . . ." She hesitated, and red blotches dotted her cheeks. "We are having a family reunion on Bay Island next weekend, and I was wondering if you do private group readings. I attended a couple of your group readings last year, and I'd love to do one for just my family."

"Sure. I could do that." She often did both small and large private groups. "How many people?"

She sucked in her top lip and closed her eyes for a minute. "I guess around fifty. And some of them are children. Is that okay? You know, to bring kids with us? We don't know anyone on Bay Island who could babysit."

"You can bring them if you'd like." Jess Ryan, Sara's daughter, was always looking for babysitting jobs, and she was amazing with kids. "If you're comfortable, I know a girl who could watch them down here while we do the reading upstairs. That way, everyone can fully participate and the kids won't be bored."

"We could do that?"

"Sure."

"That would be perfect. Can I schedule it now?"

"No problem." Cass grabbed her appointment book from beneath the counter and scheduled the reading for the following weekend, grateful for the upstairs room. Without it, she'd never have been able to accommodate fifty people.

Luke helped himself to coffee and took a seat at the table while she rang up a couple of gift baskets for the couple.

"Thank you so much," the woman gushed. "This is going to be so amazing. I can't wait for everyone to get to see you in person. I've told them all so much about you and how accurate you are."

"Thank you." Apparently she'd made an impression on her, but try as she might, Cass couldn't remember her. "I'm looking forward to it. And if you'd like to make a night of it, you are welcome to have it catered too. Bella's on the Bay is amazing. They cater all of my group readings."

"Oh, that would be perfect."

Cass wrote the appointment time on the back of a business card and handed it to Kyleigh, along with one of Isabella Trapani's catering cards. She always tried to support other Bay Island businesses, and Bella was also a friend. She walked Kyleigh and Wade to the door and said goodbye, feeling better than she had in days. Repeat customers who loved attending her readings always made her feel good, but today she'd really needed the boost. Smiling, she closed the door and turned, and ran smack into Luke's broad chest.

He caught her arms and pulled her close. "I sure hope that smile's for me."

Her heart stuttered. Darn him. He always managed to send her pulse racing, even when she was determined not to melt into a puddle at his thick Southern drawl.

She laced her hands together behind his neck and kissed him. "I always have a smile for you, but I don't think you came in for my smile, or for that kiss."

"It was a very nice kiss." He traced a finger along the side of her cheek, down her jaw.

"Mm-hmm . . ."

He stepped back and released her, to her disappointment. "But you're right."

"I usually am."

He laughed. "Who sounds like Bee now?"

"Yikes!" That was all she needed. "So, to what do I owe the pleasure of this visit?"

"Can you sit for a few minutes?"

"Sure." She led him to a small seating arrangement and sat beside him on the couch. When he rested his arm along the back of the couch behind her, she snuggled closer and laid her head against his shoulder, only for a minute. It would look totally unprofessional for a customer to walk in and find her snuggling with her boyfriend on the couch. If only they could find more time to sit together like this outside of work. After a moment or two of indulgence, she straightened and turned to face him. "What's up?"

"I spoke to prison officials upstate first thing this morning, and according to them, Malcolm King was a model prisoner."

"So that's a dead end?"

"Not completely. According to their records, he used to have a regular visitor, said she was his sister and provided a New York State driver's license as ID."

"Why do I sense there's more to that story?"

"The driver's license turned out to be a well-done forgery, which they apparently didn't realize until I called to question them. Ironically, once the DMV changed their driver's licenses, the woman stopped coming."

He stood and pulled a folded piece of paper out of his shirt pocket and handed it to her. "Does she look familiar?"

The woman's dark hair hung long and limp in front of her shoulders, plastered close to her head. Something seemed vaguely familiar about her, but it could just be she had one of those faces people thought they recognized. She read the name on the copy of her driver's license. "Connie Smith. Is that her real name?"

"I doubt it, but I just started searching, so we'll see. There is no record of her that I've been able to find so far."

Cass handed the picture back to him. "I don't remember going to school with a Connie Smith, or any Connie, to be honest."

"We've already requested records from several local agencies, but I'm not optimistic."

"Is it still possible that's her real name?"

He paced, only stopping long enough to grab his coffee mug from the table. "It could be, but it's not likely, and I find it strange she'd stop coming once the licenses changed. Could be she wasn't able to obtain a forgery of the newer, more secure document."

"Or it's possible something happened between them, a falling out maybe?"

He nodded and sipped his coffee while he paced. "She could have passed away too, or moved. We just don't have enough information yet. On another note, when I looked into Malcolm's original conviction, it turns out he had a partner in crime, a friend he swore was with him the night he robbed that mansion, though the friend denied being there, and no witnesses ever came forward to corroborate his testimony."

"Oh?" Cass didn't remember seeing anyone with Malcolm or anywhere else in the area that day, but the weather had been awful. It was very possible she'd missed someone. "Who was that?"

"Dirk Brinkman."

Chapter Twenty

Cass reeled. Dirk had been friends with Malcolm? Had possibly gotten away with something Malcolm had gone to prison for? "Are you serious?"

He shrugged. "We can't connect them in any way, other than Malcolm's statement, so I have people trying to look into it. In the meantime, I paid Aiden Hargrove and his brother, Blake, a visit."

"You talked to Aiden's brother?" Cass had specifically told Luke she didn't want to press charges for the incident in the shop. "You didn't arrest him, did you?"

He rolled his eyes. "No, I didn't. Not that I agree with your decision not to press charges, but I do respect your wishes."

Cass already shouldered enough responsibility for the incident with Aiden, she didn't need any more. She wasn't about to ruin his brother's life by saddling him with a permanent criminal record. "What did they have to say?"

Luke sat in one of the armchairs across from her, set his coffee mug on a coaster on the coffee table between them, and rested his elbows on his knees. "Tough guy wasn't as intimidating once he was face-to-face with a detective."

A small niggle of compassion for Hargrove tried to surface, but she tamped it down. She couldn't blame Luke for being angry, and if Blake and his buddies showed up again, it would be a different story, but for now, Luke would have to understand. "Did he admit what he did?"

"Yeah, and he agreed to pay for the damage." He stared at her, daring her to argue.

She simply nodded. "That sounds fair. And what about Aiden? You said you questioned him too?"

"Yeah. He says he didn't know anything."

That didn't surprise her.

"He was lying."

That surprised her even less. "Do you think he had anything to do with Dirk's death?"

Luke raked a hand through his thick dark hair, leaving a small tuft sticking up on the side. "His brother gave him an alibi."

"Do you believe it?"

"No reason not to, but I don't know. Aiden says he was upset when he left here that night, got into a fight with his date, and went to his brother's for a drink. Is it possible? Sure."

"But also convenient."

"It would have been better for him if they'd gone to one of the bars."

The fact he had only one witness to his whereabouts, a witness who had gone to bat for him once already . . . Wait. Bat. Stephanie had said they'd found a bat, but Tank had told her that in confidence. "Do you know how Dirk was killed?"

A smile played at the corner of his mouth.

Maybe that hadn't sounded as innocent as she'd hoped.

The hint of a smile quickly disappeared. "We found a baseball bat at the scene. It's been confirmed as the murder weapon."

If they could figure out who the bat belonged to, maybe Emmett would go free. "Do you know whose it is?"

"It belongs to Emmett, and his are the only fingerprints we found on it."

Her stomach turned over, and acid bubbled up her throat. "What did Emmett say?"

Luke shrugged. "Says he uses it to hit balls for the dogs to chase when he's not busy."

That made sense. Emmett had been very athletic growing up, had played all kinds of sports, but his son Joey didn't share his athletic ability or interest. "Do you believe him?"

He spread his hands wide then dropped them into his lap. "I don't really know what to think, Cass. I'm trying to believe him, and he will remain innocent in my eyes until something definitive proves otherwise, but it's not looking good."

"Maybe I could—"

"No. I mean it, Cass, you have to stay out of this. I'm worried you're in too deep as it is."

"What do you mean?" She hadn't even gone to the hotel yet.

"The victim was last seen by anyone other than Emmett and the killer, assuming they're not one and the same, at a public event you hosted. By all accounts, he spent the evening heckling you. Your friend Emmett intervened and then Dirk went after him. Blake

Hargrove targeted you specifically, and rumor has it his brother's out for blood. Yours. And, to top it all off, you seem to think Emmett's wife is trying to contact you from . . . wherever."

Okay, when you put it all together like that, it did seem she could be somewhat involved.

"I don't want to have to worry about you while I'm trying to investigate this case."

"I understand." It was the best she could do since she wouldn't lie to him, but she had no intention of backing off until Emmett was cleared. Whatever happened after that, she'd stay out of. Probably. As long as it didn't involve any of her friends. "How is the art theft case going? Are you any closer to solving it?"

He stared at her a moment longer, then sighed. "Knowing Jay Callahan is back on Bay Island may have been the break we needed. We're checking out his known contacts."

"What about Ellie?" As long as Jay was around, Ellie could be in danger.

"We can't justify protective custody, because he hasn't made any threats, not that we know of . . ." He held eye contact, turbulence darkening his deep blue eyes.

"That you know of?"

"When we spoke to Ellie, it was clear she's terrified, but she won't say a word against him."

And she never would, no matter what he did. She was too terrified of him to ever ask for help. "You can't just leave her out there unprotected. She—"

"Don't worry." He held up his hands. "We're keeping an eye on her, increasing patrols past her house and when she's at work. At the first sign of Jay, we'll put her under constant surveillance and try to get him."

"I don't like it." Despite the great lengths Ellie had gone to to hide her bruises when they'd been together, everyone had known she was being abused. "I'm worried about her."

"I know. I am too, but she's tied our hands by refusing to cooperate."

"Yeah, I know." Cass still beat herself up just a little over saying anything when it was clear Ellie had shared Jay's return in confidence, but her loyalty was to Ellie, and if it meant breaking her confidence to keep her safe, then so be it. She was no longer bound by doctor-patient confidentiality. "But I don't have to like it."

Luke looked at his watch, then stood. "I'm sorry, I have to run, but do you have plans for tonight?"

Go home and fall flat on my face in bed. "Not yet."

"I'm taking the night off. Would you like to do something? We could go out somewhere, if you want, or I could just bring dinner and we could stream a movie."

The last thing Cass wanted was a night out on the town. Unfortunately, past experience had taught her that if they snuggled on the couch with a movie, at least one of them would be sound asleep before the opening credits finished. At least if they went out to dinner first, she'd get some time with him while they were both awake. "Why don't we go out to dinner and then stream a movie."

He held out a hand and pulled her up, then wrapped his arms around her. "Sounds like a plan."

"Are you sure you can take a night off right now?" She didn't want him to feel like she'd pressured him into spending time with her or think she didn't understand the demands of his career. "I'm not that needy that you have to set work aside for me. I was just going through something because I kept having a bad feeling."

"Has that subsided now?"

She hadn't given it any thought lately, but that constant prodding in her gut seemed to have receded, if not completely disappeared. "I think it's better than it was."

"Could it be Dirk's murder that was grating on you?"

Could it be? Maybe. "It's possible that was at least part of it."

He threaded his fingers into her hair, cradling her face between his hands. "I need this as much as you do, Cass, not only because I need to spend time with you, but because I'm exhausted. I need a break. Hopefully I can come at everything with a clear head tomorrow."

Wind chimes interrupted the moment, and they jerked apart.

Flustered, she whirled to greet her customer. "What are you doing here?"

"I could ask you the same thing, honey." Bee pointed back and forth between her and Luke.

Heat flamed in Cass's cheeks. "Uh . . ."

"Don't worry about it." Bee laughed. "I'm just messin' with ya. I couldn't sleep, so I came back to see if you wanted to close up for an hour and go . . . uh . . ." He stopped short, staring at Luke, and held up a finger. "You know what? I'm sorry. I didn't mean to interrupt. Why don't I just grab a cup of coffee while you two finish up there?"

Luke propped his hands on his hips. "What are you two up to, Bee?"

"Up to? I don't know what you're talking about." He made a beeline for the coffeepot on the counter toward the back of the shop.

"Cass?"

She popped up on her tiptoes and kissed his cheek. "Don't worry about it. I promise I'll stay out of trouble."

"You'd better." He tapped the tip of her nose with his finger. "I'll see ya later."

His words held a hint of promise that sent chills skittering along her spine.

"Yeah, see you later."

The minute he walked out the door, Bee was at her side, fanning himself with one hand. "Good thing Emmett fixed the air-conditioning, because the temperature just shot up about twenty degrees in here."

"Ha-ha. Very funny." She watched Luke climb into his Jeep, then turned to Bee. "So, what's up?"

"Sorry about almost blurting your plans in front of Detective Steamy, but in my defense, I haven't had any sleep."

"Join the club."

Bee practically vibrated. Nervous energy? Excitement at the thought of whatever gossip Elaina might impart? Probably too much caffeine. "So, do you want to close up for an hour lunch break and take a ride out to the hotel?"

It would probably take a little more than an hour at this time of day to drive out to the hotel, find Elaina, question her, and return, but the shop wasn't swamped at the moment anyway.

As if reading her mind, Bee rubbed a hand up and down her arm. "Stop worrying. You know there're fewer customers during the week. Besides, you'll probably be more crowded later when the beach gets too hot to be comfortable."

The fact he was right didn't ease her worries. "I know you're right, but still . . ."

"Come on. If we get done at the hotel quickly, I'll call an order into the deli, and we can come back and have lunch. I'll even drop you off to pick up your car so you can head back here while I pick up the food. At least then you won't have to walk home alone later."

And there it was, the real reason Bee couldn't sleep. He was worried about her.

Chapter Twenty-one

The drive to the hotel took less time than expected, since most people had flocked to the beaches to beat the heat. Since Beast wasn't allowed in the hotel, and it was way too hot to leave him in the car, Cass had left him at Mystical Musings, though she probably should have gated him in the back room rather than letting him roam free. Hopefully, everything would still be intact when she returned.

Waves of heat shimmered across the parking lot as she climbed out of Bee's Trans Am. "Where do you think we'll find Elaina?"

Bee checked his watch. "She's probably cleaning rooms right now. I'll text her and see if she can meet us in the lobby."

Cass searched the lot for Luke's Jeep but didn't see it. He was more than likely chasing down some lead or another. Several news vans clustered in one corner of the lot.

"Okay, she'll meet us in the lobby in a few minutes."

"Great."

"Just out of curiosity, why didn't you ask Luke, or even Tank, about the surveillance cameras?"

Yeah, right. Like those two were going to give her any information on the investigation. "I mentioned it to Luke in passing, and he hedged, told me to stay out of the investigation, and blah, blah, blah . . ."

"Ahh . . . and naturally your response to that order was to come out here and interrogate the poor housekeeper?"

"I'm not interrogating her. I'm just asking a few questions."

"Mm-hmm . . ."

She stopped walking and started to turn around. "We could just leave."

He grabbed her arm and whirled her back toward the hotel entrance. "And have to hear whatever Elaina knows from Emma Nicholls? Not a chance, sugar."

"It's not like I want to insert myself into the investigation, but Emmett came to me for help. Besides, all I'm really doing is talking to a friend. It's not like I'm doing anything dangerous."

Bee snorted. "You got that right, honey. No way I'd be tagging along if you were."

"Says the man who's helped me through more than one danger-ous situation."

"Yeah, well, that's changed now. From now on, if you are going to get yourself into trouble, I'm out."

Cass stopped walking to stare him down.

"What?" He studied his fingernails.

Bee always had her back, without fail, no matter what kind of mess she got herself into. "Since when?"

He yanked the collar of his T-shirt down away from his neck. "Since Luke asked me so nicely, with that thick, sexy drawl and all, to keep an eye on you."

"And?"

Bee swallowed hard, his Adam's apple bobbing, then leaned close and whispered, "And everyone knows Luke is staying at the hotel, so for all I know he could be somewhere around here right now. Listening."

Cass laughed and hooked her arm through Bee's as they resumed their trek across the hot blacktop. "Come on, you. And if you're good, I'll tell Luke you were true to your word."

Bee yanked her to a stop. "You wouldn't really tell him I repeated that, would you?"

"No, Bee. I promise, your secret's safe with me."

"Whew." He pulled a handkerchief from his back pocket and mopped the sweat from his brow. "I would not want to be on that man's bad side."

"Don't be silly. How could you ever get on his bad side when you take such good care of me?"

"That is true, and if you want to remind him of that, without spilling the beans that I slipped and told you about his request, I'm totally on board."

"You got it, Bee."

By the time they strolled through the front doors, Elaina was already seated on a couch in the far corner of the lobby. She waved them over, then recapped her water bottle and pointed to two water bottles on the table. "I figured you'd need it after the heat in that parking lot."

"Thanks, Elaina." Cass sat in an armchair across from her, the air-conditioned air chilling her skin after the heat outside. "Do you have a few minutes to talk?"

"Sure. I was actually just finishing up when Bee texted."

"What have you been up to?" Cass opened her water bottle.

"Nothing much besides working. You know how it is here during the summer."

"Yeah, I do. In some ways, I wish it was like that all year long."

"Bite your tongue." Bee plopped down in the armchair next to hers. "No way I'd want to keep up this pace all year long. I'd never get anything else accomplished."

Easy for him to say. Most of his work was commissioned or through appointments, so he didn't have to worry about generating income for the rest of the months.

"Oh." Bee held up a finger. "Speaking of the summer season ending, you're going to do the fashion show this year, right, Elaina?"

"Of course. I wouldn't miss it for the world."

Attendance at Bee's annual fashion shows had increased dramatically over the past couple of years, and even brought buyers from New York City out to Bay Island. Since he used local merchants for everything, including modeling his amazing dresses, and filled up the hotel and restaurants during the off-season, his shows had become quite popular.

Cass took a long drink, the ice-cold water racing down her throat.

"Cass is going to be modeling something from my new lingerie line."

Cass choked. She covered her mouth to avoid spraying water all over the place.

"Oh, dear, are you okay?" Bee jumped up and patted her back.

She glared at him over her shoulder while she sucked in air and tried to regain her composure.

"What happened?" He feigned innocence.

"Very" — *wheeze* — "funny."

"I'm sorry." He sat back down in his chair and batted his long lashes at her. "I guess maybe I could have chosen a more opportune moment to spring that one on you."

"Ya think?" She recapped the bottle and put it on the table.

"Don't worry, honey, don't I always make you look beautiful?"

Actually, he did. Bee had an incredible eye for what designs would look best on whom. He'd designed dresses more than once with her in mind, and she was always amazed when she tried one on and looked in the mirror, especially his gowns. He was famous for gowns with elaborate strappy backs. Even so . . . "But lingerie?"

"Nothing revealing. You know me: I believe in understated elegance rather than trashy, in-your-face garments that don't leave anything to the imagination."

"We'll see, but I'm not promising anything."

Apparently appeased by her answer, Bee crossed one leg over the other and settled with his hands folded on his knee. "You'll look stunning. Trust me."

She did. Mostly. But she still had every intention of worming her way out of modeling anything referred to as lingerie. "Anyway, I wanted to ask you about something, Elaina. It's about the murder at Emmett's."

With a quick glance around the lobby, Elaina scooted closer to the edge of her seat and leaned forward. "What's up?"

"I was just wondering if there are surveillance cameras on the hotel that catch any of Emmett's lot or garage?" She held her breath, hoping they'd caught something, anything, that would exonerate Emmett.

"Apparently there are two that have a view of the road in front of the garage and the entrance to Emmett's lot, but the detectives already confiscated them."

Cass had expected as much. "Do you know what they showed?"

"Seriously? My uncle owns the place, remember? Of course I heard what was on them."

Her heart raced.

Bee leaned forward, his knees bouncing up and down in anticipation of new dirt.

"Nothing." Elaina sat back and finished off her water bottle. "Not even one car went by on the road between the time Emmett pulled in and the time the first police car showed up."

No wonder Luke had avoided telling her what was on the surveillance footage. He must have known she'd feel the need to investigate further if the evidence suggested Emmett's guilt. She closed her eyes and rolled the cool water bottle across her forehead.

"You okay?" Elaina capped her empty water bottle.

What could she say? She needed time to process that. "Sorry, I'm fine. Um . . . I also wanted to see if you have a guest named Olivia Wells?"

"Olivia Wells?" She shook her head. "It doesn't sound familiar, but if you give me a few minutes, I can look her up and let you know."

"Thanks, Elaina. I'd appreciate it." She had to try to get in touch with Olivia. But what would she say to her? A shadow crossed her vision while doing a reading? The woman hadn't seemed particularly impressed with the premise of communicating with the dead, nor with Cass's ability to do so. And when Cass had tried to warn her, Olivia had not only dismissed but threatened her.

"Hey." Bee nudged her arm with his elbow. "You know who that is?"

Cass opened one eye. "Who what is?"

"The guy who just sat down at the desk over there."

Cass opened her other eye and followed Bee's line of sight with her own. The last thing she needed just then was a gossip session with Bee. She had to figure out what to do about Emmett.

A man sat at a desk in the small office area that provided office equipment for hotel guests. He gestured with one hand while speaking urgently into his cell phone, though she wasn't close enough to make out what he was saying. "Who is he?"

"Bruce Brinkman."

She sat up straighter. "Dirk's son?"

"One and the same." Bee nodded.

"I wonder why he's staying at the hotel." Seemed he'd have stayed at his father's house.

"The two didn't speak to one another, and Bruce arrived on Bay Island while his father was still alive, so it makes sense he'd have stayed somewhere else."

"Unless they were reconciling." What other reason could Bruce have had to return? "Who do you suppose he's talking to?"

"I don't know, but he sure does look aggravated." Bee stood and smoothed his linen pants.

"Where are you going?"

"I want to get close enough to hear what he's saying."

"You can't just walk over there and eavesdrop."

"Watch and learn, honey, watch and learn." He tucked his hands into his pockets and strolled across the lobby, saying hello to a couple of people as he passed and nodded greetings to a few others. When he reached the office space, he sat down at one of the desks and put his phone against his ear, people-watching as if he hadn't even noticed Bruce.

Bruce Brinkman spared him one quick glance, then turned his back toward Bee and continued his conversation. He dug through the center desk drawer and pulled out a notepad and pen, then jotted something down.

Bee's chair came precariously close to tipping as he craned his neck to see over Bruce's shoulder, all while trying to maintain his air of discretion.

As soon as he was done writing, Bruce jammed the page he'd written on and the phone into his shorts pocket, shoved the pad back into the drawer, and strode across the lobby and out the door.

Cass jumped up and hurried over to Bee. "Well?"

"That's it? Well? Not even a word of praise at my incredible prowess?"

She punched his arm. "You were amazing, Bee. Now, pretend I gushed and tell me what he said."

Bee laughed, thankfully dropping the drama-queen routine. With Bee, you never knew. It could go either way. He'd either snap out of it or spend the rest of the day sulking. Since he'd snapped right out of it, the dirt must be good.

"He was arguing with someone. I don't know what about, because he changed tactics once I sat down, but I did overhear him say he listed his father's house for sale."

"Already?"

"I know, right. Doesn't it seem too soon?"

When Cass had returned to Bay Island after her parents passed away, she'd spent hours walking through their home, staring at different things that evoked memories of her mother and father and their lives together. Every time she'd opened a dresser drawer, the aroma of rose-scented sachets enveloped her in memories of her mother. She'd often sat in her father's reclining chair, just to feel close to him while she poured through old photo albums. She couldn't imagine coming home and listing their home for sale after only a few days. As it was, she'd never been able to leave and had, once again, made Bay Island her home. And still, she could never shake the regret that she hadn't done it while they were still alive.

"Hey, Cass?" Bee shook her arm. "Are you okay?"

"Huh?" She wiped a tear that had slid unnoticed down her cheek. She'd have to go by the florist and pick up some flowers later. It had been a few days since she'd visited the cemetery. "Yeah, sorry. Just got lost in thought for a minute."

Bee's phone played a jungle drum rhythm, and he pulled up his text messages. "Elaina says she has to get back to work. Some kids spilled soda all over the carpet in their room, but there's no Olivia Wells, or any other Wells, listed in the hotel registry."

Just what she needed, another dead end. Somehow, she had to find this woman, to reach her and let her know she or someone close to her could be in danger. She should have been more insistent when she'd tried to warn her after the reading.

"Don't worry about it. We'll find her, and it's not like you didn't try to warn her. You did. Who knows? Just because she appeared to blow it off doesn't mean she did. She may be more careful because of it." He held out a hand to help her up. "Come on. Why don't we get out of here?"

"I have to get back to the shop now, anyway. I don't want to leave Beast alone any longer than I have to." She stood and started toward the door. "Oh, by the way, were you able to see what Bruce Brinkman wrote down?"

"Nah, and not for lack of trying."

"I noticed that. Hang on a minute, I have an idea." She ran back to the desk and opened the center drawer. Three pads with the hotel's logo, address, and phone number embossed on the top sat side by side. With no way of knowing which one Bruce had used, and desperate to find a way to clear Emmett's name, Cass ripped the top sheet off each pad and stuffed them into her purse's front pocket, careful nothing would crease or dent them. With any luck at all, she'd be able to figure out what Bruce Brinkman was up to.

"What are you doing?" Bee asked.

"Shh . . ." She grabbed Bee's elbow and urged him toward the door. "I'll explain when we get outside."

Bee followed along without arguing. "Hey. Is that Stephanie?"

"Where?" Cass slowed.

"In the second office on the left."

Stephanie sat at a conference table in one of the private offices she often rented at the hotel when she had a client she didn't want to meet with at her home office and who didn't own a shop on Bay Island.

She sat with her hands folded on the table while a paunchy man in a full suit, despite the almost hundred-degree heat, paced behind her twisting a ring around his pinky.

Cass and Bee angled themselves toward the door, trying to appear casual.

When Stephanie spotted them, she glanced sideways at the man without turning her head, then rolled her eyes.

Cass frowned at her.

Stephanie gave one discreet shake of her head, a warning not to interfere.

The man turned and started another circuit behind Stephanie, then marched to the door and slammed it shut.

Apparently Cass and Bee were not as stealthy as they thought.

"Well, I never," Bee huffed.

"Do you think that's her new client?"

"She didn't say anything about meeting with him today, only Friday, but she did say he might come to Bay Island. Maybe he moved the meeting up."

Cass bit her lip, unsure what to do. "Do you think she's all right?"

"She seemed to be." Bee propped his hands on his hips and stared at the door, then started forward. "But we can check."

Cass grabbed his arm. "What are you doing?"

"What? I was going to knock first."

"You can't barge in there while she's working."

He scowled. "Why not?"

"Bee, how would you like it if you were meeting with a client and Stephanie and I came bursting in?"

He grinned. "It would be interesting."

"Ha-ha."

"Oh, all right. I see your point." He slid to the side of the closed door, then peeked into the narrow window beside it. He waited until the man turned his back, then shot Stephanie a thumbs-up.

She glanced at the man's back, then returned the gesture.

Satisfied Stephanie was okay, they headed out to the parking lot.

Though she scanned the lot as they hurried to Bee's car, Cass found no sign of Bruce Brinkman. Wherever he'd disappeared to, Cass had no hope of following him. Not that she would have. Probably. But the choice was out of her hands.

"It's probably for the best, anyway," Bee said.

"Huh? What is?"

"The fact Bruce disappeared before you could follow him."

"How did you know —"

"Oh, please, I don't have to be psychic, or even particularly observant, to see you looking for him, or to notice the look of disappointment when you didn't find him."

"That transparent, huh?" She laughed.

"More transparent than those ghosts you're always claiming you don't actually talk to."

"Touché."

Chapter Twenty-two

Bee opened the car door for her, then went around to the driver's side.

She slid in, grabbed the seat belt buckle, burnt her hand and yanked it back. She should have known better with the sun beating down so hard.

"You all right?" Bee started the car and blasted the air-conditioning.

Cass sulked and rubbed her fingers. "Your car burned me."

He caressed the dashboard. "She must think you brought spirits with you."

She huffed out a breath. Bee's constant references to her haunting his car in some way were beginning to grate on her nerves. She turned, ready to lay into him.

"Touchy, touchy. Don't worry, I'm just funnin' with ya." He winked. "This time."

Bee headed out of the parking lot. "I should have taken the T-tops off. Do you want me to stop and do it now? It's a gorgeous day."

"Sure." A ride along the beach road with the wind whipping around her might be just what she needed to clear her head.

He pulled over in the empty lot at Emmett's garage, got out, and popped the trunk, then grabbed the pouches the T-tops would slide into.

The car Dirk had been found in had been removed, though all of the other cars Emmett had lined on the lot still remained. A *Closed* sign hung crookedly in the garage's front window.

Cass climbed out of the car and started across the lot.

"Hey." Bee stood beside the car, one hand on his hip. "Where are you going? I'm almost done here."

"I'll be right back. I just want to have a look around." She ignored his token protest and took a deep breath of the salty air. She only wasted a moment staring at the empty garage, which had already begun to feel abandoned. Emmett must not have gone back to work yet. Maybe the police hadn't allowed him to open. If the yellow crime scene tape hanging limp in the still air was any indication, they still considered the garage a crime scene.

By all accounts, nothing had happened between Emmett and

Dirk inside the garage, so there wasn't likely to be anything in there to help her. Besides, the doors had to be locked, and Bee would undoubtedly offer more than a token protest if she tried to break in. She refocused her attention, homing in on the spot where Dirk had been found.

Windblown sand grated beneath her feet as she circled the empty parking spot. Obviously Emmett hadn't swept the lot since his arrest. Cass paused. Even if some of the sand had been blown onto the lot after the murder, some sign of bloodstains should have remained visible. She walked around the spot again, more slowly, then crouched where she estimated the crime scene tech had stood the night of the murder. Nothing, not even a mark on the blacktop or a disruption in the piles of sand that had settled in the crevices.

Cass closed her eyes. The softest of breezes rippled her hair. Seagulls screamed. A foghorn sounded in the distance. Footsteps intruded on her concentration. Probably Bee. If not, he'd have yelled a warning or stopped whomever it was from sneaking up on her. She pushed the sound away, unwilling to lose an opportunity to open herself fully without the vulnerability of being alone.

Where could the killer have come from that wouldn't have shown up on the cameras? She opened her eyes and turned in a circle. The cameras had a view of the road, and no cars had passed, so she dismissed that direction. Even someone walking would have shown up on the video. The garage took up the other side of the lot. That left two directions. One led into the thick stand of woods lining the road for several miles, the other through the woods to the shoreline.

Clearing her mind, Cass started walking. She didn't consciously choose a direction, simply started walking whatever way felt right. She stepped into the woods, careful to avoid a pricker bush. Unlikely a killer would have entered the lot through that spot, especially at night when he wouldn't have seen the prickers. She studied the bush, searching for any clue someone had passed through—blood, a scrap of fabric, trampled or broken vines. Nothing. If there had ever been any, the police had already removed them.

She pushed deeper into the woods, trudging through the thick undergrowth. Fear skittered across the back of her neck, raising goose bumps despite the suffocating heat. Movement in her peripheral vision. She gasped and whirled toward it.

A squirrel jumped from the trunk of a tree beside her, chased by another, and ran up the next tree it came to.

Cass pressed a hand against her chest, willing her heart back under control, but the feeling of being watched didn't abate. She paused and turned in a circle, searching for any sign of an intruder.

Bee stood scanning the area, far enough away to give her privacy, close enough to keep an eye on her and intervene if she needed help. Had his presence caused the sensation?

Sunlight poured through the trees, a soft breeze off the bay rippling the leaves, sending dappled shadows skittering throughout the area. Would the motion be enough to hide someone, conceal them in the shadows? The moon had been near full the night of the murder, and moonlight would have caused the same effect. Could it have provided cover for a killer's retreat?

Something's here. She could sense it, feel it deep in her gut. But what? Had the police already found whatever it was? Though she hadn't searched the entire lot, and it was still possible Dirk had been killed at Emmett's, he hadn't been killed beside the car he was found in. Could he have been killed in the woods and taken back to the lot? But what would he have been doing in the woods?

She pressed forward. A fallen tree, caught and suspended by another, blocked her path. Probably not safe to go under, but she couldn't climb over it, either. Around then. She skirted the tree. Prickers scratched her legs. Shorts probably weren't the best attire for traipsing through the woods. The detour forced her to change direction, angling more toward the beach.

Hiking through the woods for only a few minutes in broad daylight had been difficult. It would have been near impossible to do so at night, even with the light from the moon. She inched forward, crept toward the edge of the woods.

Beach grass encroached, pushing out some of the thicker vegetation, and the dense trees and underbrush opened up to the empty shoreline. Though Bay Island boasted miles and miles of shoreline, not all of it was suited for beachgoers. Algae-covered sand, spotted with thick patches of wet seaweed, led the way to sharp, jagged rocks where the beach met the bay. A beautiful spot to walk, if you brought a beach chair with you in case you wanted to sit down. Which was easy enough, since they made chairs that folded up and slid into a bag you could sling over your shoulder. Cass had done it herself numerous times when she'd wanted some space.

But would a killer have come this way? Maybe. If it hadn't been high tide, when the water would have risen past the edge of the sand and into the trees.

Sunlight glinted off a yacht anchored in the bay, and Cass shivered, the feeling of being watched blasting through her with a vengeance. She took a few steps back and turned around again, searching everywhere.

Bee stood at the edge of the woods, clearly visible, but she'd already known he'd be there, so he hadn't elicited the fear stalking her.

The beach stood empty but for the seagulls foraging for whatever they might find. She turned and headed back to where Bee stood.

"Are you done now?" he asked.

She looked around one last time. "I guess, but something feels . . . I don't know . . . off. You know?"

"I'm taking the fifth." He turned and started back into the woods. "Let's go. I left my car on the edge of Emmett's lot with the tops off."

Yikes. Bee never did something like that. Guilt tugged at her. "Sorry, Bee."

"Don't worry about it. I didn't have to follow you. It was my own choice." He paused and looked around for a minute to get his bearings, then changed direction. "But now I need to get back, and so do you."

No kidding. She'd left Beast alone at the shop way too long. With a new sense of urgency, she hurried back to the car.

As Bee started to pull out onto the road, he slowed. "Hey, is that Emmett?"

"Where?" Cass didn't see him anywhere by the garage or in the parking lot.

"Right there. By the hotel." He pointed. "Quick."

Cass caught sight of a man through the chain-link fence surrounding the back of the hotel just as the service entrance door swung shut behind him. "I couldn't tell. Are you sure it was Emmett?"

Bee inched forward, his gaze still on the hotel door. "How many other men do you know with long, crazy gray hair and a red baseball cap?"

Point taken. Emmett's look was somewhat unique.

"Do you want me to swing around and park and see if he comes back out?"

As curious as she was about what Emmett might be doing sneaking into the hotel's back entrance, she didn't have time to sit around. She'd already been gone longer than she should have. "No, thanks, Bee, but if it's okay with you, I just want to get back and get the shop open."

"Sure thing." He headed down the long stretch of road past Emmett's.

Even though Emmett had been released on bail, the garage remained closed. If he didn't open up soon, while tourists still flocked to Bay Island, he'd have an especially tough winter.

Bee flipped on the radio, the volume turned low. "You really should hire someone, you know."

"We've been over this before." And now wasn't the time to rehash it.

"I know, but Tim is working out so well for me in the shop, I'm thinking of hiring someone full-time."

"Really?" That surprised her. Bee had never talked about taking on help before.

He shrugged. "I don't know. It's been kind of nice not having to worry about what time I get there every day or if I want to run out for something."

It would definitely be nice to be able to get a day off, or even a few hours off, without having to close. "I don't know. I don't think I'd trust anyone enough."

"So, don't hire a stranger. Hire someone you already know. You're in the shop most of the time, anyway."

Bee also generated a much larger income than Cass did. She'd be lucky to make it through the winter months as it was. Hiring someone might tip her into the black.

"Jess Ryan is graduating in June. Maybe she'd want to work in the shop next summer, just to help out until she goes off to college."

"Is Jess going away to college?" As much as Cass had wanted to get off Bay Island when she'd left for college, she'd come to regret the decision all these years later. She could have had so much more time with her parents if she'd stayed and pursued her dream sooner. "Sara will be crushed."

"I know. I was talking to Sara about it the other day, and she's torn. As much as she wants to see Jess do everything she wants to do, she'd miss her terribly. She even mentioned relocating in passing." Bee eased into a curve, and the trees parted to a view of the dark blue water of the bay.

"Oh, no. Emmett would be devastated."

"Yeah, but his situation is kind of up in the air right now, so . . . uh . . ." Bee's eyes went wide. "Not that I think he's going to jail, and Sara certainly didn't say any such thing, it's just . . ."

"Don't worry about it, Bee. I know what you meant."

He nodded. "You do have to admit, it's not looking too good."

Cass shrugged. What could she say? He wasn't wrong. "You can't possibly think he did it?"

Bee squirmed beneath her gaze. "It's not that I think he did it, but you weren't that close to him that night. When I stepped between him and Dirk at the reading, well, let's just say the anger in Emmett's eyes surprised me. Before that, I wouldn't have thought he had it in him, but now . . . I don't know. I think maybe anyone can be pushed far enough to snap."

"I thought you said Emmett didn't have it in him to kill someone?"

"I did, and I don't, not really. It's just . . ." He swallowed hard, his Adam's apple bobbing with the effort. "After going through the woods up there and finding out what's on the video cameras, it's hard to believe someone ghosted their way up there, killed Dirk, and disappeared, all without leaving any kind of evidence or getting caught on the cameras."

How could he have changed his mind so fast? "Yeah, well, just remember how it felt to be on the receiving end of that kind of thinking."

Bee clamped his mouth shut and stared straight ahead out the window.

Great. Now she'd hurt his feelings. "I'm sorry, Bee. I didn't mean—"

"No. You're right. I don't know what I was thinking. I'm sorry."

"Bee . . ."

He pulled into her driveway but didn't shift into Park. "Don't worry about it, Cass. It's fine."

"I'm sorry. I didn't mean to hurt you or dredge up bad feelings."

He studied her for a moment. "It's fine, Cass. Really. I'm the one who's sorry. I shouldn't have said that."

How could she have jumped down his throat like that just because he voiced a concern? "I'm your friend, Bee. You should be able to say anything to me without fear of judgment."

"You're right, and I can, but that doesn't mean you shouldn't call me out when you don't agree with me." He offered a tentative smile. "Besides, you're right, I did say I didn't think he had it in him, and I meant it."

Cass leaned her head against his shoulder. "Thank you."

"Of course." He kissed the top of her head. "Now, shoo. Get back to the shop before the customers bang down the door or Beast eats something important, like your table."

They both knew the second scenario was far more likely.

"I'll see if Stephanie wants to join us and pick up lunch, then meet you there."

She hadn't liked leaving Stephanie with that client either. It didn't sit right in her gut. Apparently, Bee suffered from the same apprehension. Cass climbed out of the car. No sense going inside, since Beast was at the shop, so she just fished her keys out of her bag and headed for her car.

"Hey," Bee called out the window.

She stopped.

"Don't you check those pages without me."

"I'll wait. I promise." Actually, she'd forgotten all about them, but now that he mentioned it, it was a promise that might prove difficult to keep. "But you'd better hurry before my curiosity gets the better of me."

Chapter Twenty-three

Cass opened the door and flipped the sign to *Open*, then stopped in the doorway. Half-chewed colored pencils and splinters covered the floor. She'd been wrong about Beast eating the table. Instead, he'd knocked her basket of colored pencils off the table and spent the hour and a half she was gone chowing down. Luckily, the pencils were nontoxic, at least according to the box. "Why do you do these things, Beast?"

He sat and lowered his head. At least he had the decency to look ashamed.

"One of these days, you're going to get into something that can hurt you, and then what? Huh?" Though Doc Martin had assured her it wasn't unusual for large dogs to get into things, she couldn't help feeling irresponsible every time it happened. And with Beast, it probably happened more often than with most dogs.

Beast whined and scooted closer to her. When she didn't respond, he nudged her leg with his nose.

"Oh, boy, what am I going to do with you?" She cradled his face between her hands and kissed his head. "I'd never forgive myself if something happened to you."

He tilted his head into one hand and closed his eyes, apparently content all was forgiven.

"Come on. Let's get you some water to wash them down while I clean up this mess." She filled Beast's bowl with water and left him in the back room so he couldn't eat any more of the pencil remnants, then she took the broom and dustpan out of the storage closet and started sweeping up. Luckily, she always kept a few spare boxes of pencils on hand. Once she cleaned up the mess and refilled the basket, she jotted a note to order more pencils and stuck it beside the register. Then she looked up Doc Martin's number in her cell phone. It couldn't hurt to give him a call and see if he needed to check Beast out.

Before she could dial, an elderly woman walked in. "Good afternoon."

"Hello. I'm Cass Donovan."

"It's a pleasure to meet you, Cass." The woman shuffled across the room and extended a hand, veins visible through almost paper-thin skin. "I'm Rosa Dupree."

"It's nice to meet you." Cass shook Rosa's frail hand, careful not to squeeze too hard. "I don't recall seeing you before. Are you new to Bay Island?"

"Born and raised here, but I don't get out much anymore, haven't in a very long time."

"I'm glad you came in." Cass guided her toward a seating arrangement near the front of the shop. "Would you like a bottle of water or a cup of tea or coffee?"

"No, thank you. I don't plan to take up much of your time." Though she stopped near the love seat, she made no move to sit.

"Can I help you with something today, or did you just want to browse?"

"I'm hoping you can help me. You see . . ." One hand fluttered to the side of her cheek. "I've been robbed."

"Oh, no." Where had she put her cell phone? Cass wrapped an arm around her. "Are you hurt? Do you need me to call the police?"

She pressed her hand against Cass's. "Oh, dear, no. I didn't just get robbed; I was robbed last week, but I need help to find who did it."

Relieved, Cass gestured toward the love seat. "Please, sit. Let me see what I can do to help. You have reported the robbery to the police, right?"

"Of course, but they haven't been able to find who robbed me or retrieve any of my stolen belongings." She finally sat and twisted her fingers together. "Honestly, I don't even care about most of it. Whoever took it can keep it if they need it bad enough to come into my home and risk going to prison to steal it."

Cass didn't have the heart to tell her the thieves most likely hadn't robbed her out of necessity but out of greed.

"But there was a small blown-glass figurine. I kept it in a case beneath a spotlight, not because of its monetary value, but for the sentimental value it held." Tears shimmered in her eyes and tipped over her bottom lashes.

Cass set a box of tissues on the coffee table.

"Chance, well, Chancellor, actually, though he hated that name. Anyway, Chance, my late husband, made it for me as a gift when my first daughter was born, two flowers twined together, one for each of us." She laughed and used a tissue to wipe her tears. "It wasn't even very good, his first attempt at a new hobby, but it means the world to me. Please, can you help me? I just have to get it back."

Cass sat beside her on the love seat and took her hands in hers. "I'm certainly going to try."

"Oh, dear, thank you."

She left Rosa on the couch to collect herself while she took her crystal ball from the back counter and set it on the coffee table. She sat in the chair across from Rosa, needing a bit of space from her grief to be able to focus. "I can't make any promises, but I will do my best."

"That's all I ask."

"Make yourself comfortable. Would you like anything before we start?"

Rosa scooted back into the corner of the love seat, slid her sandal off, and tucked one leg underneath her. "No, thank you, I'm fine."

"Okay, tell me about the piece you're missing." Cass took a deep breath and stared into the crystal ball, looking past its surface, searching its depths for focus and aid.

"It's all glass, on a small stand. Two pink flowers with glass leaves and stems, intertwined to represent the beauty and joy our new baby would bring us."

Cass tried to picture the piece, tried to imagine it sitting beneath the spotlight.

"Help her."

She gasped and lurched back. Was Rosa in trouble?

"Help her, help her."

"Okay, I'm trying, but let me concentrate."

She waited a moment, but the voice didn't return, so she once again focused on the ball. The image re-formed easily, the glass case, the spotlight glinting off the figurine, drawing your attention. In a flash, the glint of light retreated. Another image replaced the first, sunlight glinting off an anchored yacht. It faded out of focus, and a third image quickly took its place, shimmering, unclear, a woman, lying on the floor it seemed, her long brown hair covering her face. "Help her."

"Pardon me?" Rosa's voice sounded so far away.

Cass's eyes shot open. She hadn't even realized she'd closed them. *"Help her."*

Rosa frowned at her. "Is something wrong?"

"I . . . uh . . ." She shook her head, trying to dislodge the fog that had come over her. Who was she supposed to help? Rosa? Or the woman in the vision? "I'm sorry, I have to make a call."

She grabbed her cell phone from her bag beneath the counter and hesitated. Luke or Tank? Who was more likely to believe her, or at least be convinced enough to check it out? And who was more likely to forgive her for being somewhere she shouldn't have been? She dialed Luke's number. *Sorry, Bee.*

Rosa studied her from across the room but remained where she was.

Cass was going to have to offer some kind of explanation, but she needed answers first.

He picked up on the third ring. "Hey, there."

"Luke?"

"What's wrong?" Of course, he'd immediately pick up the sense of urgency in her tone.

"I'm sorry. Everything's okay, but I need you to do something for me. And then I need you to forgive me. And definitely Bee. It wasn't his fault."

"Calm down, Cass. What do you need? Hang on." His muffled voice came through the receiver, but she couldn't make out what he was saying. Probably telling Tank she'd lost her mind. "Okay, sorry, what do you need me to do?"

"There's a yacht anchored off the beach behind Emmett's garage, at least it was there a couple of hours ago. Is there any way you can send someone to check it out?"

Silence. Had she lost him? Had he hung up?

"Please, Luke, I can't really explain, but would you do it?"

"Tank's taking care of it right now."

Relief rushed through her. "Oh, thank you."

He only paused a moment. "Do you want to explain now?"

"Is not explaining an option?"

"Cass?" Though he phrased it as a question, she had no doubt it was a command.

Principle had her starting to bristle at the order, but she tamped it down. He had done as she'd requested, immediately, no questions asked. He deserved an explanation. "I'm at the shop with a woman named Rosa Dupree."

"That name sounds familiar." The sound of paper rustling came over the receiver.

"Several art pieces were stolen from her house."

"Yes, kind, elderly woman, worried about reclaiming a piece her husband made for her."

"That's her. She came into the shop to see if I could help her find whomever had taken the figurine and retrieve it. When I did her reading, something happened. I saw an image of her piece, then it sort of transformed into . . ." Now for the tricky part. "A yacht I saw when I was out by Emmett's earlier."

"Bee was with you out there?"

She bit the inside of her cheek. How could she tell the truth without Luke getting angry at Bee? "He begged me to leave things alone, but when I refused, he followed me to keep an eye on me."

A scratching sound came over the line, and she could envision him stroking a hand over his five-o'clock shadow. "All right. I'll call you as soon as I know something."

"Luke? Wait."

"Yeah."

"In my vision, there was a woman. She seemed to be lying on the floor, her hair covering her face. There's something familiar about her, but I can't tell who it is." She paused.

"All right. Hang tight until I call you back." He disconnected.

Cass held the phone in her hand and stared at it for a moment.

"I knew you'd be able to help me." Rosa wrapped her arms around Cass and squeezed, with more strength than Cass would have thought possible when she'd first walked in. "Thank you."

"Don't thank me yet." They'd have to wait to find out if Cass had actually been able to help or if she was losing her mind.

"No matter how things turn out, I'm truly grateful. You understood how important it was to me, and you tried your best to help." She nodded and stepped back, then dug her wallet out of her bag. "How much do I owe you? There is no price too high for me to get that figurine back."

"Nothing. Don't worry about it, please. Let's just hope I was able to help." She didn't often refuse payment but, sometimes, readings became personal, and it just didn't feel right to charge.

"Thank you again, my dear, you truly are a good woman."

Bee and Stephanie walked in just then but didn't interrupt. Instead, they set the bags and cup holder on the table and started setting up for lunch.

Beast turned in circles by the back door and whimpered.

Bee pointed to his leash, and Cass nodded, grateful he'd understood he needed to go out.

"Thank you for coming in, Ms. Dupree. I really hope things work out, and I'll get in touch with you as soon as I hear anything."

"Thank you, again, for your help."

Cass watched her go before joining Stephanie at the table and flopping into her chair. "I am so beat I can barely even function."

"Is everything okay?"

Her hands shook as she pulled her hair back and knotted it at the back of her head. "I'll tell you about it as soon as Bee gets back."

She nodded, knowing he'd never forgive them if he missed something juicy. "Bee said you're worried about Aiden keeping customers away."

She shrugged. She hadn't thought about that in a while, but it definitely was a concern. She'd hoped Luke's talk would stop him.

"Don't worry, business will pick up again. With the festival this weekend, you're bound to get a ton of tourists," Stephanie said.

"I sure hope so." The last thing she needed was a slow summer. And to think, only a few days ago she'd been complaining she couldn't get a break. "Anyway, what's going on with you? Was that a client you were meeting with at the hotel?"

"Yes." Stephanie took a large Caesar salad out of the bag and handed it to Cass. When Bee said he'd bring lunch, she'd been hoping for something a bit more substantial, maybe a nice Italian hero, since he'd said he was going to the deli.

Stephanie set out two more salads.

"Salad? For Bee?" What was the world coming to?

Stephanie grinned. "Do me a favor and don't say anything. I promised I'd help him with his diet, since he gained another pound this week. And I had a heck of a time convincing him fast food from a drive-thru wasn't the most nutritious lunch choice."

Cass's mouth watered. An order of loaded nachos and a couple of tacos sure would hit the spot. She removed the lid from her salad. At least it had grilled chicken and croutons. "Thank you."

"For?" Stephanie's brow furrowed.

"Not bringing me something I could stress eat and have to feel guilty about later."

Stephanie laughed. "Thank Bee, not me, though he wasn't happy about it."

No, she didn't imagine he would be.

Bee returned just as Stephanie removed the Diet Cokes from the cup holder and set them out beside the salad dressing.

Beast ran to Cass, tail wagging wildly.

"Good boy, Beast." She petted him and looked up at Bee. "How was everything?"

"Colorful."

Cass groaned and went to the sink to wash her hands.

Bee beat her to it. "What did he get into this time?"

"My colored pencils." She'd have to remember to call Doc Martin right after lunch, though Beast seemed to be his usual perky self.

Bee shook his head, but to his credit refrained from saying I told you so. He used a couple of paper towels to dry his hands. "Did you figure out what was written on the papers you swiped from the hotel?"

"What papers?" Stephanie asked.

"Bruce Brinkman was on the phone at the hotel, and he seemed agitated. When he wrote something down on a notepad, Cass took the top page off each one so she could see what he was up to." Bee poured dressing from a small plastic cup over his salad, then looked in the empty bag. "Is that all there is?"

"Yup." Stephanie pointed at him with her fork. "That's all you need to give it a little flavor."

"I don't want a little flavor." Bee pouted. "I want a whole lot of flavor. Preferably, the flavor of beef. And cheese. Oh, and bacon. Definitely bacon."

"Eat your salad, Bee. It doesn't help to think about what you can't have."

"Yeah, yeah." He took a big bite, chewed, and swallowed, a pained expression marring his features through the entire process. "Why don't you get the papers out and distract me."

"I will, but first I have to apologize."

He frowned. "What for?"

She ran through what Rosa had told her, then explained her vision. "I had to call Luke and tell him what happened so he'd check it out."

"Who do you think the woman is?"

"I don't know. The angle she's lying at and the haze covering the image . . . I just couldn't tell."

He nodded and crunched his salad.

That was it? "Am I forgiven?"

"For what?" he asked.

"Telling Luke you were out there with me?"

"There's nothing to forgive, Cass. If you think a woman might be in danger, you couldn't have made any other choice." He nibbled a crouton. "But how about that distraction now, so I can get through this salad?"

Cass dug through her purse for the papers from the hotel, then pulled a dark blue colored pencil from the basket. She scribbled back and forth lightly over the top sheet of paper from the first pad, hoping the indentations would show her what had been written on the page above it. It only took her a minute to recognize directions from the hotel to the Bay Island Lighthouse. Probably a tourist who'd used the notepad to jot them down.

Stephanie's cell phone rang, and she checked the caller ID, then groaned. She swallowed the bite she'd taken and answered. "Yes, Mr. Morris?"

A man's voice barked what seemed like an order.

"No problem. I'll be there in a little while." She hung up.

"What's he want now?" Bee asked.

She waved him off. "I have to meet with him again this afternoon. He says he found invoices to cover some of the money that's not adding up."

"This guy sounds like a real mess." Which would be hard for Stephanie to deal with, considering she kept her books meticulously. Cass had no doubt she'd straighten him out quickly or drop him.

"You don't know the half of it."

The top page off the next notepad yielded a date and time but nothing to indicate what it meant. Cass checked the date on the page against her phone calendar. Whatever it was would take place this Friday evening at seven. The same day and time as her next reading. Coincidence? Maybe. It could be perfectly legitimate, as many hotel guests attended her readings, or it could have nothing to do with her and simply be a dinner date. Friday at seven certainly was a common enough time to go for dinner, especially while on vacation.

"Anything?" Bee craned his neck trying to see what she'd found.

"Not that I can tell." She started on the next page, scribbling back and forth. The letters on that one showed up better than the others. Perhaps Brinkman's anger had him pressing down harder with the pen. An address appeared. "Bingo. Thirty-five West Main Street. Hmmm . . . Why does that sound so familiar?"

Stephanie stopped eating and lay her fork down on her plate. "That's the antique shop just outside of town."

"The one where Ellie works?" Bee fumbled his fork. "Are you sure?"

"Yes."

No wonder it sounded familiar to Cass, she'd just been there to see Ellie.

"Positive. The owner is a client."

"Does anyone know what time Ellie gets off?" She couldn't explain the sense of urgency prodding her, but she had a strong feeling she needed to get in touch with Ellie.

Bee frowned. "What would Bruce Brinkman want with Ellie?"

"We can't be sure that's the pad Bruce wrote on. He could very well be visiting the lighthouse while he's in town, or he could have an appointment on Friday evening with anyone at all, including a perfectly legitimate meeting to get his father's affairs in order." Cass dialed Ellie's cell phone number.

"Or?" Bee asked.

An image of Ellie, her long brown hair splayed around her, popped into Cass's head. "Or it could be Jay Callahan had the nerve to show up at the hotel and used that pad to track down Ellie."

Ellie answered on the first ring. "Hey, Cass, is something wrong?"

"Uh, no, not at all. Um . . ." Okay, that was lame. She hadn't thought past getting in touch with Ellie and making sure she was okay. Now she had no clue what to say. "I just wanted to check in and see how you were doing and thank you for sending Willie over with the chairs and barrels."

"I'm fine, thank you, and you're welcome." Silence stretched between them.

Should she tell her about the notepad? Probably not. With Ellie on the line, apparently fine, the urgency subsided. It was possible she'd overreacted. The antique shops on Bay Island often drew tourists who stayed at the hotel. "Okay, then. Just remember, I'm here if you need me, okay?"

"Sure thing, Cass, thanks."

"You're welcome." She disconnected and lay the phone on the table.

"She's okay?" Bee asked.

"Seems like it."

"Okay, so what do we know that we didn't already know?" Stephanie asked.

Cass shrugged. "Absolutely nothing."

Chapter Twenty-four

Cass brushed highlighter beneath her eyebrows for the third time, then accepted her attempts weren't going to yield any better results. Giving up, she stuck the palette back in the vanity drawer. She didn't often wear makeup, and she admired women who could put their faces together in a way that looked both sultry and natural. She didn't share their talents.

Luke had said he was taking her out for dinner, but he hadn't said where. He also hadn't called back since she'd asked him to check out the yacht. In some ways, she hoped it turned out to be a dead end, that the woman with the long dark hair would turn out to be a figment of her overactive imagination. No use thinking about it. Not like she could do anything other than wait.

She studied herself in the bathroom's full-length mirror and smoothed the clingy black dress. Hopefully, the dress wasn't too casual, especially since she'd dressed it up with jewelry and a belt. She grabbed her high-heeled sandals and the lint roller from the closet shelf and carried them with her to the kitchen. "Still not here yet, huh, Beast?"

If she sat down, she had no doubt she'd fall asleep within minutes. That's all she needed, to have Luke finally get a night off, walk in to pick her up, and find her passed out on the couch, probably snoring with a line of drool running down her chin.

She picked up a romance novel she'd started before the summer rush had begun and flipped through the pages. Though she could have used her e-reader, she preferred the weight of a real book in her hand when she curled up to read, and it definitely made it easier to skim the chapters and remind herself what had been going on.

Satisfied she remembered the main characters and plot line, she turned on all the living room lights and sat on the couch, curling her feet beneath her.

Beast curled up against her side.

If Luke took too much longer, she might just decide not to go out after all. She started to read, tried her best to concentrate on the words, but her mind wandered back to the yacht and the woman in her vision and Rosa Dupree. After reading the first paragraph for the third time, she increased her efforts to focus. Maybe reading hadn't been the best idea. Maybe she should get up and clean something. With her luck, she'd splash bleach all over her dress if she tried. As it was, she'd have to run the lint roller over the black dress on her way out the door to remove the coating of Beast's hair.

She rubbed her eyes. Exhaustion beat at her. Reading, or trying to anyway, was only adding to the problem, burning her eyes. She opened the book and tried again. The words jumbled on the page. Her eyes fluttered closed. Her body jerked, and she dropped the book onto her lap, then shot straight up on the couch. So much for reading. If she allowed herself just a minute or two to close her eyes, she'd probably get a second wind.

Liar.

Her mind drifted, beyond her control. Darkness tunneled her vision, and her eyes slid closed. Fragments of images flickered through her mind. A woman. Long brown hair fanned around her as she lay on what looked like concrete, her body bent at an awkward angle. Wait. Concrete? That wasn't right. Was it? Not on the yacht then.

The woman's features swam in and out of focus, never quite clear enough to discern. Her eyes remained closed.

"Help her."

"I don't know how." Safe in her own home, Cass reached for the voice, immersing herself fully in the vision. *"Who is she?"*

"Help her."

Darkness swirled around the woman, obscuring any chance of recognition. *"I can't see – "*

"Help her, help her. Help her! Helpher, helpherhelpher . . ."

Hands gripped Cass's arms, tightening their hold, squeezing, vise-like, lifting her . . .

Cass screamed and tore herself from the vision.

Her book flew across the room, slammed into the wall, then dropped onto the floor with a thud.

"Cass!" Bee held on to her arms, gripping her tight enough to keep her from falling to the floor when her legs gave out. He pulled her into his arms. "Cass, talk to me."

"What?" She shook her head and closed her eyes. She had to get the vision back, had to know who the woman was. Dark hair.

Familiar. Someone she knew. Ellie? "Let go of me. I have to go back."

Bee gently lowered her to the couch and stepped back, hands up in a gesture of surrender. "Cass, you're scaring me a little here."

She lay her head back against the couch cushion and closed her eyes. She searched for the vision, tried to recreate it, pulling up every detail. It was no use. The image, never fully formed to begin with, faded, distorted, then disappeared completely. She opened her eyes.

"Honey, I have no idea what's happening here, but you're not going to spin your head around or anything, are you?" Bee's hands shook, and what he'd managed of a tan so far this summer had vanished, leaving him ghostly pale. He glanced between Cass and the paperback that had landed on the floor beside an armchair.

Tears streaked down Cass's cheeks, no doubt destroying her painstaking makeup job. She half sobbed, half laughed. "Oh, man, Bee. I'm so sorry."

He pursed his lips and backed across the room. When the armchair hit the backs of his knees, he dropped straight down onto it and lowered his head into his hands. He blew out a breath and shoved both hands through his hair before finally making eye contact. "What on earth was that?"

"What was what?" She wasn't even trying to feign innocence. She was fully aware something had just happened, but she honestly had no clue what had him so freaked out.

He pointed at her and spun his finger around and around. "That thing. Episode. Whatever it was. You were babbling, the same phrase over and over again. 'Helper' or something like that. I'm not gonna lie, that was some freaky stuff."

"I'm sorry, Bee. I didn't mean to scare you. I don't know what happened exactly. I was reading, waiting for Luke to pick me up for dinner, and I must have drifted off for a second."

"Oh?" He shot out a breath and smiled. "A dream, then."

"Not exa—"

"A dream I can live with." He stared hard, willing her to shut up and let it go at that.

She buttoned her lips. If he wanted to think it was a dream, so be it. If she left his delusion alone, maybe he'd help her figure out what it meant. "I guess I must have dozed off for a minute or two, and I dreamed about a woman. It wasn't 'helper' she was saying, it was 'help her.' She kept repeating it over and over again."

"Help whom?"

"Isn't that the million-dollar question." And she wished she had an answer.

Bee glanced at his watch. "Since when do you and Luke go out to dinner so late?"

"Late? Says the man who eats dinner in the wee hours of the morning."

"Ha-ha."

Beast lay his head in Bee's lap and gazed up at him.

Bee petted his head. "I know exactly how you feel, boy. That was really weird."

Cass stood and stretched her back. "Anyway, Luke was running a little late, I guess. He hasn't called, but he said the dinner reservations were for eight o'clock, and I—"

"Eight? Cass, that was more than two hours ago."

She lurched back. "What?"

"It's quarter after ten. I hate to be the one to tell you, but apparently you've been stood up."

"What?" Two hours? Pressure squeezed Cass's chest. She'd lost two hours? How could that be?

"Listen, hon, since you're all dressed up anyway, and I'm starved since all I ate for lunch was a . . . ahem . . . salad, why don't you go freshen up, and I'll take you somewhere nice for dinner?"

Since she had no intention of going back to sleep anytime soon—or maybe ever—she agreed. "Just let me call Luke and see where he is."

She dialed Luke's number as she headed for the bathroom, then left a message when his voice mail picked up. So much for a night off. Hopefully he'd gotten a break in the murder investigation or the art theft case and he'd get some free time soon. Not only because she missed him, but because he was clearly exhausted and needed the break. He'd admitted as much earlier. Giving up on salvaging her tear-streaked makeup, Cass washed her face, lined her lower lids with black eyeliner, swiped on a little mascara and called it a day.

She took Beast out, then settled him with a peanut-butter-filled treat and petted his head. "You be a good boy for me, okay? No eating anything you're not supposed to."

She poked her head into the living room to let Bee know she was ready. "You ready, Bee?"

He jumped and whirled toward her, one large hand pressed against his chest. "Don't do that to me."

"Do what?"

"Startle me like that." He fanned himself and tugged at his collar.

"What is wrong with you?"

He waved his hands. "Nothing, nothing. Let's just go."

"Are you sure you're all right?"

"Yes, I'm fine. I just . . ." Patches of red popped up on his cheeks. "I just . . . I get a little spooked when . . . well . . . you know . . . *that* kind of stuff happens."

Cass clamped her lips tight to keep from teasing him, though it wasn't easy when he made such an easy target of himself with all his proclamations that anything supernatural didn't exist. Usually, given such a prime opportunity, she'd have pounced on him for being so afraid of something he didn't believe in, but not tonight. Tonight, he'd been so sweet about taking her out for dinner after Luke hadn't shown up that she went to him instead. She hooked his arm with hers and leaned her head against his shoulder. "You don't have to worry, Bee. I won't let anything bother you."

He looked down at her. "Really? You can do that?"

"Of course I can. If I can communicate with . . . whatever . . . why wouldn't I be able to protect you from them?" And even if she couldn't, she'd step between him and danger in a heartbeat without a moment's hesitation.

"Seriously?" He straightened up and patted her hand, then gripped it against his arm "Well, why didn't you tell me that sooner?"

All right, maybe a little teasing. She looked up and widened her eyes in pretend innocence. "Because you didn't believe in ghosts."

"Yeah, well . . ." He ran a hand through his already sticking-up hair. "That's kind of like me saying these blond locks didn't come from a bottle. You can't admit it if you're going to keep up appearances, you know?"

"You never have to worry about keeping up appearances with me. I already know how kind you are and how brave. You have more courage than anyone I know, and you always look out for the people you care about, even at risk to yourself. Why do you think I love you so much?"

He hugged her close and kissed the top of her head. "I love you too, Cass, more than you know."

She leaned into him for a moment, comforted by his strong embrace, by his broad chest beneath her cheek, by his faithful friendship, and was disappointed when he stepped back.

"I'll always take care of you, Cass. You know that, right?"

"I do know it, and I appreciate it so much, appreciate you so much. Just don't forget that street goes both ways. Don't ever be afraid to share your feelings with me, or anything with me, because I will always have your back."

"Thank you, Cass. You are one of the first people in my life who's ever simply accepted me for who I am, the good and the bad, and I can't tell you how much that means to me." His voice hitched, and he turned away for a moment. "Now, let's go eat before I waste away. I asked you to help me with my diet, not starve me to death."

Satisfied he understood the depth of her feelings for him, she let it drop. Bee showed how he felt about his friends in so many ways, but he wasn't always comfortable discussing his feelings, a trait probably borne of so many years trying to hide them. "Waste away, huh? It's not like you didn't eat lunch."

"Ha! You call that lunch? For a rabbit, maybe." He waited for her to lock the door. "You want to take my car? I didn't put the tops back in yet."

"Actually, let's take mine." She dug her keys out of her bag and held them out to him. Exhaustion had begun to encroach again, despite the nap—or whatever—she'd had earlier. The last thing she needed was to fall asleep driving.

He paused. "Why do I have the feeling there's an ulterior motive here?"

The downside of having such a close friend. He knew her too well. "I'll tell you in the car."

He considered her another moment before taking the keys.

They'd barely started backing out of the driveway before he pounced. "Where am I going?"

"I just wanted to ride by Ellie's house quick and make sure everything looks okay."

He nodded. "That I can do."

The fact that Ellie had eventually sold the house she and Jay had shared and moved into the home that had been her mother's, which just so happened to sit directly across the street from Malcolm King's parents, was just icing on the cake.

The thought of cake made her stomach growl. As much as she hated to admit it, Bee might be right. The salad she'd had for lunch definitely wasn't filling enough to last so many hours.

Bee slowed as they approached Ellie's house.

A lone light shone from the living room window, and everything looked quiet. None of the cars lining the street appeared to be occupied. She didn't see anyone lurking, nor did she get any kind of sinister vibe in her gut. "I guess everything looks okay. Would you mind turning around and driving down the road one more time?"

He made a U-turn two blocks down and headed back down the road.

The two-story colonial where Malcolm King had grown up was dark. There were no cars in the driveway or out front, although they could well be in the garage.

Bee followed her gaze with his own. "Want to tell me what's going on, since Ellie's house is on the other side of the street?"

"I did want to check on Ellie, and everything looks okay there."

"So, who does the house across the street belong to?"

"Malcolm King's parents."

"Are you crazy?" Bee sped up. "What are you trying to do, get me killed?"

"Oh, please, I highly doubt Malcolm killed a man just to get even with me."

"Who's talking about Malcolm? If Luke or Tank find out I'm assisting you in trying to investigate on your own, they're going to kill me."

She laughed and relaxed. He was probably right.

Her cell phone rang, and Luke's name popped up on the screen.

She swiped the screen. "Hey, Luke, what's going on?"

"Where are you?" His voice sounded strained.

"I just left with Bee to get something to eat. When you didn't show up and I couldn't reach you, I figured something was going on with your case. Are you at my house? We could swing by and pick you up if you want?"

"I need to talk to you. And Bee. Now."

How could he know they'd driven past Malcolm's house? He couldn't. Could he? Maybe Bee was right to be afraid. Or maybe he'd found out something about the yacht. "Do you want to meet up with us for dinner?"

"No, I need to see you somewhere private and discreet."

"Bee was planning on going into Dreamweaver after dinner to work, do you want to meet up with us there?"

"That'll work, but not after dinner. I need to see you both immediately. We need to talk, Cass, and I'm concerned for your safety." Something had happened. It must have. Had they found the woman with the dark hair? Could she have been on the yacht? She couldn't think about that right now, couldn't think about what it would mean if they had.

While she might have blown off his concern for her, since he tended to worry excessively, she'd never take a chance of putting Bee in danger. "We'll be there in about ten minutes."

"Don't stop anywhere, you hear me? Go straight there, and if you get there before us, go in and lock the door. Got it?"

Did the yacht and the woman have any connection to each other? To Dirk's murder? Was the woman alive if they'd found her? "Sure."

"Cass, I mean it."

"Okay, Luke. I will. I promise." She disconnected the call and looked at Bee, reeling from the urgency in Luke's tone.

He glanced at her. "What's going on?"

"I have no idea, but whatever it is, it can't be good."

Chapter Twenty-five

When Bee pulled up in front of Dreamweaver, Tank and Luke jumped out of an unmarked car and jogged toward them.

Cass froze with her hand on the door handle.

"Why are they running?" Bee made no move to get out of the car.

"I don't know."

Luke reached her door and opened it. "Come on inside."

Tank guided Bee out of the car and followed him to the shop door, his head swiveling between Bee, Cass, and both ends of the street.

Cass followed Bee into the shop, but the instant Luke closed the door behind her and Bee locked it at Tank's instruction, Cass turned on them. "What is going on? And I don't want to hear you'll tell me after anything else. I want an answer."

"A woman named Olivia Wells was found dead tonight."

Bee gasped.

Cass staggered back. She should have done more to warn her. The image of the woman lying on the ground surrounded by a fan of dark hair assailed her. "Was she on the yacht?"

"No. In the woods beside Emmett's garage. I'll explain what happened with the yacht after." Luke held out a plastic evidence bag with a paper inside. "Did you know Olivia Wells?"

"Uh . . ." Cass took the bag from him and turned it over in her hands. The familiar color blobs Cass had made while doing Olivia's reading stared back at her. She tried to tell herself she'd made every attempt to warn Olivia of the potential danger she was in, but had she really done all she could?

"Cass." Luke tapped the bag she still clutched in her shaking hands. "Do you know her?"

"I do." *And I should have saved her. I should have worked harder to find her.*

"How?" Though his eyes held some measure of sympathy, his tone demanded answers.

"I gave her a reading earlier today. Or, I guess, yesterday now."

"Was that the first time you'd seen her?"

Bee moved beside Cass and wrapped his arm around her

shoulders, then shot Luke a warning glare. "It's okay, Cass. Why don't you come sit down?"

Cass moved automatically toward a chair behind the counter with Bee. "Thanks, Bee."

"Of course, dear. Sit. Do you need anything?"

"No, thank you." What she needed most was a moment to collect herself, and he'd given her that. "I'm good now, Bee. Thank you."

He nodded and took a step back but still hovered.

Luke crouched in front of her chair. "I need you to tell me what you know, okay, Cass?"

"Yes, I'm okay now. I'm sorry, the news just came as a shock." And brought with it a wave of guilt so horrendous she'd thought it might drown her. "Olivia Wells came to my reading the other night. When I inadvertently embarrassed Aiden Hargrove, Olivia is the woman I thought he was in love with."

Luke flipped through his notebook. "Didn't Hargrove bring a date?"

"Yes." Could Aiden have killed Olivia? But what purpose would that serve? "Nanette Coldwater, who came to see me the following morning. Monday. She was his date."

He lay a hand on her knee. "Tell me what happened."

She relayed the events of that evening, even though they must have heard them a thousand times after Dirk had been found. "Then, Nanette came into the shop, and when she left, she was angry, very angry. She said she was going to Aiden and Olivia and demanding answers."

"Do you think she confronted Olivia?" Tank leaned over Luke's shoulder.

"I know she did. Olivia said as much when she came in for her reading yesterday." Though she hadn't seemed too concerned about the confrontation.

Tank straightened and wrote something in his notepad. "Did she say if Nanette was still angry when she'd confronted her or what she told her?"

"No. Olivia simply said she'd told Nanette the truth, but she didn't elaborate."

"The reading is where you did this coloring?" Luke indicated the bag she'd placed on the counter when she sat down.

"Yes, the individual reading I did for her." She told him everything she could remember telling Olivia. "And toward the end of the reading, a shadow crossed my vision."

Luke's gaze crashed into hers. At least he understood the implication, since it wasn't the first time a shadow had preceded a death.

"When I tried to warn her to be careful, she told me I was the one who needed to be careful and that I'd fallen right into his master plan."

Luke frowned. "Whose master plan?"

"I have no idea. She wouldn't elaborate."

"Did she say anything to indicate she was afraid?" Tank asked.

Cass was already shaking her head. "Nothing."

"Okay. What else can you tell me?"

"Nothing I can think of." She racked her memory, but nothing stood out. They already knew everything else that had gone on.

"You're going to have to be careful, Cass." Luke's strength seeped into her as he took her ice-cold hands in his warmer ones. "It's very early in the investigation, but so far, we haven't been able to find any connection between Dirk Brinkman and Olivia Wells except for your reading on Sunday night."

"You think someone is targeting Cass's customers?" Bee wrung his hands together.

Luke nodded. "We think it's a good possibility."

"But for what purpose?" If Luke was right, she would have to cancel the reading she had scheduled for Friday night. Otherwise, she'd be painting targets on the backs of a roomful of people.

"Who knows? You said Malcolm King is back in town and threatening to ruin you. Aiden Hargrove is certainly out to cause you trouble. And, by all accounts, Jay Callahan is back on Bay Island. I don't need to remind you of the implications his presence brings."

No, he didn't. Yet another man who blamed her for his poor choices. Like it was her fault he'd committed any number of crimes then had to run when multiple warrants were issued for his arrest. Just because Cass had been instrumental in proving his guilt didn't mean she was at fault for his bad decisions.

"And don't forget Bruce Brinkman is back in town." Bee's cheeks flared red. "I mean, well, not that he'd have any reason to harm Olivia Wells, but you said she was found by Emmett's, which is also by the hotel, and Cass and I saw Bruce at the hotel when we went by there earlier."

Bee's gaze slid to Cass, a discreet reminder of whom else they'd seen by the hotel. Emmett, sneaking in the service entrance. Thankfully, he remained silent.

Luke wrote something in his notepad, then looked over his shoulder at Tank. "Can you think of anything else?"

Tank held his gaze a moment longer than necessary before shaking his head. "Not right now."

Something was brewing between the two. Though their tension was warranted under the circumstances, Cass couldn't help but think there was more going on than they were saying.

Someone knocked on the shop door.

Luke used the key Bee had left hanging from the lock to unlock the door, then opened it and stopped short. "What are you doing here?"

An older, handsome woman with striking features and wearing a navy blue suit, despite the heat and the late hour, leaned a hip against the front window ledge, arms folded across her chest. "Is that any way to address your commanding officer?"

"I'm sorry." Luke nodded toward her. "What are you doing here, ma'am?"

Chief Rawlins made an imposing figure standing toe to toe with Luke. "Good evening, Cass."

"Good evening, Chief Rawlins." Cass had met her before, and she'd seemed nice enough at the time, even insinuated she'd worked with psychics in the past.

"I'd like a word, if you have a moment." Her tone, despite the laid-back Southern social grace, indicated she was going to have that word regardless of whether or not Cass had a moment. And no matter how Luke felt about it.

Luke sighed and stepped aside.

Confused, Cass waited for him to send her some sort of signal, but he remained silent, so she returned her attention to Chief Rawlins. "What can I do for you?"

"I've come to ask what Luke and Tank won't."

That piqued her curiosity. "What's that?"

She ignored the question and gestured for Cass to sit. "What made you ask Luke to check out that yacht sitting off the island?"

Luke and Tank hadn't yet told her what they'd found on the yacht but, apparently, they'd found something. "I don't know, honestly. It just occurred to me that something wasn't right about it."

"When was that?"

She glanced at Luke from the corner of her eye, but when no help was forthcoming, she answered the question as best she could. "A woman came to see me. Rosa Dupree. While I was doing her reading, a series of images flashed through my mind; the yacht was one of them."

Chief Rawlins pulled up a chair and sat directly across from Cass. "What other images did you see?"

"The figurine Rosa was searching for, then the yacht, then a woman with dark hair fanned around her lying on a floor. Is that how Olivia Wells was found?"

"No." Chief Rawlins frowned, deep furrows creasing her forehead. "If I'm not mistaken, her hair was up, though some tendrils had escaped."

Cass shook her head. That wasn't right, not what she'd seen. "The image I saw was hazy, but I'm certain a mass of frizzy or wavy brown hair surrounded the woman."

The chief's gaze held Cass's, steady, confident, never wavering for an instant. "Then I do believe we have a problem, ma'am."

The knowledge poured through her even as Chief Rawlins uttered the words.

"Unless we can figure this out, I fear there's going to be another victim."

Cass shared the chief's concerns, but she wasn't sure why she was sharing them with Cass rather than a roomful of detectives.

"If Olivia Wells wasn't found on the yacht, can you tell me what was?" Because she had a sneaking suspicion it had everything to do with why Chief Rawlins was sitting across from her.

She pursed her lips, sat back, and crossed one leg over the other. "Rosa Dupree's missing figurine for one."

"You found it?" A small niggle of joy surfaced, but it didn't last long.

"Among other things." The chief nodded once. "You pretty much broke our art theft case wide open. But there was no one on board."

Luke and Tank shared a look Cass couldn't interpret.

"Apparently, the thieves were storing the artwork they'd stolen on the yacht until they could transport it wherever it was headed, which we have people looking into."

Although that was certainly good news, she was missing something. "So, what would you like me to do?"

Chief Rawlins clasped her hands around her knee. "I'm hoping you'll agree to try to contact whatever or whomever reached out to you before in an effort to figure out who the woman from your vision is before anything happens to her."

"Wait, what?" Bee stood up straighter. "Are you talking about like a séance or something?"

To her credit, Chief Rawlins appraised Bee quickly, apparently recognized his fear, and nodded. "Or something."

Bee smiled. "Well, it sure has been nice havin' y'all in for a visit."

"Bee—" Cass started.

He held up a hand in protest. "Cass, you know I love you, and I'll do anything I can to help. I'll even come to Mystical Musings and assist with your séance in any way I can in order to try to save whomever it is you're seeing, but you are *not* contacting anything otherworldly from my shop. Period."

"But—"

He ushered them all toward the door. "Besides, you don't have any of your voodoo stuff here, anyway."

That was true, though she wouldn't refer to it as voodoo stuff. Besides, she'd never put Bee in a position that would make him uncomfortable. At least, not that uncomfortable. "Bee's right. I do have tools I could use at the shop."

Bee mouthed *Thank you.*

Of course, she had no real clue how to go about contacting the dead. It's not like she could just ask a question and a ghost would answer. Most often, the dead reached out to her when she was just about to fall asleep or was lost in her crystal ball. Somehow, going to the shop and taking a nap didn't quite seem like what Chief Rawlins had in mind. But she'd had luck with the crystal ball, so maybe she'd try that.

She waited while Bee locked up, thankful for a few minutes to decide how best to proceed. With Luke and Tank flanking her, Bee walking just behind her, and Chief Rawlins bringing up the rear, they headed down the boardwalk like some kind of somber parade. Not exactly inconspicuous if someone was watching them.

Bee leaned close to her ear. "Thank you."

"Sure." She searched the boardwalk for any sign of a stalker.

"And for the record, you are going to look amazing in that blue negligee."

Cass groaned. How could she argue? Bee attending a séance was no less uncomfortable for him than modeling his new lingerie line would be for her. Now she was going to have to spend the rest of the summer watching what she ate and somehow squeeze in time to get a tan.

As soon as they arrived at Mystical Musings, Cass lit a white candle and set it on the table, then settled in her chair with Bee and Chief Rawlins on either side of her. The candle flames flickered, reflecting in her crystal ball's depths.

The floor creaked beneath Luke's weight as he paced the front of the shop, stopping every so often to peer out the window.

Tank's mumbled voice intruded on her concentration as he spoke into his phone, his voice too low for her to make out the words.

Chief Rawlins remained quiet, her silence as distracting as Bee's harsh breathing.

Cass tried to block everything out, to focus on the task at hand, but each sound came to her magnified by the weight of this moment's importance. If she couldn't get her act together, a woman might die.

Okay, she could do this. But instead of using the crystal ball, she dug through her bag and pulled out the crystals she'd found in the register. Setting the black tourmaline aside on the table, she focused on the fire agate, staring deep into its core.

An image formed, hazy at first, insubstantial. A woman. The same woman? She tried not to project her expectations into the vision, instead waiting for the image to come to her. The woman lay on something gray. Concrete, maybe? Or it could be a carpet. The background remained fuzzy.

She tried to center her focus on the woman. Her long dark hair spread around her, the same as it had last time, covering her face, hiding any features Cass might use to identify her.

A chair scraped as Chief Rawlins stood and approached Tank, then whispered something in his ear.

He nodded and returned to his call.

Cass closed her eyes. She could do this. She had to do this. The woman floated in her mind. Dark hair. Something familiar about her.

"Help her."

"Tanya?" Cass concentrated on the voice, blocking out everything going on around her. The rest of the world ceased to exist as she focused on the woman lying on the floor. *"You have to help me. I don't know how to find her."*

A rush of adrenaline shot through her. Her own anxiety? She didn't think so. Tanya's maybe?

"Help her."

As much as it seemed Tanya wanted to help, her abilities were apparently limited.

Cass searched the vision. How could she find her? There was nothing in the background to indicate where she was. Nothing stood out about the woman. She wore black slacks, a pink blouse. Business attire, maybe. Not dressy. Black shoes, though the edges of the vision were too murky to make out the style.

Someone stood behind her, a man's slacks. She refocused her attention on him, sliding her gaze up. She couldn't reach his face. His hands moved, and she shifted her attention to them, watched as he twirled his pinky ring around and around his finger.

A glint of light flashed in Cass's eyes, blinding her for an instant. Her gaze shot to the woman's hand lying next to her head. To her wedding ring. Cass shifted all of her focus to the ring. A double gold band, the engagement ring set between them. Familiar. She knew that ring. Her blood ran cold. "Stephanie!"

Chapter Twenty-six

"Stephanie?" Tank whirled toward her. "Where?"

Cass's eyes shot open and she jumped from the chair. "It's Stephanie. The woman in my vision."

Luke was at her side in an instant. "Are you sure, Cass?"

"I'm positive. As soon as I saw her wedding ring, I knew." She rummaged through her bag for her cell phone, then searched for Stephanie's number, her hands shaking violently. "And I think Calvin Morris is the one who has her."

"She's not answering." Tank ran for the front door.

Luke kissed her head, then glanced at Chief Rawlins.

"Go, I'll stay here."

He ran out after Tank.

Cass waited through five rings then got Stephanie's voice mail. She hung up and dialed again.

"Someone, lock that front door, please." Chief Rawlins barked orders into the phone.

"You have to do something. She's not answering." Cass disconnected and dialed again.

Bee locked the front door, then leaned his back against it, gaze locked on his phone as he dialed.

"I already have officers en route to the house. Do you know if that's where she's supposed to be?" The chief typed frantically into her phone.

"No."

"When was the last time you saw her?"

Bee straightened and jammed his phone into his pocket. "At lunch. She got a call, said she was going to meet with Morris."

"Full name?"

"Calvin Morris. She's met with him several times, but something seemed off."

"What do you mean, off?" she demanded.

Bee shook his head. "I don't know, exactly. Cass?"

"Huh?" She couldn't just sit there dialing Stephanie's number all night.

"I said, what was off about Calvin? I don't know much about

189

bookkeeping; that's why Stephanie handles all of mine." Bee's voice shook, but he held himself together.

"I don't know. She wasn't specific, just said things didn't add up."

Rawlins turned her attention to Cass. "What makes you think she's with him now? The fact she was supposed to meet him?"

"No, I . . . uh . . . I saw them together at the hotel this afternoon. He was standing behind her turning a ring around his pinky." They had to get to her, had to find them, fast. "In my vision, he was standing behind her, feet apart. I couldn't see his face, but I could see his hands, and he was twirling the ring around the same way he had earlier."

"Okay." Chief Rawlins held her hands up. "Let's all calm down. It's very possible she's just sound asleep and didn't hear the phone."

"This many times?" Cass held up her phone. She wanted to throw it against something, but then she'd have no way to contact Stephanie or get word if someone else did. At least she felt like she was doing something each time she dialed her number. "Besides, her husband is a detective on an active murder investigation, with not one but now two bodies. Stephanie isn't sleeping that deeply anytime soon."

Cass sat and put her phone on the table, then shoved her fingers into her hair and squeezed. There had to be something she could do besides sit there at the table with her head in her hands and wait for news. She'd tried to contact Tanya but was met with only silence. The vision would no longer appear to her no matter how hard she tried to focus. It seemed any psychic skills she may have once possessed fled with the realization Stephanie might be in danger.

Bee dialed Stephanie's number again, then slammed the phone down onto the table.

Cass already knew he wouldn't reach her.

Chief Rawlins barked orders into her phone, then she hung up and stared at Cass.

"Anything?" Cass held her breath.

She shook her head, her expression guarded. "They can't find her."

Tremors tore through Cass. Stephanie had been her best friend growing up, was still one of her best friends. If anything happened to her . . . She should have figured it out sooner. Should have realized Stephanie was missing and started searching so much earlier. She sobbed, not that it would do any good, but she couldn't keep the emotions pent up any longer. "What are we going to do?"

The chief squatted in front of Cass's chair, elbows resting on her knees, and stared directly into her eyes. "First, I need you to calm down."

"How do you expect me to calm down?" Cass twirled the fire agate between her fingers, desperate for something to do to help. "How can you sit here so calmly babysitting me while Stephanie's missing?"

The chief tilted her head and narrowed her eyes, her gaze on Cass intense. "I'm not babysitting you. I'm waiting."

Cass jumped up and paced. No way she could sit there with the chief's gaze drilling holes through her. She passed Bee as he paced in the opposite direction.

Chief Rawlins stood, interrupting Bee's path.

He stopped. "Well, I don't know how you can wait so calmly. Shouldn't you be out there looking for her?"

Cass wanted to intervene, to tell Bee not to take his frustration out on her, but she didn't have the energy.

Chief Rawlins ignored him and continued to study Cass. "Make no mistake, I am fully prepared to move forward with this investigation. My two best detectives, both personally invested in this case, are out there following any and all physical evidence they can get their hands on."

Cass stopped pacing. "Physical evidence?"

"That's right." She moved toward Cass, stopping when she was only about a foot away and standing face-to-face. "Are you ready now?"

"Ready for what?"

"If you've calmed down enough to proceed, you seem to be our best shot at finding her."

"Me?" A lot of good she would do. Her emotions had clearly done something to dampen any messages she might once have received. The only thing that would register for her now was fear. Gut-wrenching terror for Stephanie's safety.

"Well, so far you've provided our only clue that she is even missing. If you'll trust me, I think I can help. I've done this before."

"Done what?"

"Worked with psychics to search for missing people, but it will require your trust if I'm going to help guide you."

"Yes, yes, of course." Cass would do anything at that point if it meant finding Stephanie.

"How did your other cases work out? Were you able to find the people who were lost?" Bee's voice quivered and he clasped his hands tightly together in front of his mouth.

"We were able to find some in time."

Cass's hopes sank. If real psychics who were used to working with the police had only managed to find some of the victims, how on earth was Cass supposed to succeed?

"We can't afford to waste any time. Do you trust me, Cass?"

"Yes." There was no hesitation whatsoever, not only because she'd do anything to find Stephanie, but because this woman's confidence inspired trust.

"Okay, then, let's go." She strode toward the door.

Cass followed, with Bee right on her heels. "Go where?"

Chief Rawlins waited while Cass unlocked the door, then locked up behind them. She gestured toward her car parked in the lot. She must have had someone move it from down the boardwalk where she'd parked when she arrived. "Sit in front, Cass. Bee, you can come, but only if you can sit quietly in the back. You absolutely must not interrupt."

Bee nodded wildly and hopped into the backseat.

Cass got into the passenger side beside the chief. "Okay, now what?"

She started the car. "You tell me."

Cass closed her eyes. She had no clue which way to go. Why did Chief Rawlins have such high expectations? What is it she wanted her to do? "I don't understand."

"Let your instincts guide you, Cass. I don't know how your abilities work, but you do. Reach out in whatever way usually works, and give me your gut instinct. Which way?"

She tried to relax, to gain focus, but fear for Stephanie muscled its way into her thoughts, crowding out everything else, threatening to consume her.

The chief shifted into Drive and crept down the boardwalk. The tires crunched against the drifts of sand that wind and people inevitably dragged from the beach to the road, despite its being swept back often. A siren wailed in the distance. Something related to Stephanie's disappearance? Most likely not, since the chief hadn't been notified.

Bee shifted, the leather seat creaking beneath his weight.

"Are you there, Tanya?" Cass smoothed her fingers over the fire agate. *"I could use a little help right about now."*

A sound intruded, soft, barely noticeable, repetitive. Cass reached for it. Whirring, followed by a soft squeak. Again and again. *Whir, whir, whir, squeak. Whir, whir, whir, squeak.*

Where was it coming from? She tried to block it out, to concentrate only on Stephanie. The image returned. Stephanie lying on the ground, gray surrounding her, hazy. Calvin standing over her, twirling the ring around his finger. *Whir, whir, whir, squeak.*

Louder this time. "What is that?"

"What's what?" Chief Rawlins hit the turn signal and slowed to make a left off the boardwalk, headed toward the center of Bay Island.

Cass tried to concentrate on the sound. "Turn the signal off!"

The chief immediately did as instructed.

Bee slid forward in his seat.

Cass latched on to the sound. Something to do with Stephanie? She listened closer. Repetitive. Something to do with Morris's ring turning. Turning. Turning. *Whir, whir, whir, squeak.* Like a wheel. An image flashed beside Stephanie. Only for an instant, barely anything. "Make a right and head out of town."

Cass held tightly to the image of the tricycle, its front wheel spinning, *whir, whir, whir, squeak.* A tarp lay crumpled on the porch beside it where a stack of paintings had once stood. Stephanie, surrounded by gray. Not concrete. Driftwood. Old, weathered, scarred.

She sat up straighter, gripping the agate tightly in her hand. Its warmth spread up her arm, burned through her chest. "Make the next left."

Chief Rawlins followed her directions, this time without signaling.

The sound grew louder, grating on her nerves until she was ready to scream, as they turned onto West Main Street. "Slow down."

Rawlins let off the accelerator but didn't hit the brake, allowing the car to coast past the small antique shop where Ellie worked. A shadow shifted behind the front curtain.

Cass held her breath and waited until Auntie V's Closet was no longer in sight. Someone was there. She was sure of it, could feel their presence. But even if she was wrong, she had to check, and there wasn't much time if whoever was in there got spooked by them passing.

"Do you want me to keep going or turn around?"

Not many cars would head through this area at night. One maybe, but not another heading the opposite direction a moment later. "No. Stop the car."

She checked the rearview mirror then hit the brakes and pulled over. "What is it?"

"That's the shop where Ellie Callahan works. There's something. I think someone's inside there."

Rawlins lifted a microphone from the dashboard.

Cass blocked out whatever she was saying and directed every ounce of her concentration to the building they'd just passed. Terror enveloped her again. Only this time, with her emotions crammed into a neat little box at the back of her mind, she recognized the sensation for what it was. Someone else's fear. "Stephanie."

Cass flung the door open, jumped out, and rounded the back of the car.

An instant later, Chief Rawlins stood in front of her, blocking her path. "I've already called for backup."

Cass's heart pounded painfully, racing so hard she thought it might burst. She rubbed her chest, trying to ease the sensation. The pain gripped tighter, squeezing. She shook her head, dispelling the vision. If she didn't cut the connection to whomever or whatever was so frightened, she'd never get to Stephanie in time to help her. "There's no time to wait."

Chief Rawlins barely hesitated for an instant before turning and heading toward the shop. "How sure are you?"

"We can't wait. We're out of time." Cass jogged toward the shop.

Bee huffed beside her.

Rawlins spoke quietly to someone else as she kept pace with Cass. When the shop came into view, she held out a hand to stop Cass, then gestured toward a small patch of trees on the corner of the lot. "Wait here."

Fully expecting her order to be obeyed, Rawlins crept forward toward the shop, gun in hand.

Bee gripped Cass's shoulder, and she barely bit back a scream. "Is she in there?"

Was she? Cass could be totally off base, and then she'd be pulling officers who could be searching elsewhere to follow up on what might be nothing. This time the pain gripping her heart was her own fear. She kept her voice low. "I don't know, but I think so."

Rawlins had reached the shop's side window. She grabbed an empty crate and turned it upside down, then climbed up and peeked in. If her stiffening posture was any indication, Cass's hunch had been right. The chief backed away from the shop and spoke into the microphone on her shoulder.

A chorus of insects filled the night, their songs blocking any whisper of sound Cass might have overheard from Chief Rawlins or anyone inside the shop.

"Help her."

There was no mistaking the sound of Tanya's voice inside her head. *"I'm trying."*

"Help her, help her."

The fear gripped Cass again, and she realized it wasn't Stephanie's fear she was feeling but Tanya's.

Cass crouched beside a large tree trunk, her sense of urgency increasing while they waited. No sound of sirens pierced the night. Either they were too far away or Chief Rawlins had instructed them to come silently. Either way, they were almost out of time. *"I don't know what to do."*

"Helpherhelpherhelpher . . ."

Cass stood. She only hesitated for an instant before the urgency beating at her prodded her forward. Ignoring the chief's gestures for her to stop, Cass crept closer to the shop.

Bee followed but hung back just a bit, much as he had when they'd moved through the woods by Emmett's garage, probably giving her room to decide what to do.

She ducked into the shadows beside the front porch.

An instant later, both Bee and Chief Rawlins were at her side.

"We can't wait," Cass whispered.

The sound of tires humming against pavement halted any response from the chief.

A car pulled into the small dirt lot and stopped. Ellie climbed out and looked around.

From her position beside the porch, Cass couldn't see if anyone looked out the window, but she couldn't let Ellie go in there, couldn't give Morris two hostages. But was Ellie actually a victim? Why would she be there at this time of the morning?

Before Cass could move, Rawlins reached Ellie. She whispered frantically in her ear, then led her to the side of the porch.

Ellie sobbed softly, shaking so badly she looked like she might fall apart.

"What are you doing here, Ellie?" Cass whispered.

"It's Jay. He called and told me to come. He's waiting for me, and then he and Mr. Morris are going to disappear." Her breathing hitched. "And so is Stephanie."

"Helpherhelpher . . ."

Cass stood. As much as she wanted to know what was going on, needed to know, they were out of time.

The shop's front door whipped open, and Jay Callahan strode onto the porch. "Ellie? Is that you? You get in here right now."

Rawlins tensed.

Before she could move, Cass moved out of the shadows and into the small pool of light cast by the shop's porchlight. "It's not Ellie, Jay. It's me, Cass Donovan."

Chapter Twenty-seven

"You? What are you doing here?"

Hopefully, since he stood on the lighted porch, and Ellie's car was parked in the dark lot, he couldn't tell it was hers. Maybe he'd think it was Cass who'd pulled up. She held her hands up where he could see them. All she needed to do was buy a couple of minutes. Surely Luke and Tank were almost in place by now, creeping closer with more stealth and self-control than Cass had mastered.

"How did you find me? Ellie called you, didn't she?"

"No, Jay."

"Then how did you find me?" He kicked the tricycle Ellie had turned into a planter, the one whose wheel squeaked with every fourth revolution, and sent it flying off its stand. "It was you, wasn't it? Who told the police about the yacht? Don't deny it. I saw you standing on the beach, staring out at me. But how did you know?"

"Why don't we talk, Jay, and I'll see what else I can tell you?"

Another man yelled from inside the shop, "Kill her and be done with it, Callahan. We have to get out of here."

"No."

"What did you just say to me?" Calvin Morris poked his head into the doorway.

Jay used the bottom of his shirt to wipe the sweat running in rivers down his face. "Get in here, Cass, now."

No way was she going inside. She couldn't, had to keep them outside talking until Chief Rawlins could get to them or Luke and Tank showed up.

"I said kill her. And then the other one. Or my next bullet will go in you."

"Just wait a second, will ya, Morris? This one can help us. She sees things. Knows things she shouldn't know. She might be able to tell us how to get out of this and off the island."

Calvin Morris stood in the doorway behind Jay, a convenient shield if a sniper waited in the woods for a chance to take a shot. He twirled the pinky ring around and around. "Fine. Get her in here. Now."

Jay lifted a handgun and aimed it at Cass.

Cass fought fiercely against the urge to look around for help. They had to think she'd come alone. She climbed the steps to the front porch.

Stephanie lay on the gray hardwood floor, her hair splayed around her.

"Stephanie!" Cass ran to her. She crouched beside her and pulled her hair away from her face. She pressed one wildly shaking hand against her neck, and a strong pulse fluttered beneath her fingers. Relief flooded her.

"Stephanie, wake up." Cass turned her over and examined her.

A trickle of blood ran from a cut on her forehead. Not bad enough to have knocked her out, so why was she unconscious? Drugged?

"All right, enough of that." Morris grabbed Cass's arm and hauled her to her feet, then shoved her into a chair. "Start talking. How do we get out of here?"

Jay stood behind him, studying her. "How did you find us?"

May as well be honest, since the only reason she was probably still alive right now hinged on them believing she had psychic abilities. She gestured toward the porch. "The tricycle. When I was here to get chairs for the shop, Ellie was filling the basket with soil to plant flowers. One of you must have knocked into it on your way in and made the wheel spin. When I was trying to find Stephanie, I heard the sound over and over again, the wheel turning, turning, turning, and then squeaking, and I recognized it."

Jay ran a hand over his mouth then propped it on his hip, the gun still hanging from his other hand.

"It doesn't matter how she found us." Calvin Morris narrowed his eyes at her. "Just tell us how to get out of here without getting caught."

Jay turned on him. "If you'd have listened to me in the first place—"

Calvin backhanded Jay across the mouth. "Enough out of you. You were the one who insisted we come to Bay Island. You were the one who said this time of year you'd be able to score big and get out quick."

Jay wiped a trickle of blood from the side of his mouth. "Yeah, well, I also told you we had to keep this one busy and out of our business too."

"And what did I tell you?" Spittle flew from Morris's mouth as he screamed. "I told you just kill her and be done with it, but you had to play head games with her, ruin her reputation, destroy her and everyone around her before you killed her. If you hadn't come back here bent on revenge against her and everyone else in this place who wronged you in some way, we wouldn't be in this mess, and my yacht wouldn't be crawling with cops. Now, how are we supposed to get out of here?"

Jay looked down at his feet. "Yeah, well, it's not my fault."

"Not your fault?" Calvin's face turned purple. "What do you mean it's not your fault? You were supposed to kill her, rob the mansions along the beach, move the merchandise to the yacht, and get out of here. How hard was that?"

Jay shrugged but remained quiet.

"But you had to bring that Wells woman back here with you, had to go along with her scheme to get revenge instead of just doing what you were told."

Guilt nudged Cass. Even though it had probably not been intentional, Olivia had inadvertently saved her.

Jay got up in Calvin's face. "What'd you want me to do? Let it all go? Let Dirk get away with screwing me? And let Emmett go on about his business after firing me without even as much as asking me if I was guilty? And what about Cass here?"

Morris shoved him back a step. "You were supposed to do what you were told."

Jay grabbed Cass by the hair. "And let her get away with ruining my life, costing me a fortune, siccing the cops on me, making me run from Bay Island like some kind of a coward?"

"If you hadn't let Wells lead you around like some kind of lost puppy, talking you into playing games you weren't smart enough to win, we'd already be out of here." Morris shoved Jay back, and he released his hold on Cass. "You'd better just hope your smear campaign worked and no one listened to her if she told them where to find us."

"Well, she's here alone, isn't she? That oughta show you something."

Morris grunted. "Just get on with this. Get it done, and let's get out of here."

Jay bristled for a moment, but then turned his attention to Cass. "Start talking. Now."

"You have to sit over here by me for me to read you and tell you what to do." She had to draw him away from Stephanie and give Tank and Luke an opening. She had no doubt they were out there by now, and that had nothing to do with any sixth sense.

Jay dragged a chair from across the room and sat it in front of her.

Close enough for her to try to wrestle the gun from him? Probably not. Besides, she had no way to know if Morris had a gun. Just because he wasn't waving it around didn't mean he didn't have one in his possession. "Could you put the gun away, please? I can't concentrate with that thing pointed at me."

Jay considered her a moment, then glanced at Morris.

He nodded from where he stood beside Stephanie.

Jay stuffed the gun into his waistband. "Start talking."

She reached into her pocket.

Jay launched himself from the chair and yanked the gun back out.

"Whoa, sorry." She held her hands out, palms up so he could see the fire agate and black tourmaline she'd pulled from her pocket. "They help me focus."

He nodded, righted the chair, and returned to his seat, the gun still held tense across his lap. "Fine. Talk."

"What are you doing here? What does Ellie have to do with all of this?"

"I didn't tell you to ask questions."

"I need to have some answers if I'm going to help." She thought of trying to turn her cell phone to record, but after his reaction last time, she wasn't about to stick her hand back into her pocket.

"Dirk Brinkman, that rat, sold me a bunch of paintings, supposedly from his father's estate. He wanted to unload them cheap, but they were supposed to be worth a good amount."

"And I told you to wait for the appraiser to get here, but no, you had to go ahead and buy them." Morris pointed at Jay, moving a step away from Stephanie.

"His old man was worth a fortune, so I figured it was legit." Jay shoved a hand through his hair, leaving it sticking up straight on one side. "Anyway, I brought the paintings to Ellie and told her to unload them on some unsuspecting tourist for as much as she could get. She's supposed to be meeting me here with the money."

"She should have been here already." Calvin glanced at his watch, then moved to the front window, shifted the curtain aside, and peeked out.

"She'll be here. She wouldn't dare cross me."

"We'll see."

Jay let it go and returned his attention to Cass. "Now, how do we get out of here?"

"I'll make you a deal."

"You are in no position to make deals, sweetie."

"Let Stephanie go. Just leave her here, and I'll go with you and show you the way out."

"Sorry, Cass, but I can't do that. Calvin here thought it would be okay to let her take care of his books when his regular guy kicked the bucket, but she turned out to be smarter than anticipated, and she figured out a good portion of his income was illegal."

Cass shrugged, feigning a calm she most definitely did not feel. "What does that matter now? The police already have the yacht full of stolen merchandise, and presumably they'll be able to connect it back to Mr. Morris. So, what does it matter if you leave Stephanie here? If it's a hostage you're looking for, you'll still have me."

Jay studied Stephanie for a second, then turned to Morris.

Cass held her breath. If she could get them outside with Stephanie out of the line of fire, the police might be able to take them down.

Morris looked out the window again, then turned to Jay and nodded. "Leave her. Let's just get out of here. By the time she comes to, we'll be long gone."

Jay jumped up and pointed the gun at Cass. "Go."

She stood and crossed the shop, praying the police would stop them before Jay realized it was Ellie's car outside and not hers.

Jay yanked the door open and looked around.

Could he sense the same fear and rage that slammed through Cass the instant the door opened?

He shoved her from behind. "Go."

Apparently not.

"Straight to the car. No tricks."

Calvin Morris stepped out onto the porch, then gestured Jay to move with her.

Jay shoved her toward the stairs, and she stumbled and went down hard on her hands and knees. She rolled to the side, getting out of the way as fast as she could.

"Freeze, police!" Footsteps pounded over the porch.

"Don't you move, Callahan," Luke yelled.

Cass pushed up onto her knees.

Luke held his gun pointed at Jay.

Jay glared at Cass but made no move to lower his hands, which he held high above his head.

Chief Rawlins held Calvin Morris face-first against the side of the shop while she cuffed his hands behind his back.

Tank ran in the front door.

Bee's strong arm wrapped around Cass from behind. "Come on, Cass. Move back and let the police do their jobs."

"I have to get to Stephanie, Bee, please." She had to get to her, had to see for herself she was okay. "She's hurt."

"All right, honey, come on." Bee helped her to her feet and wrapped an arm around her waist, hugging her close as he guided her toward the front door. "Girl, I am going to knock some sense into you later, if Luke doesn't beat me to it, but right now I'm just so grateful you're okay."

She leaned into him. "Thanks, Bee."

Tank was on his knees at Stephanie's side. Tears tracked down his cheeks as he smoothed her hair away from the cut on her head and murmured softly to her. He took her hand in his and pressed it against his lips.

A paramedic had arrived to examine her and started an IV.

Cass knelt by her head, unable to stem the flow of tears that had built up throughout the ordeal. "It's okay, Steph. It's over."

"Are you okay, Cass?" Tank squeezed her hand.

She nodded.

"Are you hurt?"

She took stock. Her knees would probably be sore for a few days, but she was otherwise unharmed. "No, I'm okay."

"What you did was incredibly brave, and I cannot begin to tell you how grateful I am to you for saving her."

Her gaze shot to his. She hadn't known what to expect from him. Anger, maybe? A lecture about how she should have waited for backup before rushing headlong into danger and putting Stephanie at risk. "Stephanie is my best friend in the world, Tank. There's nothing I wouldn't do to save her."

He swallowed hard. "If you hadn't come in, we wouldn't have made it in time. They'd most likely have killed her when Ellie showed up."

Even though she suspected the same thing, the confirmation sent a chill up her spine.

The paramedic gestured for a stretcher, and Tank lifted Stephanie onto it.

"I'll meet you at the hospital," Cass said.

Tank nodded and walked beside the stretcher toward the waiting ambulance, Stephanie's hand still clutched tightly in his.

Bee helped her to her feet. He wrapped an arm around her shoulder and kissed her temple. "You did good, Cass. You're amazing."

She leaned against him, suddenly exhausted and shaky as the adrenaline rush subsided.

"Cass!" Luke strode across the shop toward them.

"I'll meet you outside," Bee whispered.

Luke squeezed Bee's shoulder as he passed him, then yanked Cass into his arms and clung to her like his life depended on it. "Are you all right?"

She nodded against his chest.

"Are you hurt?"

"No, I'm good."

He finally loosened his hold and looked down into her eyes. "What am I going to do with you, woman?"

She laughed. "First you're going to take me to the hospital to make sure Stephanie's okay, and then you can take me out for that dinner you promised. Or I guess breakfast at this point. Turns out confronting a killer makes you hungry."

Chapter Twenty-eight

Cass tilted her face toward the sun, enjoying the warmth of the late afternoon. She'd already closed Mystical Musings and now sat with Bee in rocking chairs on the back deck, waiting for everyone to arrive for the volleyball tournament. She held her chair still so as not to rock on Beast's tail, since he sat right beside her chair, enthusiastically gnawing a rope toy.

The scent of barbeque filled the air, and her mouth watered. "So, you promised you'd tell me your good news, and you still haven't."

The deck creaked beneath Bee's chair as he used his foot against the railing to rock it slowly back and forth. "It's been a busy couple of days."

And he'd used that to avoid answering her question. "We're not busy now."

"Okay, fine." He sighed and sat up straighter. "But you have to promise you won't be upset with me."

"Why would I be upset with you?" The curiosity was killing her. So was the fact he'd either deflected or completely ignored her every time she'd asked since he'd told her he expected to have something exciting to share.

He sipped his iced tea, contemplating the lighthouse standing watch over the island. "Aiden Hargrove reached out to me."

"What?" When had that happened, and why would he not have told her?

Dark sunglasses covered Bee's eyes, preventing her from reading anything. "During his attempt to ruin your career, Aiden called me, said he wanted to invest in a line of designer gowns."

"You didn't tell me that."

"No, I didn't."

"Why not?" It hurt that he hadn't trusted her enough to tell her, that he might have thought she wouldn't support him. "I'd never have asked you to say no to a chance like that, Bee, and I wouldn't have been upset with you for jumping at it."

He set his iced tea on the small table beside him. "Maybe not, but you'd have been upset that I told him no."

"What? Why would you say no?" He'd wanted that so badly.

"I told him I couldn't agree to any kind of partnership with him unless he dropped his vendetta against you." Bee shrugged. "Considering everyone on Bay Island knows what good friends you and I are, going into business with him while he was actively trying to destroy you would have looked bad, like I maybe agreed with him or something, you know?"

She didn't know what to say. "Thank you, Bee."

"Yeah, well, don't be too thankful. I wanted his funding badly, so once the situation was resolved I called him and asked if he'd still like to consider doing a line with me." He stared out over the water, resting his head against the back of the chair.

She reached over and gripped his hand.

He squeezed her hand then smiled. "I told him what happened at the reading wasn't your fault, pointed out that you'd actually been right about his feelings for Olivia."

Cass laughed. Leave it to Bee to make something good out of her mistake. "So, you got the line with him, then?"

He nodded.

"Congratulations, Bee, I'm really happy for you."

"Thank you. And that's not all I got." He pointed toward the beach, where a small group of people had started setting up the volleyball nets. They'd be starting soon. "I also got a promise from him to leave you alone."

"How in the world did you manage that?"

"Seriously? The instant he found out you were instrumental in solving the case and that he was one of Jay's targets, his whole attitude changed." Bee laughed. "I'd be surprised if he's not falling all over himself to apologize next time he sees you."

"Somehow, I doubt that." Unless Bee had anything to do with it. Then, all bets were off. But finding out his name was on Jay's hit list had to have come as a shock. Cass still couldn't wrap her head around the lengths Jay was willing to go to in order to hurt everyone on Bay Island who'd ever wronged him.

Ellie had told the police Jay had a grudge against Aiden because he'd asked her out after Jay had disappeared. Apparently Jay had kept better tabs on Ellie than anyone had realized. The thought sent a chill skittering up her spine.

"In the end, I think he truly loved Olivia, and he wanted to see

Jay punished for killing her. Since you played a role in that, I think he was more willing to forgive and forget."

That made sense. Though they couldn't have known each other long, Aiden had obviously fallen hard for her, despite her insistence the relationship remain secret. Olivia had played on his feelings to manipulate him into attending Cass's reading, just as Jay had appealed to Dirk's hatred with the promise of a shot at Emmett if he showed up at the reading. Too bad Dirk's loathing for Emmett had clouded his perception too much for him to figure out Jay was playing him.

And once Dirk and Emmett went after each other at the reading, Jay realized his plan had come off even better than expected. Dirk had played his role, and now Jay could kill him and implicate Emmett. His and Olivia's plan, after all, was to discredit Cass by ensuring that all the victims and suspects could be connected to her in some way. Jay admitted as much to the police when they'd questioned him afterward. "Do you think Aiden and Nanette will get back together?"

"Nah, I heard she left Bay Island the day after Olivia was killed. Who knows? Maybe she was afraid she'd be implicated in the crime."

Could be. She'd been rude to almost everyone before Cass's group reading and had pretty much threatened the woman before storming out of Cass's shop when she'd come in alone, so it made sense she'd run.

"Besides, after Friday night's reading, I'd be surprised if anyone could do anything to harm your reputation."

Warmth surged through her. The reading had been packed on Friday, and it had gone flawlessly. "I can't believe how many people showed up."

He shot her a grin "Once the news hit the rumor mill that you helped the police solve the art theft case as well as Dirk's murder investigation, no one dared miss it."

It felt good to be there with him, relaxing, enjoying the gentle breeze drifting across the bay, bringing with it the salty scent of the sea. The scent of home. This is what she remembered of summers on Bay Island. "And how did that rumor get started?"

"A little birdie passed the info to Emma Nicholls."

"A little birdie, huh?"

"Yup." He rocked back and forth.

Cass lay her head back and closed her eyes, content to just sit together in comfortable silence.

"Hey, there." Stephanie's footsteps vibrated against the deck. She sat down in the rocking chair on Cass's other side and crossed her ankles on the deck railing.

"Hey." Cass tilted her head to study her. "How are you feeling?"

"Better." The drugs Calvin Morris had used to knock her out had worn off, leaving her nauseated and groggy for a day or so, but her color had returned, and she had begun to look more like herself. "But Tank's hovering is wearing thin. He hasn't left my side since you found me."

"You love it, and you know it," Bee said.

"You're right." Stephanie laughed.

"Speak of the devil." Bee slid his sunglasses onto the top of his head.

"What are you talking about?" Tank slid behind Stephanie and rubbed her shoulders.

Stephanie winked at Cass.

She laughed. Bee was right; Stephanie was loving every minute of the attention Tank was showering her with.

"Hey, there, beautiful." Luke kissed Cass hello, then leaned against the railing facing her.

She smiled up at him, happy to see him so relaxed. "Have you learned anything new?"

He nodded toward Stephanie. "Looks like Stephanie was right about Calvin Morris. His books didn't add up."

Stephanie had already told them, as soon as she'd woken up in the hospital, that she'd confronted Morris about his numbers right before he'd knocked her out. She didn't remember much after that.

Tank squeezed Stephanie's shoulders tighter. "Apparently, he and Jay were working together, Jay stealing the artwork, Calvin selling it. Calvin was trying to hide the money from the illegal art sales."

Ellie waved from the beach. With Jay behind bars on the mainland, and the promise he wouldn't be getting out anytime soon, she'd begun to regain some of her confidence. She'd even highlighted her hair again, though it would surely take some time before she could get over the emotional toll Jay's presence had taken on her. The fact he'd been watching her without her knowing it had nearly broken her. She'd apologized to Cass a million times for not telling her everything, but Cass couldn't blame her. She'd been terrified of him. That Ellie had come to Cass and given her any warning at all showed a tremendous amount of courage. Cass had given her the name of a therapist she hoped would be able to help.

Cass waved back. "I still can't believe Jay had the nerve to come back here, knowing there was a warrant out for his arrest."

Luke shrugged. "He didn't know anywhere else as well as he did Bay Island. He knew exactly where to find what he wanted and could sell. I'm sure he figured he could stay under the radar, and who knows? He probably would have if not for his need to seek revenge. And if he hadn't been so afraid of you. If he'd have been content to rob the mansions before they closed up for the season, he'd probably have been sitting on a beach somewhere with Olivia come winter."

"Did he say why he killed her?" Her death still weighed heavily.

"When she told him what she'd said to you, about his master plan, he lost his temper. He was afraid you'd figure out what was going on because of it."

"I'd never have thought he'd fall for a woman like that." Confident, independent. Jay's tastes ran more toward women like Ellie, easily controlled, meek, subservient.

"I don't think he did. He didn't seem too upset over her death, seemed more upset she'd interfered with his plan to destroy you. And given his history of abuse, it's not surprising he killed her in anger. He'd worked hard to put all the players in place, rile Dirk up to heckle you, have Olivia win Aiden over."

Bee shivered. "I never figured Jay was smart enough to engineer something like that."

"Ironically, we don't think he did. Seems Olivia was the calculating one, the brains behind the scheme."

That didn't surprise Cass. Jay using Olivia made more sense than him loving her. She was pretty sure Jay Callahan held no capacity for love.

"On another note, Chief Rawlins has officially given permission to consult you on cases." Luke folded his arms across his chest, crossed one leg over the other, and shook his head.

She wasn't quite sure what to make of that. He didn't seem particularly disturbed by the idea, nor did he seem happy.

Tank massaged the bridge of his nose between his thumb and forefinger, probably concerned about what kind of trouble Stephanie would get into with her next. Cass couldn't blame him.

"Just wait until that one hits the gossip mill," Bee said. "You'll be swamped with customers."

Luke gave him a hard stare. "Why don't we just keep that one under wraps for now, Bee?"

As much as she wanted the increased business, she could definitely understand Luke's concern.

Bee sulked. Nothing irked him more than having good dirt he couldn't share.

"By the way, Bee," Luke added, "I did check into Bruce Brinkman, as you suggested."

He perked back up. "You did?"

"Yeah, and you were right, he did come in on the ferry the night before Dirk was killed. Unfortunately, it wasn't to see his father. A group of his old friends were getting together for the week, and he agreed to come."

"So, he never saw Dirk before he was killed?"

Luke shook his head.

Bee rubbed his chest as if it ached. "Thanks for letting me know."

"Hey," Sara yelled as she and Emmett waved from the beach. "You guys playing?"

"Yup, and guess who's going to be treating us to barbeque after?" Bee yelled back.

Because his garage was closer to Main Street, Emmett played on the opposing team. "Don't be too sure about that, buddy."

"Oh, I'm quite confident we'll win. We have a secret weapon this year." Bee nudged Cass's arm with his elbow. "Show him, Cass."

She held up the two stones she'd found in the register, the only occurrence throughout the entire ordeal still unexplained. No one had taken credit yet for leaving the stones in her register drawer. Who knew? Maybe she'd never know how they'd gotten there. Either way, Cass was glad they had. Without the fire agate, she might never have gained enough focus to find Stephanie. Maybe Tanya had helped more than anyone realized.

Emmett started up the deck steps, then stopped and leaned against the rail. He looked around at the assembled group, then took off his hat and smoothed his hair back. "I just wanted to say thank you to all of you."

Tank clapped him on the back. "No need to thank us, Emmett. You were innocent; everyone knew that."

"Well, I still appreciate everything you guys did, so I just wanted you to know." Emmett nodded and put his hat back on. "It's been nice to be able to go back home and open the garage without reporters camping out on my doorstep. I was getting tired of having to sneak in the back door of the hotel to avoid them. Grateful, mind you, that Henry let me stay and didn't even charge me, but I wanted to go home, ya know?"

"Yeah, I do." Cass stood and wrapped her arms around his neck.

Not one for public displays of affection, he gave her a quick hug. "Could I speak to you alone for a second?"

"Of course." Cass led him around the side of the building. "What's up, Emmett? Is something wrong?"

"No, I just . . ." He smoothed a hand over his goatee, then rested his hands on the railing and looked out over the bay. "Did you really see her? My Tanya?"

"I did, Emmett."

He turned his gaze on her, his chin quivering. "And she was okay."

"Yes, she was, and she is clearly still watching over you and Joey."

A sense of pride surged through Cass, and she had no doubt it was not her own. She lay a hand on Emmett's arm. "She's proud of you, Emmett. Of how you've raised Joey. She's happy."

Emmett lowered his gaze and nodded. Tears tipped over and slid down his cheeks, and he spoke in a harsh whisper. "Thank you for that, Cass."

Joey jogged up beside him. "You ready, Dad?"

Emmett swiped the tears away quickly and turned to his son. "Sure thing, Joey."

Cass squeezed his arm on her way past and returned to their

friends, who were getting ready to head down to the beach. This promised to be one of the best tournaments ever.

Beast danced in circles in their midst, wound up by all the excitement.

"You're playing, Joey?" Bee asked.

"I'm gonna give it my best shot." A younger, lankier version of Emmett showed in Joey's appearance, posture, and mannerisms.

"Good for you." Bee gave him a high five and grinned. "But, no matter how much I like you, don't expect me to go easy."

"Come on, Beast." Cass clipped the leash to Beast's collar as they all started down the steps to the beach.

Beast trotted on one side of her, while Luke fell into step on her other side.

"Looks like they're getting ready to start." Bee rubbed his hands together. "Who's ready to whoop some bootie?"

"You wish!" Emmett nudged his shoulder.

Laughter filled the air.

Luke slung an arm around Cass's shoulders.

She leaned into him. "Now, this is what summer on Bay Island is supposed to be."

About the Author

Lena Gregory is the author of the Bay Island Psychic Mystery series, which takes place on a small island between the north and south forks of Long Island, New York, and the All-Day Breakfast Café Mystery series, which is set on the outskirts of Florida's Ocala National Forest.

Lena Grew up in a small town on the south shore of eastern Long Island, where she still lives with her husband, three kids, son-in-law, and five dogs, and works full-time as a writer and freelance editor.

To learn more about Lena and her latest writing endeavors, visit her website at www.lenagregory.com/, and be sure to sign up for her newsletter at lenagregory.us12.list-manage.com/subscribe? u=9765d0711ed4fab4fa31b16ac&id=49d42335d1.

Made in the USA
Middletown, DE
05 June 2019